A GAME OF
GROANS

A GAME OF GROANS

GEORGE R. R. WASHINGTON

THOMAS DUNNE BOOKS
ST. MARTIN'S GRIFFIN
NEW YORK

THOMAS DUNNE BOOKS.
An imprint of St. Martin's Press.

A GAME OF GROANS. Copyright © 2012 by St. Martin's Press. All rights reserved. Printed in the United States of America. For information, address St. Martin's Press, 175 Fifth Avenue, New York, N.Y. 10010.

www.thomasdunnebooks.com
www.stmartins.com

Design by Steven Seighman

ISBN 978-1-250-01125-1 (e-book)
ISBN 978-1-250-01126-8 (trade paperback)

First Edition: April 2012

10 9 8 7 6 5 4 3 2 1

A GAME OF
GROANS

PROLOGUE TO THE PROLOGUE

Watch it with the wand, Specs," breathed the tall man in black, rubbing the area on his backside where the boy in the round glasses had accidentally poked him.

The boy, who could not have been more than ten, yet spoke with the confidence of an eleven-year-old, grumbled, "*You* watch it," then, under his breath, added, "Y'probably wouldn't be so tough without that helmet, would you, mate?"

The man in black growled, "Speak up, young one. Can't hear you," then rapped his be-gloved knuckles on the side of his own head and noted, "The Death Star R&D department didn't exactly do a bang-up job on the ear amplifiers."

"The Death Star R&D department doesn't exactly do a bang-up job on *anything* . . . especially the Death Star," the boy pointed out. "I mean, how hard would it have been to make a retractable cover for the thermal exhaust port? Even Weasley could've figured that one out."

"Is that right?" the man in black snorted. "Well, you tell this Weasley to come up with a budget that'll cover uniforms and weapons for 251 stormtroopers *and* a retractable cover, then we'll talk."

"Both of you, please lower your voices," monotoned the pointy-eared man in the skintight blue and black suit. "It is highly illogical to engage in this sort of heated discussion before we attempt this ambush . . . which is illogical enough to begin with." Gesturing at the leafless trees, the muddy ground, and the snakes snaking around their ankles as if they were snakes, he claimed, "This is not a logical launching area. There are only five of *us* and this Lion, who represents Jesus Chryst—and you know he represents

Jesus because *Lion* is capitalized—and we do not know how many of *them*. We are not ready for battle."

A bearded man in a brown robe shook his head and sighed, "He is correct. We are not ready for battle. You have not *studied*. You are not *learned*. You have not absorbed the teachings of the F—"

"Don't say it," interrupted the man in black. "Don't say the *F* word!"

"—orce," finished the bearded man.

The four other men, the golden android, and the Lion all groaned.

"The Force is foolishness," the bespectacled boy complained. "You know it, and I know it, and everybody at Hogfarts knows it."

"Hogfarts?" growled the Lion.

"That's right, mate, Hogfarts. Spelling Hogfarts with a 'w' could get us in trouble."

"You mean Wogfarts?"

"No, I mean Hogw—"

"Don't say it," interrupted the man in black. "Don't say the *H* word!"

"—arts," finished the bearded man.

The four other men, the golden android, and the Lion all groaned.

A noseless man with a shiny bald head snarled, "I concur with the boy. The *F* word is foolishness. I believe this is the first time the young magician and I agree on something." He glared at the boy. "You are learning. And that is unfortunate for me." Addressing the rest, he loudly added, *"That is unfortunate for us all!"*

After the echo from the bald man's cry dissipated, the man in black said, "Way to keep our location a secret, Lord Bigmouth."

"This surprises you?" the droid asked. "His Lordship isn't exactly known for his subtlety, is he?"

The pointy-eared man said, "Not to worry, robot. The acoustics here behind the Wall are such that we could sing the Vulcan Anthem at the top of our lungs without giving away our position to the Fraternity of the Swatch."

"Know-it-all," the man in black muttered.

The pointy-eared man grumbled, "I swear to Hephaestus, I will mind-meld you with an ant."

The man in black glared through his helmet at the pointy-eared man and hissed, "Mind-meld me? Mind-meld *me*? Like that'll ever happen. Set your phasers to *give me a break*."

The boy pointed out, "I should point out that it's impossible to mind-meld somebody who doesn't have a brain."

The bearded man raised his hands to the sky and groaned, "Others, Others, Others, please control yourselves. I feel a great disturbance among you. If we are to take what is rightfully ours, we must band together, or else . . ."

"Hold on a sec," the man in black interjected. "Can we discuss this 'Others' business?"

"What is there to discuss?" the bearded man inquired.

The man in black sat down on the muddy ground—killing six snakes in the process—and stretched out his legs, then gestured at the Wall and asked, "Shouldn't *they* be the Others? Why are *we* the Others?"

Shrugging, the bearded man explained, "Some chucklehead from House Barfonme named us the Others several Summers ago. It stuck."

"Well, how about we *unstick* it?" Again gesturing to the Wall, he suggested, "How about we call *them* the Others. I bet they'd hate that." Raising his voice, he yelled, "Hey, all you Swatch dummies! We're no longer the Others. I decree that from now on, *you* are the Others! We're the . . . the . . . the *Awesomes*!"

A belch like sound drifted over the Wall. The droid asked the pointy-eared one, "Did you hear that?"

"Of course he did," snarled the man in black. "What with those stupid triangles on the side of his head, the guy could probably hear a baby dragon taking a leak against the wall of House Barker."

"Dragons are extinct," sneered the pointy-eared man.

"*You're* extinct."

"Why don't you go make an obscene phone call, you mouthbreathing psycho?"

"Who're you calling psycho, nerdling?"

"Who're you calling nerdling . . ."

Again, the bearded man lifted his arms to the sky and, pointing at the sun, kvetched. "Gentlemen, please, we're losing the light. Can we get down to business? Maybe a weapons check?"

The pointy-eared man pinched together his thumb and index finger. "Check."

The glasses-wearing boy twirled his wand between his fingers as if it were a miniature baton. "Check."

The droid made two brassy fists. "Check."

The man in black shook his head at the droid and snarled, "Fan*tas*tic. That'll have 'em quaking in their boots."

The bald man pointed his finger at the glasses-wearer, who transformed into a pony, then back into a human. "Check."

The Lion stuck his paw in front of his mouth, roared, smelled his breath, squinched up his face, and growled, "Check."

The man in black removed a small cylinder from his pocket, pushed a button, nodded at the beam that leapt from his weapon, and said, "Check, double check, and triple check, bitches."

The bearded one said, "Alright, Others . . ."

"I told you, we're not the Others! *They're* the Others! *They're* the Others!"

". . . may the you-know-what be with you!"

PROLOGUE

The Wall was melting.

It was not melting quickly by any means—Easterrabbit's continental meteorological experts estimated it would take at least six Summers for there to be a significant loss of mass—but if, like Broheim Jarhead and Broheim Airhead, you were forced to guard the Wall day in and day out, night in and night out, you noticed.

The two sworn members of the Fraternity of the Swatch were sitting on the Earth's muddy surface, legs crossed, eyes glazed. Jarhead passed Airhead a large green bottle, and belched, "This sure isn't what my mother had planned for me."

Airhead took a deep drink, then leered, "Probably not. But I have something planned for your mother."

Jarhead sarcasticked, "Boy oh boy, I sure haven't heard *that* one before from you."

"Boy oh boy, your mother sure has," Airhead retorted.

"Shut up and take a drink," Jarhead commanded.

"My pleasure."

After a lengthy guzzle, Jarhead pulled the bottle from Airhead's grip and said, "Quit bogarting the grog, Bro."

"I have seniority, and I can bogart as much and as often as I'd like, just as Lord Borgar of Castle Blanca once did." Airhead burped. "By the time you turned four, I already owned three swords, and had eight kills under my belt."

"Yes," Jarhead noted, "you've mentioned that. Several hundred times."

"And I pulled myself up from nothing. *Nothing*," Airhead whined.

"That has also been mentioned," Jarhead pointed out. "But I suspect that won't stop you from telling me . . ."

"I never knew who my father was, Bro," Airhead interrupted. "I was a . . . a . . . a *jerkoff*."

"Of course you were."

"That's what folks around most of Easterrabbit call boys who don't know who their fathers are: jerkoffs."

"I know."

"I understand they call them bastards up on the other side of the Wall, but here, they call them jerkoffs."

"They sure do."

"You understand that? For the sake of this discussion—and any discussions following—the definition of *jerkoff* is the definition of *bastard*."

"Got it."

"Forget everything you know about the word *jerkoff*. Right now, and for the next two hundred or so pages, a jerkoff is a child who was abandoned by his father."

"Check."

"And I was the biggest jerkoff in all the land."

"And you still are."

Airhead finished off the bottle, then stood up and threw it straight ahead, as hard as he could; the bottle stuck to the Wall as if it were covered in Velcro, and the Wall was covered with more Velcro. "That's why I joined the Fraternity, Bro. Because I'm a jerkoff. A stupid jerkoff, with a stupid life that's now even more stupid, because I spend every minute of every day watching this stupid Wall, wearing this stupid armor in this stupid heat. I'm sweating my onions off in here."

"You think you had it rough just because you don't know who your father was?" Jarhead questioned. "I grew up on the border of Dork. All our food came from Dork. All our clothes came from Dork. All the smells came from Dork. *That's* a stupid life."

Airhead raised himself to his knees, stood up, then fell down again. "I'm sorry, Bro," he apologized. "Jerkoffs tend to focus on the fact that they're jerkoffs, and that is *not* how a Frat brother should act." He reached his hand under his armor, scratched his shoulder, then added, "It's just that it's hot, and I'm bored."

Jarhead nodded his understanding, then said, "I understand. You want another drink?"

"I do," he agreed, "but what I'd like more is to use my training. I want to fight." He picked up his sword and whooshed it to and fro. "We trained to fight. We took an oath to fight." He faced the Wall and yelled, *"We're ready when you are, Others!"*

A voice came over the Wall: *"You're the Others!"*

Airhead and Jarhead gawked at each other. "Did you hear that?" Jarhead asked.

Airhead nodded.

"What do you think we should do?" Jarhead queried.

"I think we should go and . . ."

Before he could finish the thought, a bald man with no nose called from the top of the Wall, *"I think you should go and suffer!* Ahoy, Others! It is time to begin our takeover of the entire continent of Easterrabbit!"

A man wearing full-body black armor and a black cape leapt over the Wall, landed directly in front of Airhead, and pointed out, "In case anybody asks, regardless of what baldy back there says, we're not the Others. We're the Awesomes."

At once, three or four voices called from the other side of the Wall, *"That's not official yet!"*

The man in black yelled, "I hate you all!" Then he picked up Airhead by his neck, held him three feet above the ground, and spiked him into the mud.

Jarhead drew his weapon and approached the man in black. When he was a sword's thrust away, the man in black held up a finger and Jarhead came to a sudden halt, holding his throat with his free hand and gagging, unable to speak. The man in black breathed, "This is *it*? This is all they've got? This is the big, scary Fraternity we've been hearing about for the last, what, zillion Summers? We've been sitting here with mud up our bum cracks, and nothing's been happening—not that we should be surprised by that, because if you know anything about Easterrabbit, you know there's often pages and pages and pages and pages of nothingness—and this is *it*?"

A bespectacled boy riding a Lion—who anybody with any sense would recognize represented Jesus Chryst, if only because the word *Lion* is capitalized—materialized out of nowhere and corrected, *"Seven* Summers.

We've been waiting seven Summers to make a move. Seven. Seven long Summers in the heat, and the sun, and the rain, and the heat, and the tornados, and the heat, and the . . ."

"Okay, Specs," the man in black said, "we know, we get it, it's hot, but put a sock in it. I'm wearing way more crap than you, and do you hear me bitching? No. So how about less whining, and more mauling." The man in black turned to the Wall and roared, *You guys coming, or what?"*

In the blink of a dragon's eye, a hole appeared in the Wall, and through it climbed the members of the group formerly known as the Others. The hole closed as quickly as it opened, and then the battle began.

A bearded man in a robe stomped on the fallen Airhead's head, sending brain matter flying in all directions. Directly in the path of the brain shrapnel, the golden droid took several hits; he flicked a blop of gooey gray matter on his chest and uttered, "Dear me, what time does Ziebart close?"

Ignoring the effeminate-sounding robot, the noseless man ripped a tree from its roots and smashed it into Jarhead's back, sending the Swatchman flying. "How'd that taste, you Easterrabbit bastards?" he asked.

Airhead sat up, picked up a fistful of brain, jammed it back into the hole in his head, and grunted, "I'm not a bastard, I'm a jerkoff!" Then he threw a handful of mud at the noseless man.

The noseless man easily dodged the salvo and called to the bespectacled boy, "Care to have a go at him, magician?"

The boy grinned wolfishly, snarled, "Bloody right I would," then threw his wand at Airhead. The stick went into Airhead's left eye and boomeranged out his right, then floated easily into the magician's awaiting hand.

The Swatchman poked his fingers into his empty eye sockets, roared, "The Fraternity of the Swatch shall not be vanquished," then pulled himself to his feet, took a single step forward, tripped on a snake, and collapsed onto the mud, looking deader than the deadest of dead snakes who had died.

During the commotion, the pointy-eared man bent over Jarhead and pinched the back of his neck. All four of Jarhead's limbs detached themselves from his torso and flew into the Wall, where they stuck as if they were covered in Velcro, and the Wall was covered with more Velcro. The noseless man then twisted off Jarhead's head and took a drink from his skull.

The bearded man declared, "We are done here. We have done what we needed to do. We have made our point. If we continue on this path, we will find ourselves heading toward the Dark Side."

"You have a problem with the Dark Side, you old fart?" the man in black asked. "It's *fun* on the Dark Side." He ripped off Airhead's arm and flung it over the Wall as if it were a twig that was blown from a tree during a Summer storm. "Now *that* is how we roll on the Dark Side, baby. It's a pile of piss. You might want to . . ."

Before he could finish his thought, Airhead whispered, "We'll be back, Bro. We'll be back." And then he bled out.

The pointy-eared man gave the dead Swatchman a nervous glance, then murmured, "He's right, you know. All logic dictates that if he says he'll be back, then he'll be back, probably right before the end of the tale."

"Whatever you say, space cadet," the man in black said. He clapped once, then said, "Okay, I'm starved. Plenty of time to eat, because nothing ever happens in this freaky-ass continent. Nothing. *Nothing.* So who's up for some onions?"

ALLBRAN

Allbran Barker broke wind.

Fortunately for Allbran's sake, the wind from the sky dissipated the wind from his hindquarters to the point that he was the only person who heard the foulness. Unfortunately for Allbran's sake, the wind was such that he was forced to inhale the foulness, a foulness that somebody with a sharp sense of smell would accurately surmise was born of a combination of onions, wild boar, raw oats, and more onions.

The seven-year-old scrunched up his nose with self-loathing, and his father, Lord Headcase Barker, noticed. Lord Barker inquired, "What's with the face, Allbran?" Gesturing to the scene in front of him, he asked, "Is *this* too much for you?"

Allbran said, "Oh, of course not, Father. I look forward to *this*!" The *this* Allbran and Lord Barker spoke of was the weekly Deserter Demolition.

Some believed Deserter Demolition to be barbaric, but even Allbran understood it was a necessity. Due to its horrible climate—brutal cold one day, deadly heat the next, even hotter than that the next—Summerseve, the town in which House Barker was housed, was a less-than-ideal place to live. Angered by the broken promises about universal air-conditioning service, the townspeople began an exodus from the region—most of those who left relocated to Caelifornea, while a small contingency escaped to Paeresfrance—and Summerseve nearly went bankrupt. In order to salvage the region, Lord Barker instituted a strict no-deserters policy, the penalty being beheading. That did not stop people from trying to leave Summerseve on a daily basis. Some made it out. Most did not.

In order to cut costs, Headcase—Head to his friends—scheduled all his beheadings for Monday afternoons, and to Allbran, those Mondays tasted as good as a plate of lemon cakes. Lemon cakes with a healthy coating of deserter blood, granted, but lemon cakes nonetheless. The beheadings were enjoyable in and of themselves, but part of the fun was the opportunity to spend time with his father, his older brother, Bobb, and his not-quite-as-old-as-Bobb-but-still-older-than-Allbran jerkoff brother, Juan Nieve. For one day a week, the Barker boys were on an equal plane, and Allbran wanted to keep it that way, thus his concern about the windbreaking.

Head smiled at his son and uttered, "I look forward to these days too, son. It's a pleasure to have you boys here by my side." Looking at Juan, he said, "Even you, jerkoff."

"Gracias, Padre,"[1] Juan said.

"I apologize to you boys that we only have one deserter. It was a slow week. I feel horrible. I have let you down. Down I have let you. If somebody were to ask me, 'In which direction have I let you,' the answer would be 'down.'"

Allbran—who was uncomfortable with his father's predilection for self-flagellation—farted, then coughed to cover up the air tulip. "That's alright, Father. One beheading is better than no beheadings."

Head's smile widened, and he said, "Ah, Allbran, you are growing into a fine young man." He pulled the bloodstained axe from his tool belt and said, "When I die—and I will die, probably soon, because characters like me, we always die—this will all be yours. Well, not yours, but your older brother's, who might lend it to you once in a while. And now, to the business at hand." He lifted the axe above his head and called, "It is decreed by me, Headcase Barker, the Seventy-Eighth of His Name, King of the Swordfish and the Hemorrhoids, Lord of the Eight, no, Nine, no, wait, Six Kingdoms, and Protector of the Protractor, that this nameless deserter's head be removed by mine hand with one whack, and one whack only." He asked the deserter, "Have you any final words?"

The deserter mumbled, "I do have a name, you know."

"Of course you do," Head agreed, then—as Bobb yelled, *"I loves me*

---

1. Thank you, Father.

some violence!"—brought the axe down upon the back of the deserter's neck.

Halfway through Head's downswing, Allbran's hindquarters emitted a sound so thunderous that he who supplied it could not deny it. It so disconcerted Head that his typically straight and sure axe chop was a tad wobbly, wobbly to the point that the axe did not slice all the way through the deserter's neck. Head attempted to remove his weapon from the deserter, but it was so embedded in the man's spine that the handle popped free of the blade, and the blade stayed put, half in his neck, and half out.

While the three full-blooded Barker men and the one jerkoff watched blood gush from the deserter and onto their respective shirts, Bobb pulled out his sword and asked, "Would you like me to finish him off, Father?"

Juan unsheathed his sword and declared, *"Dios mio, Padre,*[2] give me the chance to prove myself. My swordwork has become *muy*[3] impeccable."

Head chuckled, "My son, my jerkoff, I appreciate the sentiment, but the law is clear: One whack, and one whack only. I know, I know, in the story outline, it was suggested that we should be as violent as possible, but once in a while, subtlety is called for, and what's more subtle than one whack?" He turned to the deserter and said, "You are free to go. But I would advise you to stay in Summerseve. I think if you give it a chance, you'll find it to be a wonderful place to live."

The deserter stood up, bowed, gingerly touched his gushing wound, and said, "Yes, my Lord. Thank you, my Lord."

Head nodded. "My pleasure." He tapped the blade embedded in the deserter's neck and said, "Hey, if you get a chance, could you return this thing to my castle?"

"Yes, my Lord."

"Fantastic. Give it to my assistant, Maester Blaester, and he'll get it to me."

"Yes, my Lord," the deserter repeated, then staggered off.

As he watched the wounded man walk away, Allbran complained, "Father, I'm covered in deserter blood."

---

2. My Gods, Father. (Now that you know what *padre* means, we'll stop footnoting that word.)
3. Very. Duh.

"We all are," Head pointed out. "Let's get ourselves cleaned up. I think a trip to the pond is in order."

With each muddy step, Allbran's piffles became more and more pronounced; his companions, being polite sorts, did not comment on the increasingly loud, increasingly odiferous emissions. He sped up his pace, in hopes that he could get out of earshot (and noseshot), but the faster he moved, the louder his cheese cut. By the time he jumped into the pond some ten minutes later, his insides felt as if somebody had scooped out his guts and replaced them with onion juice.

At the pond, the other Barker men stripped down to their undergarments—Head's, Bobb's, and Allbran's were made from chainmail, the preferred undergarment of the royals, while Juan's consisted of a piece of string and two feathers—and dived in. Bran watched his family rinse themselves in the soupy water, hoping against hope that he would soon outgrow his stomach issues. He let out a sad sigh, and a sadder fart.

While the others dried themselves off and put back on their bloodstained clothes, Allbran remained in the pond, floated on his back, and stared at the overcast sky. He almost drifted off to sleep, but a significant ripple in the water jolted him from his trance. Standing up, he peered toward the other side of the pond, and his jaw dropped. He pointed to the South and burbled, "Over there." He could barely get the words out.

The rest of the Barker clan followed Allbran's finger, and were greeted by a sight so shocking that they were shocked. There, frolicking in the water, were six animals, rare animals, animals that were thought to be extinct for generations, animals that nobody in Easterrabbit thought would ever be seen in their lifetimes, or their children's lifetimes, or their children's children's lifetimes.

Those animals? It might be better to tell you what they were not. They were not direwolves, because they would be too obvious, too common, and too close to a tale told by a man with the most absurd white beard you'll ever see. They were not direpenguins, which might upset some because direpenguins are beloved beasts. And they were not direbananas, because direbananas were a fruit.

No, they were direpandas.

And not only were they direpandas, they were tiny, fluffy baby direpandas, smaller even than Allbran, and Allbran wanted them all. He jumped out of the water, splashing his family in the process, and galloped toward the other end of the pond, screaming, "Direpandas! Direpandas! The Barker family symbol! Direpandas! Direpandas!" And then he broke wind so loudly and sharply that the direpandas froze with shock, fear, or admiration.

"Allbran," Head called, "get back here! Direpandas are vicious killing machines! And they probably haven't gotten their shots!"

Allbran ignored his father and continued his beeline to the animals. Bobb smirked at his brother, then took off in a sprint. After Juan followed suit, Lord Barker sighed and trekked after his brood.

The baby direpandas were romping as only baby direpandas could—gaily—and Allbran was enchanted. He gently reached out his hand to the smallest one and let the bear inhale his scent. The animal made a quiet hooting noise, then licked Allbran on the arm, covering the boy with bubbly direpanda saliva, a liquid that, for some, was the nectar of the Gods, and for others, was as deadly as it was gooey. For yet others, it was simply gross.

Giggling, Allbran exclaimed, "These direpandas, they are ours! They are on our land, and they are drinking our water, so they belong to us."

Ignoring his son's enthusiastic fart, Head pointed out, "They are not ours, son. They belong to their parents."

Juan noted, "*Padre,* I see no direpanda *mamacita* or *papacita*. It appears to be just the little ones. Is it possible that they, too, are jerkoffs?"

Shrugging, Lord Barker said, "It certainly is possible, Juan. If anybody would recognize a bunch of jerkoffs, it's another jerkoff."

"Then they need parents," Juan said. "They need care. They need love."

Bobb pointed at the viscous direpanda saliva congealing on Allbran's arm and said, "They need a trip to the dentist."

"They need *us,*" Allbran insisted, picking up one tiny direpanda and squeezing him to his chest. He asked Head, "Can we take them home, Daddy? Can we? Can we? Huh? Can we? Can we? Huh? Can we? Please please pretty please? I promise to feed them, and walk them, and clean up their poop, and I'll do my homework, and eat all my vegetables, and pick up my room, and I'll stop doing Dutch ovens to Dickoff. Please please please please please?"

After a moment, Head sighed. "If I see one piece of direpanda poop inside the house, I swear to the giant parakeet in the sky that they will all be beheaded."

"Giant parakeet?" Juan asked.

"Here in Easterrabbit, the religion stuff is a bit, um, er, let's say *nebulous*. In book one, when we're cursing something, it's always all Gods this and Gods that, but we're never told who or what the Gods are. It's a different story in books two through five, but I won't bore you with that, because they're Godsdamn boring enough. So for now, I'm going with the parakeet."

Disregarding his father's admittedly pointless aside, Bobb queried, "You would behead the animal who graces the House Barker sigil?" For centuries the Barker Flag had borne the image of a direpanda peeing on Calvyn from Calvyn and Hoakes.

Waving a dismissive hand, Head grinned. "Just kidding, Bobb. I would never simply behead them. Like any good ruler, I'd behead them and turn them into direpandaburgers. But a mere beheading? Never."

"Waste not, want not," Juan said.

"Well put, Juan," Head said. "Spoken like a true jerkoff." To Allbran, he added, "There are six direpandas, and I have five kids, and one jerkoff. One animal for each of the seeds of my loins; black and white pets for all but the jerkoff, who can have the white and black beast. It's almost as if it was meant to be. Well done, son."

"Thank you, Father," Allbran said, then let one rip. And if ever a fart sounded and smelled contented, it was that one.

GATEWAY

Until King Magoo M. Magoo outlawed healthy debate, religion—especially the giant parakeet—was the most discussed topic throughout the continent of Easterrabbit. The nonbelievers outnumbered the believers by a ratio of ten to one, but the believers were loud, thus the debates, though they were seldom resolved, were deafening, so deafening that the Earthbound Gods themselves stopped listening, and were forced to find other ways to occupy their time.

During Easterrabbit's third Summer, Nestamarley, the dark-skinned God of greenery, was concocting a plant that he hoped would survive the eternal Summer heat and nourish the citizenry of the Seven . . . no, wait, Five . . . no, Twelve Kingdoms, a plant that was at once tasty and nutritious, a plant that could be ingested without any preparation, a plant that would change the world.

He failed miserably.

Each plant was bitterer than the last, inedible and off-putting. One morning, frustrated after twenty-six consecutive hours of fruitless searching through the wet mud for useful-looking seedlings, Nestamarley set fire to his crop, a crop of nine-leaved plants that were shaped like fans. As he watched the flames destroy his hard work, a thick and herbal yet somehow pleasing scent filled the air, and Nestamarley was overcome with a deep sense of peace, and an even deeper sense of hunger. He smiled, ran his hands through his matted hair, took a deep breath, curled up on the ground, wrote the number *420* in the mud, and wished that somebody had invented television.

After several weeks of enjoyable experiments, Nestamarley determined that the plant was indeed the cause of this deep peace, and that the best way to deliver the plant's healing power was to dry it, chop it into tiny pieces, roll It up in a large leaf, light the tip of the leaf, and inhale, and inhale, and inhale some more.

Word of Nestamarley's discovery spread throughout Easterrabbit, and, after pouring down a mug of grog, it became the favored manner to unwind after a tough day of slogging through the Easterrabbitian mud. Sadly, like all the Gods of Easterrabbit, Nestamarley passed away (which begs the question, were they actually Gods, but whatever), and with him went the formula for creating this magical plant. There was, however, an abundance of the plant still in existence, the majority of it in a field in Summerseve, so Tyrannosaurus Barker, the first Lord of Summerseve, confiscated it for royal use only, and stored the remaining greenery in one of his castle's sub-basements.

The plant—which had become known as Godsweede, or simply weede—fell out of favor during the ensuing Barker reigns, and the plants were left untouched for decades, until a long-haired, free-spirited young Lady named Gateway Bully—a young Lady who happened to be engaged to Lord-in-waiting Headcase Barker—stumbled upon the stash. She had no idea what it was, but, after one whiff, somehow knew what to do with it.

Six weeks later, Gateway Bully—daughter of Hosehead and Mikasa Bully—became Gateway Bully Barker, the Lady of House Barker, and the region's sole worshipper of Nestamarley. And she prayed at Nestamarley's temple each and every day, in part because when you live in a world where one-third of the chapters have little to do with the plot, you need an escape, and in part because Godsweede is freaking sweet.

Today was no exception.

Gateway sat under her favorite tree behind the castle, inhaling a plump roll of Godsweede, unconcerned that her hindquarters were slowly sinking into the mushy, dirty earth. She closed her eyes and chanted a little nonsense tune that she had composed on the spot: "Ravens eat it, and they leave it. Turkeys eat it. Lambs love to play with it." The song was so silly that Gateway giggled, and giggled, and giggled some more.

Just as she was about to haul herself out of the mud and track down some food—a plate of raw onions with a side of cooked onions in a light onion sauce would have hit the spot—a gentle sound nudged her from her reverie: "Gateway," the beloved voice whispered.

She opened her eyes and smiled at her husband. "Head, darling." After an unsuccessful attempt at pulling herself out of the sludge, she swallowed her roach, held out her hands, and said, "Little help here?" Head smiled indulgently as he pulled his bride up from the squishy ground. After she gave him a passionate, muddy kiss, she pointed at the bloodstains on Head's chest and queried, "Tough day in the fields, big guy?"

Head looked down at his shirt and frowned. "Godsdamn it, that will *never* come out. And I was going to wear this shirt to greet Bobbert."

Gateway asked, "Bobbert's coming?"

"King Bobbert himself," Head agreed.

Gateway asked, "When? How? With whom?"

Head answered, "Soon. On horses. With everybody."

"The kids will be thrilled to see him," Gateway pointed out.

"I agree," Head agreed, "that the boys will be pleased. The girls, I am not so sure. I think he frightens Sasha and Malia."

"He frightens me too," Gateway claimed, "but I just nut up and deal with it. I'll talk to them."

Head nodded and said, "Thank you, darling." He wiped his brow with the back of his hand, regarded the sweat stains on his shirt, and added, "Summer is coming."

Rolling her eyes, Gateway noted, "You've mentioned that, darling. Several times."

"I know I did," Head admitted, "but it bears repeating: Summer is coming."

"So I've heard."

"I know you've heard it, Gateway, but do you *understand* it?"

When she was in the warm, mellow grip of Godsweede, Lady Gateway did not understand much, but she became very agreeable, so she said, "Don't be silly, Head. Of course I understand it."

"Do you?" he asked. "Then please explain."

"Okay, I mean, you're telling me, that, like, y'know, it's kinda like Summer is coming." Giving him her finest smile, she asked, "Right?"

Head draped his arm over his wife's shoulders and said, "That's right, Gateway. You've got it. Summer is coming."

She put her arm around his waist and uttered, "We know why *Summer* is coming, but why is *Bobbert Barfonme* coming?"

Head looked away from Gateway and asked, "Can't one old friend come to visit another old friend?"

"Of course he can, Head, but Bobbert Barfonme doesn't get off of his throne for any reason other than to get his grog on, and he doesn't leave Capaetal Ceity unless he's in the midst of a political disaster that could end up with one of his friends dead." Her synapses awoke to the point that she was able to put two and two together, and even though she came up with five, she knew something was amiss. "Okay, Headcase," Gateway sighed, "what's wrong?"

Head cleared his throat, looked away, and fumbled, "*Whaaaaat?* Something wrong? That's crazy talk. Wrong? *Never.* Why would you think anything's wrong? Nothing's wrong. Everything is one-hundred-percent copacetic."

Gateway growled, "Head, don't do this."

"Do what?"

"*That* thing."

"*What* thing?"

"That thing where you don't tell me about an important character getting murdered."

"Oh. Right. *That* thing."

After a moment of uncomfortable silence, Gateway asked, "So who bit it now?"

Again, Head cleared his throat, and again, there was a moment of uncomfortable silence. Finally, Lord Barker said, "Your brother-in-law."

"My brother-in-law?"

"Yes," Head sighed.

"You mean Mr. I'm-So-Cool-Because-I'm-the-Foot?"

"Right."

"Mr. Help-Move-the-Story-Along?"

"Yeah, him."

"Mr. We-Had-Several-Amazing-Jokes-About-Him-Specifically-Some-

Baseball-Oriented-Chuckles-Centered-Around-His-Last-Name-but-the-Legal-Department-Made-Us-Take-Them-Out?"

Head nodded sadly, at both the loss of his wife's brother and the genius sports humor. "He's gone, my love. Lord Functionary Aaron has passed on. The Foot of the King is dead."

A tear ran down Gateway's muddy cheek. "Poor Lysergic. Whatever will she do without her plot point of a husband?"

"Who cares?" Head mumbled. "Your sister's a queynte."

"Wow," Gateway said, "I've never heard you use the Q word. But yes, Lysergic *is* a queynte, but still." She took a deep breath, then sighed. "It was only a matter of time, I suppose."

"What do you mean?" Head asked.

"The King's Foots have notoriously short lifespans, dear."

Head exclaimed, "*Whaaaaat?* That's crazy talk. Advisers to the King live as long as anybody else. Everything is one-hundred-percent copacetic."

"What about Mayce Windu?"

"Oh, right. A mysterious death by overacting."

"And Orvylle Redynbacher?"

"A mysterious death by choking on popcorn."

"And Swyfty Lazyr?"

"A mysterious death by suffocation."

"And Stumpy Pepys?"

"A mysterious death by drowning."

"And Stumpy Joe Chylds?"

"A mysterious death by fire."

"And Petyr Jaymes Bond?"

"A mysterious death by bludgeoning."

"And Mick Shrymption?"

"A mysterious death by dismemberment."

"And Functionary Aaron?"

"Nobody knows how he died. It was very mysterious."

"And there you have it."

As they walked back toward the castle in silence, Head fingered his sword. Gateway noticed and asked, "Something wrong with Slush?"

Head removed his sword from its house and swooshed it through the air. It wobbled from one side to the other, flapping like a willow tree in the midst of a windstorm in a field of willow trees. "Slush is fine," he boasted defensively. "Slush was made from Corinthian leather, and nothing will hurt Slush, thus nothing will hurt me. *Ever*."

"I don't know about that, Head," Gateway opined. "From what I gather, nothing will stop whatever's behind the Wall. Not even Corinthian leather."

"Gateway, I know my own needs, and what I need from a sword, I know I get from Slush. I could ask for nothing beyond the quality of Slush's workmanship. I request nothing beyond the perfection of the softest Corinthian leather. Yet it is on the battlefield where Slush answers my demands. I get much more from this sword than great comfort at a most pleasant price. It gives me great confidence, for which there can be *no* price. With Slush, I have what I need."

"You sound like a car commercial."

"Maybe I do, Gateway," Head consented, "but it is a sword so fascinating, that it has captured the hearts of many. Slush is the most successful new personal-sized luxury sword in the last five Summers, and here's why: Slush combines luxury and class at an affordable price. See Slush now at your Chrysler-Plymouth dealer."

"First of all, Summerseve doesn't have a Chrysler-Plymouth dealer. And second of all, what's with the accent? You suddenly sound like that jerkoff kid of yours."

Ignoring her, Head barreled on: "Elegantly designed. Luxuriously appointed. And now is the time to buy Slush here in Easterrabbit, because it is priced to give you the value you have been looking for. You see, it is the end of the model Summer for your Chrysler-Plymouth dealer, so if you purchase Slush now, you'll get an excellent deal on the Slush you want, ready for immediate delivery. Don't hesitate. Experience Slush while it is such an unbelievable value."

Gateway Barker touched her husband's flaccid sword and said, "Whatever you say, dear." Looking up at the sky, she wondered aloud, "Hey, is it 4:20 yet?"

HEADCASE

After a rumble jarred Lord Headcase Barker out of a sound slumber, he mumbled, "Gods in hell, Allbran's queefs are getting chunkier." Then he put his pillow over his head, hoping sleep would again come. Just as he was about to nod off, there was a louder rumble, followed by a cry of "Hey Barky-Boy, drop that tiny winky of yours and get your fat ass out of bed!"

Head groaned, then elbowed Gateway awake and murmured, "Get up. Bobbert's early."

Gateway echoed her husband's groan—it was almost as if they were playing a game of groans—then reached over to her nightstand, grabbed the remnants of last night's pre-bedtime Godsweede, sparked it up, and took a hit. With the smoke still in her lungs, she held out the plant to Head and gasped, "Want a taste?"

Head—who indulged once when he was eleven, an indulgence that still elicited nightmares of yet-to-be-fought battles against bearded scribes with predilections for composing overly lengthy tomes that often included scenes in which a beloved protagonist is prematurely killed—said, "Tempting, but I'll pass. Bobbert will probably be all grogged up, and when he's grogged up, he likes to talk, so I should probably be lucid."

"Good point." She nodded. The unclothed Gateway then rolled out of bed, stumbled to her closet, and grabbed her robe. Covering herself and sauntering to the window, she added, "It sounds like a circus out there. I wonder who he brought with him." Did he bring the entire cast of characters? Did he bring people we'll see in season one or season two? Or the next book? Or the book after that? Or the book after that? Or the book after the book after the book after *The Hunger Games*?"

"I'm *afraid* of who he brought with him. Hopefully not the Queen. My best shirt is stained, and the last thing I need is Cerevix whining, *Head isn't fit to be a Lord,* and *Head doesn't represent House Barker the way it should be represented,* and *Head isn't this,* and *Head isn't that.*" Clutching his stomach, he added, "Gods, my ulcer is acting up already."

Gateway said, "Maybe Cerevix didn't come."

A cry came from outside: "Rise and shine and open the Godsdamn door, Barky-Boy! Cerevix has to take a leak . . ."

Head sighed, "Godsdamn it. Cerevix came."

Bobbert continued, "And Jagweed's gotta drop a deuce."

"Wonderful," Head gamely groaned. "That one's here too." He stood up and sighed. "Let's get this over with." He trudged to the other side of the room as if the floor were covered with the muddiest of mud, pulled back the curtain, opened the window, forced a grin, and roared, "Bobbo Slobbo!"

"Barky Burger!"

"Kingo Ringo!"

"Header Bedder!"

"Barfy Barfy Banana Fanna Fo Farfy!"

"Lordy Lordy, drink a forty!"

Head wiped the crust from his eyes and gave his friend a onceover, not impressed with what he was seeing. King Bobbert Barfonme was big even when he was little, but his years on the throne had not been kind to his waistline. The King had probably packed on thirty or forty pounds since the last time they got together, three Summers before. "You look great, Your Highness!" he called.

"I look like hell, and if you call me *Your Highness* again, I'll slap that scraggly beard off your face."

"I'm sure you will, Bobbert. I'm coming down. Tell Cerevix and Jagweed they can use the outhouse."

Queen Cerevix—blond, beautiful, regal Queen Cerevix—roared, "Head, there is no way in hell that my junk is touching a toilet that's been touched by the junk of a peasant!"

"That's all we have to offer, Cerevix."

"Godsdamn jerkwater town, full of empty-headed mud-suckers," Cerevix grumbled as she trooped to the toilet.

Head called to the King, "Looks like your way with words has been rubbing off on your wife, Bobbert!"

"That's not the only thing I've been rubbing off on her!"

At that, Gateway chuckled. Head turned around and glared at her, then hissed, "Quit laughing. You'll only encourage him."

"I can't help it. He's funny."

"He's a clown," Head complained.

"He's your oldest and dearest friend," she noted.

"I know," Head agreed, "but he's also my oldest and dearest pain in the backside."

Gateway threw a pillow at her husband and ordered, "Go down there and play with your pal. But play nice."

When Head made it downstairs and out the castle's front entrance, Bobbert jumped off his horse, fell on his rump, stood up, and embraced his friend. Head winced upon getting a noseful of Bobbert's grog-soaked breath and an eyeful of his sweat-coated chainmail. Bobbert beamed, "Heady, Heady, Heady, you got old!"

Head was not able to fully wrap his arms around the King's beefy torso, and was this close to saying, *Barfy, Barfy, Barfy, you got fat,* but he held his tongue. Instead, he noted, "I'm old? Bobbert, you're two days older than me."

The King pulled back, and said, "And two Summers wiser." He mopped his brow, then added, "It's hot. Summer must be coming."

Nodding, Head said, "Summer *is* coming."

From the window, Gateway called, "Is that right? Is Summer really coming? Because you have yet to mention that."

Bobbert laughed, then suggested, "Gateway, Gateway, Gateway, you bring that fine booty of yours down here, or else I'm coming up. And I'll tap that thing, I promise you that."

On her way back from the outhouse, Queen Cerevix noted, "I'll believe that when I see it, Mr. Big Talker. You haven't tapped anything in months."

Bobbert chuckled nervously, then told Head, "Oh, that wife of mine, always the jokester." As if to prove her wrong, he headed into the castle and up the stairs.

Head pointed to the exceedingly tall, exceedingly slender, exceedingly gawky man sitting perilously on the horse behind Bobbert's, and said to nobody in particular, "I thought he was the jokester."

The tall man grinned, and said, "Great to see you, Lord Barker. You look smashing. I'd give you a wave, but I just flew in from Capaetal Ceity, and boy, are my arms tired." After nobody laughed, the tall man straightened an imaginary tie and said, "Woof, tough crowd." He said to a passing stranger, "Hey! You! Where you from?"

The stranger stopped, and said, "Um, Summerseve."

"Ah, Summerseve. I once spent a night there. It lasted a year. *Ch-ching!*" After more non-laughter, he said, "I knew my material would go over everybody's head here. Anyhow, how's it hanging, Head? For Gateway's sake, I hope that answer is *Down in the dirt.*"

Lord Barker noted, "Ah, Tritone Sinister. The funniest of the Sinisters. And that isn't saying much."

"Look at you," Tritone grinned, "spritzing with the pros. Nice work, your Lordship." He pointed to a painfully ugly three-armed man standing beside a painfully ugly three-legged horse, and said, "You know this one?"

Head shook his head.

"Sandstorm Leghorn. Bobbert's bodyguard. Tough job, because that Bobbert has a lot of body to guard. *Hi-yo!*" After nobody laughed, the tall man said, "Well, that's all for me tonight. Tip your waitress, and try the veal with onions, and please always remember, and please never forget, wherever you go, there you are. Now I'd like to turn it over to the man of the hour, who makes the ladies wanna shower, ladies and gentlemen, *Sandstorm Leghorn!*"

Sandstorm grunted, "Grunt."

"Sandstorm Leghorn, ladies and gentlemen, give it up!" Tritone hopped off his horse and asked Head, "Say, Shecky, who does a guy have to blow to get a drink around this dump?"

Head cocked his thumb over his shoulder, toward the castle, and said, "See my assistant, Maester Blaester. Upstairs, third room to the left of the stairs."

Tritone bent down, patted Head on the cheek, and grinned. "You're beautiful, babe. Don't ever change."

After the skinny giant entered the front door—clocking his head on the top of the doorway in the process—Bobbert stuck his head out of the upstairs window and yelled, "Hey, Headmaster, as soon as I finish doing my Kingly duty to your wife, you and me are gonna talk. Somewhere private."

The Queen's twin brother, the Knight Sur Jagweed, piped up, "You want me to sit in on this one, Your Highness?"

Frowning, Bobbert asked, "You have any clue what the word *private* means, Jag?" Then, under his breath, he mumbled, "Dumbass."

Cerevix screamed, *"I heard that!"*

"Good!" he screamed back. To Head, he ordered, "Meet me in the drawing room before I show this wife of yours how a real man takes care of his business."

Once they were seated in the drawing room, sipping their drinks— Head a small glass of water, Bobbert a huge goblet of grog—Bobbert belched and said, "So. Functionary ceased to function."

Head nodded. "Yes. Heartbreaking."

"You hear how he bit it?" Bobbert asked.

Rolling his eyes at Bobbert's callousness, Head said, "No, Bobbert, I did not hear how your Foot, and my brother-in-law, passed away."

"He died laughing."

Head sighed. Dying of laughter had become a minor epidemic in Easterrabbit, but it had only affected the peasants. Royalty had avoided this terrible fate. Until now. "Do you know what he was laughing at?" he asked.

"No clue," Bobbert said. "But you can bet it wasn't at anything Tritone said. That man needs some new material."

"You aren't kidding. So who's going to take over the rule of Vailcolorado?"

"Well, your sister-in-law Lysergic isn't fit to rule a litter of cats, let alone an entire kingdom. Plus she's a woman, and Gods knows you can't put a woman on a throne. They're insane."

"Not *all* women are insane, Bobbert," Head said.

"You live with Cerevix for a few Summers, and we'll talk. As for Functionary's replacement, if I had my druthers, I'd bring in one of those Dorki idiots, because they're too stupid to make stupid decisions, if you know what I mean. Unfortunately, I can't, because it's House Aaron, and it has to be an Aaron, which means . . ."

Interrupting, Head groaned, "Bobbby."

Nodding, Bobbert said, "Bobbby."

"No. No way. No how. Bobbby's a . . . a . . . a . . ."

"Yeah, he's a prick. He's only six, but he's already a prick. I agree. But he's the next male Aaron, so we're stuck with the little freak."

"Great. So we've got a moron leading House Aaron, and a moron-in-waiting at House . . ." He trailed off.

Bobbert said, "You were going to say, *A moron-in-waiting at House Barfonme,* weren't you?"

"I . . . I . . . I . . ." Head stammered.

"You . . . you . . . you . . . you're *right.* My son *is* a moron, Head. My Godsdamn horse is smarter than that little yahoo. And lucky you, he's only a Summer away from being your son-in-law."

"Don't remind me," Head moaned. "Sasha is thrilled about the whole thing. She can't wait to marry him. And I have to pay for the wedding. The thought of it gets my ulcer burning as hot as the hottest of hot Summers."

"As well it should. So listen, I didn't come here to discuss how idiotic our respective families are. I need to ask you something, face-to-face, man to man, *mano a mano.*"

"Anything, Bobbert . . ."

"Be my Foot."

". . . except that. No. No way. No how. No sir."

"Why not, may I ask?" asked the King.

"Well, Summer is coming."

"An unacceptable answer. Next excuse."

"Um, okay, I'm not worthy to fill the Functionary's pants."

"You are. You da man. You're so money, and you don't even know it. Next excuse."

"Okay, how about Summer is coming?"

"Still unacceptable. Next excuse."

"How about Foots seem to die a whole bunch, and I have a family to consider."

Bobbert shook his head as if it were a ball bouncing in a field on a muddy day. "Tough patooties. You're my new Foot. Pack up your crap. We're outta here."

"But . . . but . . . but . . ."

"But . . . but . . . but what, Headcase? Out with it."

"But Summer is coming."

LOLYTA

Loly Targetpractice—known to those in the know as Lolyta Tornadobutt, Princess of Duckseventually—regarded the odd dress and asked her handmaiden, Magistrate Illinois, "How in the name of Gods am I supposed to get this Godsdamn thing on?" Comprised entirely of $1" \times 2"$ rectangular rectangles, it was like nothing she had ever seen. The rectangles—which were all gold and covered with numbers and letters that might or might not add up to or spell something—were connected to one another by tiny wires; thus much of Loly's skin was exposed. Loly felt the dress was too haute couture for the season, but as long as Ivan Drago, the King of Dork and her future husband, approved, her opinion did not matter.

Once she finally wriggled into the garment, her brother swished into the room and exclaimed, "My, my, my, Loly, you look most fierce."

"You think so?" she asked. "Am I showing too much skin? Or maybe not enough?"

Vladymyr—known to those in the know as Vladymyr of the House Targetpractice, the Zillionth of His Name, King of the Sandals and the Ryebread, Lord of the Who-the-Heck-Knows-How-Many Kingdoms and Protector of the Elves—gave his little sister an intense once-over and said, "No question, Loly, you will be queening out on your wedding. And thank Gods for it."

"Why *thank Gods*?" she asked. "What're you so concerned about? I'm the one getting married to that stinky manhorse."

"Because," Vladymyr explained, "manhorses have short lifespans, and when he dies, I will take my rightful place on the throne."

The dress was making her itch. Scratching her back, she said, "Okay, explain to me again why you, Vladymyr of the House Targetpractice, the Zillionth of His Name, King of the Sandals and the Ryebread, Lord of the Who-the-Heck-Knows-How-Many-Kingdoms and Protector of the Elves, will succeed Ivan Drago, a full-blooded Dorki and a native of Dork, as the ruler of Dork?"

"Because, Lolyta Tornadobutt, Princess of Duckseventually, everybody knows that the ruling families throughout Easterrabbit are all about inbreeding—it's been documented on both the page and the small screen—so when Ivan Drago dies, everybody in Dork will think that you and I are dorking, and according to the Dork constitution, whoever is dorking the Queen in Dork sits on the Dork throne."

Loly shook her head dubiously and opined, "I don't think that's the exact wording in the constitution. Nor on the page. Nor on the small screen."

"That's my interpretation," Vladymyr hissed, "and as Vladymyr of the House Targetpractice, the Zillionth of His Name, King of the Sandals and the Ryebread, Lord of the Who-the-Heck-Knows-How-Many Kingdoms and Protector of the Elves, *my* interpretation is the *only* interpretation." Patting his stringy blond mane, he added, "Besides, look at my hair. That's royal hair if I've ever seen it."

"It certainly is fabulous," Loly grunted. "Hey, if you can tear yourself away from yourself, get over here."

"Why?"

"I need to show you something." She turned to Magistrate Illinois and ordered, "Take a hike, Chicago. Me and big brother need some alone time." After Illinois departed, Loly repeated, "Get over here."

"As you wish, Queen-to-be." While flitting across the room, he asked, "What is it those Dorkis call their Queens? It's starts with a K, and they always capitalize it."

"KERBANGER."

"Right, KERBANGER in caps. Is it true they used to use italics?" Vladymyr asked.

"Correct," Loly explained. "But the Dorks' printing equipment isn't particularly sophisticated, and their italics always looked lousy, thus the caps."

"Got it."

"Good. So. In a few days, I'll be KERBANGER Lolyta. How cool is that? Youngest KERBANGER in Dork history."

"That's wonderful, little sister. Now why did you want me to come over here?"

"Quick favor." Unfastening four of the rectangles, she said, "Can you pinch the tip of this, please?" She pointed at her bare breast.

Vladymyr squinched up his face at the sight of his sister's nipple. "What's this, Loly?" he inquired.

"A nipple. You've probably seen them before. Granted, never one as perfect as this."

Vladymyr mumbled, "It's not as perfect as the ones on the queynte who'll be playing you on the HBO show."

"HB *what*?"

"Small screen," he explained, then adjusted a growing bulge in his crotch and continued, "I've seen plenty of perfect nipples before. Boys have them too, you know."

"You mean you've seen other boys' nipples?" Loly asked.

"Um, no. No. No, I've seen my own nipples, and they're perfect. And girls' nipples. And lots of them. Lots and lots of them. Lots and lots and lots of them. And I know exactly what to do with girls' nipples, that's for sure."

Loly smiled. "Perfect. I was hoping you'd know what to do with nipples, because I'd like you to do that to mine."

Vladymyr puckered his lips as if he'd jammed his tongue deep into a giant lemon. "I'd rather not. That's gross."

"Why is it gross?" Loly asked, freeing her other breast. "We're siblings. And according to the page and the small screen, that's what siblings do. Do stuff with their siblings' nipples. Among other things."

"I'd rather not."

"I'd rather you did."

"It would be gross."

"It would be lovely. As future KERBANGER, I command you, Vladymyr of the House Targetpractice, the Zillionth of His Name, King of the Sandals and the Ryebread, Lord of the Who-the-Heck-Knows-How-Many Kingdoms and Protector of the Elves, to pinch my nipple as hard as you can, and not to stop until I'm either screaming or bleeding."

Vladymyr's pale face paled to the point of translucence, and several dots of sweat materialized on his forehead. "If you insist," he whispered, then gingerly reached out his right hand and grazed his sister's right nipple with his pinky, then jerked his hand away as if Loly's breast were piping hot, which it arguably was, although not as hot as the ones on the queynte who played Loly on the first season of the HBO show.

Loly said, "Really, Vladymyr? Really? That's it? That's the best you can do? I can find a duck who'd do that better."

Shaking his head, Vladymyr said, "I don't understand your obsession with ducks. You're the only person in Easterrabbit who yammers on about ducks. With everybody else in this Godsforsaken story, it's all games, and thrones, and clashes, and kings, and storms, and swords, and feasts, and crows, and dances, and dragons, and mud, and onions. But with you, it's all ducks, ducks, ducks."

As she removed her dress, Loly said, "And I don't get your obsession with dragons."

"Dragons are fab," Vladymyr pouted.

"Dragons are extinct. And nobody cares about them. Hell, there aren't even any in *The Lord of the Rings*," Loly noted.

"Yeah, but there's one in *The Hobbit*," Vladymyr said. "Smaug."

Waving her hand dismissively, Loly said, "Tolkien's a schmuck. You can't trust anybody who has that many *R*s in his name. I mean, J. R. R.? Seriously?" She paused, then continued, "So listen, are you going to pinch the hell out of my nipples or not?"

"Not."

"Fine," she simpered. "Then get out of my face, you girly-man."

"I am not a girly-man!"

"You go ahead and keep telling yourself that, Vladymyr. And send Illinois in here. I need a bath."

After the Magistrate filled up the tub, Loly climbed in and positioned herself so her head was the only part of her body not submerged in water. Once Loly was settled, Illinois turned to leave, but before she could even take a step, the future KERBANGER said, "Don't move a muscle. I need to do the thing."

The Magistrate took a deep breath and asked, "Must you?"

Loly said, "I must."

"And with me here?"

"I must," Loly repeated, then spread her legs apart and rubbed herself in the spot where virtually all of the thirteen-year-old girls in Easterrabbit like to rub themselves. Her mouth opened, her eyes went to half-mast, her breathing quickened, and Magistrate Illinois covered her ears, because she knew what was coming next:

"Oh my Gods," she yelled, *"bring it, bring it, bring it! Right there! Harder! Now softer! Now faster! Now rounder! Rounder! Rounder! Yes, yes, yes, give me those scallions, you stud! Scallion me like you've never scallioned before!"*

After Loly finished (twice), Magistrate Illinois said, "Do you still need me here, ma'am?"

Flushed, Loly panted, "Give me a minute to recover. That was a good one. Or a good two, I guess." Once she regained her composure, she complained, "If stupid Vladymyr would've tweaked my nipple like I asked, I might've gone for a tripleheader. Can you grab my robe?"

"As you wish, Lolyta."

Immediately after Loly donned her garb, there was a harsh knock at the door, so harsh that it caused the walls to shake. Loly and Illinois exchanged nervous glances, after which Loly asked, "Who's there?"

No answer—just another knock. Except it was louder.

This time Magistrate Illinois asked, "Who's there?"

Another knock. Even louder.

Loly pulled her robe tighter, grumbled, "Screw this," and then wandered over to the door and flung it open. She was greeted by a sight unlike anything she had ever seen.

Loly looked the creature up and down, taking in his long, oily black hair, his bottomless black eyes, his bulging chest, his toned arms, his flat stomach, his creative facial hair, his four legs, his shaggy tail, and his enormous horse dong. Their eyes met, and after a seemingly endless staring contest, she said, "Ivan Drago, I presume."

The manhorse nodded and grunted, "Ooga booga. Unga bunga. Moo moo moo, poo poo poo."

She gave him a half grin and said, "That's easy for you to say, handsome. Why don't you and your tail come on in here?" As Ivan Drago hopped over the threshold, Lolyta Tornadobutt, Princess of Duckseventually, asked him, "So what's your stance on nipple pinching?"

JUAN

Being that he was a jerkoff, Juan Nieve knew he would never be invited to the feast celebrating the arrival of the House Barfonme royal family, but that did not stop him from hovering outside of the castle to get a peek at what many were calling the event of the season . . . and considering the season lasted a lengthy, yet undetermined, unexplained period of time, that was saying something.

Normally he was not the type of boy to arrive at an event such as this without asking or being asked, but A) if he did not go, he would have lost one of his few chapters, and a relatively important one at that, as without this chapter, we would not meet another character who will die a painful and surprising death, and B) he was feeling randy, so he figured that rather than stay home, grab a scoop of oily mud, and pleasure himself, he would hang out by the castle and see if his Barker bloodline would impress any unattached young ladies. If that failed, he could always use his adorable direpanda—whom he had named Fourshadow—as chick-bait. And if that failed, he would go home, grab a scoop of oily mud, and pleasure himself.

Juan positioned himself by the side of the building, peeked through an open window, and found the feast a sight to behold, and a scent to besmell. The interior and exterior walls of the castle were covered with the banners of the two Houses in attendance—you're already familiar with the Barker insignia; the Barfonmes were represented by a fluffy black and white kitty cat—and the attendees were dressed in their finest finery. There was enough food on the long tables to feed all of Summerseve: yak with boar sauce, boar with yak sauce, leg of wolf with a citrus coulis, a thick stew with some red chunks that Juan could not readily identify, onion soup, onion tarts, onion juice, onion steaks, and whole onions swimming in an onion puree.

One by one, House Barker's important characters walked the dining room's red carpet, where they were accosted by a slender, red-haired, loud woman who shoved a long stick in each of their faces and asked them odd questions like "Who are you wearing?" and "Can you tell me about your latest project?" This both confused and bored Juan to no end, so he decided to relocate.

When he repositioned himself at the front of the castle, he got a gander at Sur Jagweed Sinister, and he could not look away, as Jagweed was an Easterrabbitian legend, at once revered and feared by the continent's denizens. Over the last several Summers, Jagweed had attempted to assassinate dozens of rulers, including King Rychard DeThyrd, King Hynry De-Eighth, King Solomon DeOnly, King Kong DeGrylla, King Jarry Lawlyr, King Byskit Flowyrhour, Burgyr Kyng, and Gnat King Cohl. Jagweed's plan of attack was nothing if not brave: Storm the castle all by himself, unsheath his oddly bent sword, and take down everybody in his path until he got to the throne, where he would mercilessly mutilate the ruler and endeavor to take over the region in the name of the family Sinister.

Attempt after attempt failed spectacularly, as a wobbly sword constructed from anything other than Corinthian leather made for a useless weapon. His attacks were so feeble that, upon seeing Jagweed, the Kings who were under fire inevitably went on a laughing jag that led to them choking on an onion, which led to them dying without the benefit of Jagweed's sword. This earned Sur Jagweed the moniker of the "Not-Kingslayer."

After Jagweed tripped over the House Barker threshold, he was accosted by the red-haired loudmouth, who asked the Not-Kingslayer, "Jagweed Sinister, what was it like to work with Martyn Skursaysay?"

Again perplexed and fed up with the proceedings, Juan called over Fourshadow. The direpanda, who, in a mere three days, had grown to the size of a pony, staggered to his master. Juan gawked at his pet's face and asked, "*Santo mierda bolas,*[4] Fourshadow, what have you gotten yourself into?" He kneeled down and stared at the area around the animal's mouth, which

---

4. Holy shitballs.

was covered with some sort of pinkish/purplish stain. Foreshadow gave Juan a huge lick on his face, and the jerkoff immediately discerned the source of the discoloration. "Your breath smells like a distillery. Where in the name of *Dios*⁵ did you get the grog, Fourshadow?"

Fourshadow belched, gave Juan another lick, then collapsed to the muddy Earth, where he promptly fell asleep. Juan scanned the area, concerned that Fourshadow's loud snoring would alert somebody to their presence.

Sure enough, Juan heard a man call from the not-too-distant distance: "Who dares to intrude upon this feast of feasts? I bet it's some jerkoff!"

Recognizing the voice, Juan smiled and said, "I'm not just some jerkoff. I'm *el más grande más enorme, apestosa*⁶ jerkoff!"

Approaching Juan, the man joked, "You sure are, Juan Nieve. You sure are." And then the two embraced.

"Sinjean Barker," Juan exclaimed, "my uncle from another mother."

"That I am, Juan Nieve. That I am. So, as usual, you're on the outside looking in, I see. That's unfortunate. You want me to put together a doggie bag for you?"

Rubbing his stomach, Juan admitted, "That red, chunky stew looks mighty interesting. Do you know what it is?"

"Venison with red onions," Sin explained.

"Exactly what my stomach is calling for," he rejoiced. "A heaping serving, *por favor*.⁷ And the more, the merrier. I need my strength."

"What for?" Sin asked.

Pointing to the North, Juan exclaimed, "I must protect the Wall!"

Sin pointed to the South and explained, "I believe the Wall is that way."

"Are you certain?" Juan asked.

Sin scratched his head. "Actually, I'm not. All the maps of Easterrabbit are too small to discern. Especially the one in the mass market paperback."

"And good luck finding a hardback."

---

5. Gods. (You should have this one down, too.)
6. The biggest, hugest, smelliest.
7. Please. (Spanish 101. We shouldn't have to translate this one for you, but we figure since you bought this book, you shouldn't have to think that hard.)

"I know, right? You can't even get a trade paperback, let alone a hard-cover. And those map replications you see online are a joke."

"No kidding," Juan complained. "*Mudo*[8] bloggers."

"Anyhow, why do you even want to go anywhere near the Wall?" Sin asked.

"I want to be like you, Sin. I want to join the Fraternity of the Swatch!"

After a long sigh, Sin whispered, "I think I know why you want to be a Swatchman."

"Is that so?" Juan queried. "And why is that?"

Sin put his big hand on Juan's thin shoulder and said, "My friend, no matter how hard you work, no matter how many lives you save, no matter how many of the Others you kill . . ."

From the distance, a voice cried, *"We're not the Others! We're the Awesomes, asshole!"*

". . . you will always be a jerkoff," Sin finished.

"I understand, *compadre*,"[9] Juan said. "But why should I not strive to be the best jerkoff House Barker has ever seen?"

"Why?" Sin exclaimed, his face becoming cloudy with anger. "*Why?!* Because you don't know what it's like on the Wall, man. You don't know what it's like down there in the shit. You don't know what it's like to have Charlie breathing down your neck day after day after day, to know that some Commie sniper has his rifle pointed at your heart from the second you get up, to the second you fall asleep. You don't know what it's like to see your buddy get fragged, then hold him in your arms, and hear him say with his dying breath, 'Make sure you tell LaShonda and the kids I love 'em.'" Sin wiped a thin film of sweat from his forehead, then continued, "On the plus side, the acid down by the Wall is pretty good, so there's that."

Juan roared, "Nothing you say will change my mind! *Nada!*"[10]

Sin asked, "Is that right? Ever heard of Rush Year, young Juan?"

"No."

"Ah," Sin mused, "Rush Year. It's sheer hell. Degrading. Insulting.

---

8. Dumbass. Or something like that.
9. Dude. I think.
10. Nothing. Duh.

Embarrassing. Lots of drinking. Full of boring contests that bring the story to a grinding halt. And that's all I can say, because I took an oath of silence."

Puffing up his chest, Juan blustered, "None of that scares me, *ese*."

Sin shrugged. "It should."

"Well, it doesn't. I'm pledging whether you like it or not."

Sin clapped him on the shoulder and said, "You do what you have to do, Juan Nieve. You'll never survive, of course." He looked at the castle, said, "Alrighty then, off to onion-fest," and wandered inside.

Juan felt an anger build within his soul, an emotion unlike anything he'd ever experienced. He spun around, took three running steps, tripped over the sleeping Fourshadow, and fell onto a man who was sitting in the mud. Jumping up, Juan said, "I'm sorry. I didn't see you."

"That's the first time anybody's ever said that about me." After the man pulled himself to his full height, Juan understood what he meant.

The jerkoff gawked at the stick-figured giant and asked, "How tall are you?"

The giant shrugged. "No idea what unit of measure they use around here. Feet? Meters? Cubits? Mud balls? My balls?" He offered Juan his hand and said, "Tritone Sinister, House Sinister's resident japemeister."

Shaking hands, Juan said, "Juan Nieve, House Barker's resident jerkoff."

Grinning, Tritone exclaimed, "You're a jerkoff? Godsdamn it, I'm a jerkoff, too!"

"Stop fooling with me, *comediante*.[11] You look like a Sinister."

Tritone pointed at his long legs and said, "Do these legs look like those of a Sinister? I may be a full-blooded Sinister, but when you're the only person in your family who has to duck to get into any room, you get treated like a jerkoff. I feel your pain, Shecky."

"How can they deny you? You look just like the Not-Kingslayer," Juan noted, pointing at Tritone's blond hair.

"Gods forbid." Tritone winced. "Jagweed's so ugly, it looks like he fell out of an ugly tree and hit every branch on the way down. He's so ugly that when he was born, our mother slapped the doctor. He's so ugly that calling him ugly is an insult to ugly people."

---

11. Funny dude. Or something like that.

Juan looked toward the castle. "I don't know. He seems attractive enough to me."

"You think he's handsome? Well, I don't swing that way, but that's cool. I'll put in a good word for you if you want, but he's already spoken for. And you don't want to mess with his significant other. She's nuttier than he is. And just as ugly. Similarly ugly, for that matter."

As Fourshadow let loose with a growl, Juan gave the giant a cockeyed grin. "You amuse me, japemeister."

Tritone patted himself on the back and said, "That's why they pay me the big bucks, Shecky." He pulled a leather pouch from his back pocket and thrust it at Juan. "Want a snort? We'll get ripped and talk about the joys of jerkoffdom."

Feeling completely accepted for the first time in a long time, Juan took the pouch, took a guzzle, and burbled, "Nothing would make me happier."

GATEWAY

Eyes closed, lips parted, and chest heaving, Lady Gateway Barker moaned, "That's it. That's it. Right there. Wait, slow down, slow down."

Headcase adjusted his rhythm, then sighed, "I don't know what to tell Bobbert. Should I, or shouldn't I?"

Digging her fingernails into her husband's shoulder, Gateway breathed, "You should, lover. Do it. *Do it!*"

"Just like that?" he asked. "Leave my family behind? Leave my kingdom behind? I'm the Lord of House Barker. I can't just get up and go."

Gateway wrapped her legs around Head and groaned, "If you speed it up, *I* can get up and *come.*"

Head mindlessly grinded faster, then explained, "If I become the King's Foot, our life as we know it will be done."

"If you lean to the left and pick it up," Gateway ordered, "this act as we know it will be done."

Noticing his wife's frustration, Head said, "Apologies," then made love to his wife the way a good Lord should.

That went on for a solid three seconds until the door burst open and an elderly white-bearded man stuck his head into the room. Without preamble, he uttered, "M'Lord, m'Lady, I . . ."

In unison, Head and Gateway yelled, *"Go away!"*

The door opened wider, and the man stepped farther into the room. Cupping his ear, he called, "I'm sorry, I didn't hear that. Repeat, please?"

Gateway shoved her husband off of her naked body and onto the floor, covered herself with a sheet, and roared at Head, *"I thought you were going to put my purple scrunchie on the door when we're busy!"*

Maester Blaester, the white-bearded gentleman who had been Head-case's trusty assistant for the past two Summers, said, "I thought so too, m'Lord."

Unconcerned about his unclothed tumescence, Head said, "Forgot. Distracted with this Foot business. What do you need, Blaester?"

Blaester looked up at the ceiling and asked, "Would m'Lord like to cover himself?"

Head gave Blaester a dismissive wave and explained, "We're all friends here. What brings you to our marital room?"

Still staring at the ceiling, Blaester handed Head a small square package. "This was delivered to you. By a *raven*."

Gateway stood up, pulled the bedsheet around her chest, and sneered, "*Ooooooh, a ravengram*. Nothing's more important than a *ravengram*. Nothing takes precedence over a *ravengram*." She got down on her hands and knees and peered under the bed, then queried her husband, "You seen my stash, Head?"

Ignoring Lady Barker, Head took the package from Blaester and carefully removed the covering paper, then opened the box. Inside the box was a smaller box. Inside the smaller box was an even smaller box. Inside the even smaller box was a box that was even smaller than that. This went on for six more boxes, until Head finally came to an envelope. Without even looking at what the missive said, Head noted, "This must be from your sister."

From under the bed, Gateway said, "Did she do that thing with the boxes again?"

"Indeed," Head harrumphed, opening then silently reading the letter. After two minutes of silence, Head Barker barked, *"Ha!"*

"What?" Gateway asked.

"Get this," he snarled. "Your dear sister thinks a Sinister murdered Functionary. Lysergic actually thinks that one of those inept chowderheads made it through the woods, climbed the mountains, got past the guards at the front gate, got past Functionary's personal bodyguards, and made Functionary laugh himself to death? Tritone Sinister would've clocked himself on a branch. Sugyrray Sinister would've gotten knocked out on his way up the first hill. LaDaynian Sinister would've gotten tackled before he got anywhere near the throne."

Gateway, having tracked down what she was looking for, wiggled out from under the bed, grabbed a match, and held it to the tiny ball of weede she'd rescued. She took a deep inhale, then coughed, "I agree that it probably wasn't Tritone, Sugyrray, or LaDaynian, but it sure sounds like Jagweed's M.O."

Head's tumescence shriveled. "It does, doesn't it?" He snatched a pillow from the bed, covered up his midsection, and mumbled, "Hmm, intrigue. Suddenly, after several relatively uneventful chapters, things are becoming interesting. Perhaps I should take Bobbert up on his offer. Perhaps I should be the Foot."

Gateway mumbled, "Perhaps you should." Gazing ruefully at her unfulfilled lap, she sighed. "I can take care of myself here. Alone. As usual."

Lord Headcase Barker smiled. "Then it is settled. To Capaetal Ceity I shall go! I must spread the news!" He dropped his pillow and left the room, still naked.

Watching him go, Gateway said to Maester Blaester, "And there, good sir, goes your Lord. Makes you proud to be part of the Barker braintrust, doesn't it?"

"Yes it does, m'Lady," Blaester said. "Yes it does."

MALIA

Malia Barker glared at Sasha Barker as if her older sister were a multi-tailed rodent who had found its way into the kitchen, then gnawed through a freshly killed yak that was to be the centerpiece of a holiday feast for the squad of Knights who had saved Easterrabbit from an attack by an otherworldly being that was so huge and powerful, it could only be described and named by modern scientists, but there were not any modern scientists in Easterrabbit, so said being went undescribed and unnamed, but it was nonetheless vanquished by the Knights who eventually ate a different yak, so it all worked out in the end.

Wrapped up in her breathtaking macaroni sculpture, Sasha Barker did not notice her sister's glower.

Malia's anger stemmed in part from the fact that her macaroni art was not going as well as Sasha's. (Of course it was not going well. Up until the previous day, this had been a sewing class, but the head of the school, Pryncipal Prynce, decided that sewing was a useless skill in Easterrabbit, an understandable choice, because it was impossible to sew an outfit that would survive the ever-changing elements. Malia did not care about the weather. Malia loved sewing. Malia hated pasta. But it did not matter what Malia liked or did not like, because be it macaroni or sewing, there had to be some sort of arena in which it could be demonstrated that the Barker sisters were loving rivals . . . except without the loving.) Malia's circles were ovals, her squares were triangles, and for the life of her, she could not figure out how to make layers. Sasha, with only several hours of practice, had become a pasta magician, a craftsgirl with the skills of a noodle artist thrice her age, this despite the fact that she had never previously touched a piece of spaghetti. Right now, she was at work on what was turning out to be a masterpiece: a bust of her father Head's head. The rest of the class gazed at it adoringly, and the teacher, Sistyr Glynda Roesy Raegan Melvyn's expression was a combination of pride and ecstasy.

Malia wanted to smash Sasha's statue into a million little pieces, then use the shards to wipe that look off of the Sistyr's face. But she was a resolute little girl, so she went back to work, determined to make her statuette of Sasha's limbless body look like what Sasha's limbless body would look like, rather than an ovular rectangle. Or maybe a rectangular oval.

However, she was having trouble concentrating, as Sasha and her friends were chatting at a volume inappropriate for a fusilli lesson. (If Malia had dared speak that loudly, Sistyr G.R.R.M. would have gouged her face with her notoriously rusty sword.) The topic, as usual, was Sasha's love life.

Sasha's blond-haired friend Jennyfer squealed, "Goofrey Barfonme *so* loves you."

Her brown-haired friend Jennyfur added, "And you *so* love him."

Her red-haired friend Jennyferr predicted, "And you guys are *totally* getting married."

Her black-haired friend Boberta offered, "And you are so going to bear many children."

Throwing down a handful of ziti, Sasha said, "Oh. My. Gods. You guys are, like, totally grotty to the max. I'm gonna, like, totally puke. Like, *ewwww!*"

It took all of Malia's restraint to keep from jamming her ovular rectangle down Sasha's throat.

Sasha continued, "So I'm, like, going for a walk yesterday, and Goof comes up to me and was all like, 'Hi,' and I was all like, 'Hi,' and he was all like, 'You look lovely today,' and I was all like, 'I know,' and I could totally tell he was trying to look down my shirt, so I was all like, 'Are you checking out my boobs,' and he was all like, 'No way,' then he totally ran away. As if?"

As all five of the girls giggled like chirping baby birds asking their mama for either breakfast or dinner, Malia threw up in her mouth a little bit.

Right then, Sistyr G.R.R.M. knelt beside Malia, glared at her ditalini, and sneered, "You call that art, girl?"

"No," Malia sneered back. Pointing at Sasha's creation, she added, "And I don't call *that* art either."

"Well, then," Sistyr G.R.R.M. queried, "what would you call it?"

"Lunch."

"You do not speak to a Sistyr that way, young Lady. You do not speak out of turn."

Pointing at the gaggle of giggling girls, Malia pointed out, "*They're* speaking out of turn."

"When somebody creates a work of genius like Sasha, we make exceptions," the Sistyr humphed.

Malia raised a single eyebrow and mused, "Nobody has ever used the words *genius* and *Sasha* in the same sentence. My sister is dumber than dirt. The ditz gets by on her looks." Then, whispering, she continued, "Kind of like her mother."

Gesturing to the door, Sistyr G.R.R.M. screamed, "I don't care if you're a Barker, or a Sinister, or a Targetpractice, or an Aaron, or a Barfonme, or if you're from one of the families from books three or five whose names nobody can pronounce and/or remember! You do not speak to a Sistyr with that tone! *Out!*"

Malia tossed a handful of tricolored gemelli into the air, screamed back, "My pleasure!" then sprinted across the room, down the stairs, and out the front door, where she ran toward the comforting fur of Stinky, her beloved direpanda. Stinky gooily licked his mistress's face, then made a happy direpanda noise when he got a gander of his brother, Fourshadow. The two animals romped around and about as if they had not a care in the world, which irked Malia to no end, so she told Stinky, "*Attack!*"

Stinky gave Malia a quizzical look, then gave Fourshadow an even gooier lick than he'd given Malia. Staring disgustedly at her pet, she said, "Wimps."

"*Maniquí,*[12] how dare you disrespect my direpanda!"

Malia spun around and smiled at her jerkoff brother Juan. Running into his embrace, she said, "Thank Gods, a Barker with a brain."

---

12. Dummy. (But he said it nicely, because he likes Malia, and vice versa. Isn't that sweet?)

Juan hugged her back, then, noticing the cloudy expression on Malia's face, said, *"Mierda,* I know *that* look."

"Yes." She pouted. "Sasha is being Sasha."

Juan took her hand and said, "Come, *mi querido,* I have something that will cheer you up." He led Malia to the jousting field on the other side of the castle, where a gaggle of young men covered in armor were paired off, clumsily thrusting their swords at one another. On the far end of the lawn, a man clad in a short-sleeved chainmail shirt and too-tight chainmail shorts blew his whistle and roared, "Alright, buttercups, that's the worst display of swordsmanship I've seen in Summers! Drop and give me fifty! And if I see anybody not eating mud, he's running laps! Actually, you'll *all* run laps!" He jogged to the center of the field and bopped two of the boys on their helmets. "You two dummies, drop your cocks and grab your steel. I want to see some fighting."

In unison, the boys chanted, "Yes, Sur Anklewankle!"

As he walked away from his students, Sur Anklewankle noticed Juan, pointed at the young man, and said, "Ladies, there's a guy you should pay attention to. He's a jerkoff, but he's got serious game."

In unison, the boys repeated, "Yes, Sur Anklewankle!"

To Juan, the teacher said, "You wanna take over my class? These buttercups are driving me batshit crazy."

Before Juan could answer, one of the two boys Sur Anklewankle singled out chirped, "I'm ready to battle, Sur."

The other parroted, "As am I!"

Juan leaned down to Malia and said, "Do those voices sound familiar?"

Malia grinned. "Bobb and Goof."

"Correcto!"[13]

Her grin widening, Malia hissed, "This'll be fun. Bobb'll wipe the floor with him. Sasha's boyfriend is going *down.*"

Juan frowned. "I'm afraid not."

"You would be against Bobb?" Malia asked. "He's so much better than Goof. *I'm* even better than Goof."

"It's not about who's better," Juan explained. "It's about politics."

Before Malia could ask what politics had to do with fighting, she heard

---

13.   Correct. Duh.

the familiar sound of steel on steel. Five clinks into the bout, Bobb fell to the muddy ground with a loud squish, then, in a flat voice, said, "Ouch, ouch, ouch. Never have I suffered such an embarrassing defeat. I don't know what hurts worse, my soul or my leg."

Goof raised his sword above his head, jumped up and down, and giggled, "Yay me, yay me, yay me! I'm the greatest jouster *ever*! Yay me, yay me, yay me!"

Bobb stood up, seemingly not the least bit hurt, removed his helmet, and told Goof, "You're the greatest, Goof." Then Bobb and Sur Anklewankle rolled their eyes at one another.

Malia said to Juan, "Bobb took a dive, didn't he."

Juan nodded. *"Sí."*

"Why?"

"Because Goof is a *quejumbrosa poco perra*,[14] and if he loses to a Barker, he'll whine to his father, and if he whines to his father, his father will whine to Lord Barker, and if the King whines to Lord Barker, Lord Barker will whine at Bobb, and the cycle of whining will never end, all because Goof is a *quejumbrosa poco perra*."

Grinning an evil grin, Malia queried, "Does Sasha know her future husband is a *quejumbrosa poco perra*?"

"No," Juan explained. "The *idiota*[15] is blinded by love."

Goof stumbled over, removed his helmet, and asked Malia, "I apologize that you had to see that. It must be a great embarrassment to you to see your blood be vanquished."

Over Goof's shoulder, Malia saw Bobb flipping young Master Barfonme the double bird. Biting her cheek to keep from laughing, Malia said, "I have never seen such a performance, and for that, I'm more embarrassed than you'll ever know."

As Goof galloped away, Malia told Juan, "Goofrey Barfonme and Sasha Barker is a match made in heaven."

Juan frowned. "Or *infierno*."[16]

---

14. Whiny little bitch.

15. Idiot. That wasn't the word Juan was looking for, but apparently there's no Spanish translation for "ditz." If you know of one, please contact us at GameOfGroans@gmail.com.

16. Hell. (So dramatic. So very, very dramatic.)

ALLBRAN

Letting loose a series of prickly tush toots that were felt two floors below, Allbran Barker stared out the window and sighed. There on the front lawn stood Bobb and Juan, shooting arrows at a newly constructed mud statue that looked suspiciously like Goofrey Barfonme. Juan's aim was slightly better than Bobb's, and every time Bobb missed, he would snarl, "*Bastard*," to which Juan would respond, "You mean *jerkoff*." Allbran had no idea what they were talking about, but he did not care; all he wanted was to join his brothers in their adventures. Unfortunately, he knew that this was not to be, partly because he was a little boy, and partly because of his uncontrollable flatulence.

He tried to manage his gastrointestinal issues, Allbran did, following the advice given to him by Summerseve's best doctors: Eat lots of raw onions. To Allbran, it felt like the vegetable compounded the problem, but he did not want to anger his parents, so he choked down one huge onion with each meal. He knew it made him unpleasant to smell both coming and going, but maybe someday the treatment would work.

Suddenly bored with his bedroom, Allbran hopped out of his window and pulled himself up to the castle's roof. The roof was his home away from home, a place where he could be alone with his thoughts and his farts, a place where nobody would tease him for being small and smelly, a place where he could be himself.

Allbran noticed that Bobb and Juan had ceased their archery and were riding their respective direpandas. He shook his head, knowing that he would never mount his pet Hinky, because that would be degrading, and if anybody knew what it was like to be degraded, it was Allbran. Bobb and

Juan's direpandas eventually got fed up with the state of affairs, so they bucked off their riders and ran off toward town, with Bobb and Juan following close behind. Again bored, Allbran wandered along the perimeter of the castle roof, balancing on the ledge as if he were an expert ledge-balancer.

Right as he turned the gargoyled corner, Allbran heard two voices from below, one a man's, and one a woman's. The voices both sounded snobby, tinged with a sense of self-entitlement that made him cringe. The man said, "No way that Headcase Barker could be a good Foot. He governs like a dodo bird flies: badly."

The woman said, "Do you realize just how horrible your metaphors are?"

"My metaphors are fine," the man complained. "They're like muddy flowers on a warm Summer day."

"Just stop," the woman exhaled, then, after a pause, added, "I can't argue with your assessment of the current regime. Taxes are up, unemployment is up, and interest rates are up."

The man said, "The populace seems happy . . ."

The woman interrupted, "The populace, the populace, it's always about the populace. You can't be a good leader if you spend all your time worrying about the populace. Look at King Goerge at House Busch. He doesn't give two shits about the populace, and House Busch is the wealthiest region in Easterrabbit. When you become Goofy's Foot, you should get the little prick to emulate King Goerge."

"Good idea. Hey, have you spoken to Aunt Millye and Uncle Iryving?"

"No. I owe them a ravengram."

"Well, you don't have to worry about that."

"Why?" the woman asked.

"They're waiting for us back at the castle."

The woman groaned. "They always show up without sending us a ravengram beforehand. We're never prepared." She paused, then asked, "Speaking of prepared, what's going on down there? Something bothering you?"

"What?" the man chuckled, sounding nervous to Allbran's ear. "Bothering me? Nothing's bothering me at all. I'm good. As a matter of fact, I'm *great*."

"That what's the holdup?"

"I'm tired," the man whined. "I can't always work on command."

"Don't get defensive," the woman said. "It happens to a lot of guys."

"Not to me!" the man blustered.

"Except for that time last week," the woman pointed out.

"I was drunk."

"Whatever." After a pause, the woman asked, "Do you want me to kiss it?"

"That's what I wanted in the first place."

"Why didn't you say so?" she asked. Allbran then heard some slurping noises that made him giggle. He covered his mouth so as not to be detected.

After a minute or two, the woman mumbled, "Still nothing."

The man said, "Here, let me try something."

Allbran then heard a quiet slapping sound. He kneeled down to get a better sense of what was happening, then slipped and tumbled off the roof. He would have fallen to the ground had he not grabbed the ledge of the window of the room on which he was eavesdropping.

As Allbran hauled himself up, the man and the woman simultaneously screamed. When he peeked his nose over the sill, he saw that it was Queen Cerevix Barfonne and her twin brother, Sur Jagweed "The Not-Kingslayer" Sinister. The Queen was lying on the bed, naked except for her bejeweled crown, while the Not-Kingslayer was completely naked, gripping his shriveled, limp manhood as if it were a sword. A small sword, granted, but a sword nonetheless.

Jagweed let go of his penis, grabbed a sheet from the bed, and covered himself. "What did you see?" he demanded.

"What I saw here," Allbran claimed, "was a brother and sister doing the kind of thing that most brothers and sisters in Easterrabbit do, because, according to those who have seen this sort of thing, Easterrabbit is the land of doing your brother and sister. What I saw here has been documented in a number of mediums—on both the page and the small screen, for example—so there's no way I couldn't know what I saw here." He paused, then added, "That all being said, I'm not sure what I saw here. But it didn't look like much."

Queen Cerevix sneered, "Exactly, Allbran: nothing much."

Jagweed wheeled on his sister and roared, *You said it happens to all guys!*

"No," she explained, "I said it happens to a *lot* of guys. Don't put words in my mouth." She stood up and grabbed her robe. "As a matter of fact, don't put anything in my mouth. We're done here."

Jagweed's face turned beet red, and, if it was at all possible, his manhood shrank even more. *"We're not done until I say we're done!"* he screamed.

Pointing at her brother's crotch, the Queen said, "Tell that to him."

After a wordless scream, Jagweed Sinister spun on Allbran and accused, "This is your fault, you Barker scum. I was doing fine until you dropped in."

Cerevix barked a single laugh, then further barked, "Sure you were, brother dear. Sure you were."

Ignoring his sister, Jagweed continued, "You'll pay for this, boy."

Chuckling, the Queen pointed at Allbran and sneered, "Pull down his pants and see if he wants to give it a go, brother dear." She slipped the robe off her shoulders, exposing her firm breasts. "You like these, Allbran?"

Blushing, Allbran stammered, "I . . . I . . . I . . . don't have anything to compare them to."

In the blink of an eye, Jagweed was kneeling directly in front of Allbran, their faces inches apart. "Listen, boy," the Not-Kingslayer whispered, "first of all, my sister has the best jugs in Easterrabbit, so you best pay them their proper respect. Second of all, what you saw here, you *didn't* see here. Got it?"

"What I saw here," Allbran repeated, "was a brother and sister doing the kind of thing that most brothers and sisters in Easterrabbit do, because, according to those who have seen this sort of thing . . ."

Cerevix interrupted, "Like I said, Allbran, you didn't see much."

Jagweed roared, "You saw plenty!" then emitted a wordless growl, picked up Allbran by his neck, and threw the boy out the window.

On his way down, the strangest thought went through Allbran's head, a thought dripping with a sense of déjà vu, a thought that came from nowhere and everywhere, a thought that seemed as if it were thrown into the chapter for legal reasons: *Hasn't something like this happened before? . . . And didn't it happen some other way that was more serious and less slapstick-y? . . . And maybe not to me, exactly, but some other version of me . . . A version of me who is cute, and cuddly, and doesn't understand the concept of incest, and doesn't fart quite as much . . .*

After landing on the mud, Allbran discharged a queef that sounded like a whimper. And then his world went brown.

TRITONE

The thing Tritone Sinister hated most about being Tritone Sinister was the difficulty he had strolling the streets incognito. As far as he knew, he was the tallest man on the continent—he was certainly the tallest member of a royal family—so he was not surprised that the majority of normal-sized citizens gawked at him all day every day, but it hurt nonetheless. This morning, as he wandered through the Mall of Ameyrika in central Summerseve, he felt hundreds of eyes give him judgmental once-overs—as usual—and it irked him to no end. Just as he was about to take his leave, he stumbled onto something he knew would cheer him up: his nephew.

Goofrey Barfonme was standing in front of a vendor, clad in a white puffy pirate shirt and his trademark pink pantaloons, gawking at the towering pile of diamonds on his table. He picked up the biggest rock and held it close to his eye, inspecting the jewel as if he knew what he was looking for, after which he stuck it in his mouth and bit down, then spit out the diamond along with three teeth. He lisped to the vendor, "I'll take it."

As Goof pulled a handful of bills from his purse, Tritone quietly tiptoed toward the boy, coming to a stop a bit behind him, just to the left. He reached over Goof's head and tapped him on the right shoulder. The boy spun to his right, and was greeted by the sight of nothing. Tritone then slid over to the Goof's other side, and jabbed him on his left shoulder. Goof again spun, and again saw nothing. Realizing this could go on all day, Tritone said, "Hey, Shecky, 101 B.C. called. It wants its haircut back."

Goofrey beamed. "Uncle Tritone! You're funny."

"Good to know somebody agrees with me on that one. Even if it's somebody like you, who's so dumb that he thinks a blood vessel is a ship."

Scratching his head, Goof asked, "What do you mean?"

"Forget it," Tritone said. "So you hear about your pal Allbran?"

"He farted?"

Rolling his eyes, Tritone sighed, "Of *course* he farted, Shecky. No, he fell off his roof. He's probably going to die. Or maybe not." After a beat, he added, "Actually, I know what's going to happen to him, but I can't say, because I'm not sure how much foreshadowing I'm allowed to do here." Goof gave him a blank look. "You don't know what foreshadowing is, do you?" Goof shook his head. "I didn't think so." He picked up one of the vendor's diamonds, handed it to Goof, and offered, "Here's some dessert, genius. Enjoy."

"Thanks," Goof grinned, then popped the jewel into his mouth. Another bite, another broken tooth, and another eye roll from Uncle Tritone.

"Good Gods, Goof, you become more kingly each day. Can't wait until Bobbert bites it, and you take over." After a beat, he added, "Crap. I think I foreshadowed too much. Anyhow, go see Lord and Lady Barker and tell them how sorry you are about Allbran."

Goof picked up another diamond and said, "But I'm *not* sorry."

"Doesn't matter. You're a politician. Be political. Make nice. Now."

"I don't want to," Goof whined. "You're not the boss of me!"

"Kid, I've only got one nerve left, and you're getting on it. Go see the Barkers!"

"*No!*"

"No?"

"*No!*"

Glaring at Goof, Tritone murmured, "Don't make me zitz you, Shecky."

"Go ahead and zitz me, Uncle! You can't make me do what I don't want to do!"

"Fine. Make a mental note of this . . . oh, wait, I see you're out of paper. That's probably why you always enter into a battle of wits unarmed. Ordinarily, people live and learn, but you just live. But don't start thinking now, because it might sprain your brain. You know that we all sprang from apes, but you didn't spring far enough. I'd ask you how old you are, but I doubt you can count that high. Hey, can I borrow your face, because my ass wants to take a vacation . . ."

With tears pouring down his face, Goof cried, "Stop! Stop! I'll go!

I'll go!" And then he ran off toward the Barker castle, bawling the entire way.

Now in a cheery mood, Tritone whistled a happy little tune, then turned on his heel and crashed into the Barfonme family bodyguard, Sandstorm Leghorn. The three-armed man snarled, "I seen whatcha did to Master Goofrey, Tritone. And I don't like it."

Tritone grabbed his manhood and asked, "Is that so? Well, how do you like this, quintaped? If ugliness were a crime, you'd be beheaded. *Zzzzzzing!*"

Sandstorm hit the muddy ground as if he'd been stabbed in the heart. As he crawled away, he shook his fist at the giant and said, "You haven't heard the last of me, Tritone Sinister!"

Shrugging at the jewel vendor, Tritone said, "Foreshadowing."

The vendor nodded and repeated, "Foreshadowing, indeed."

LOLYTA

Lolyta Targetpractice was naked, and not ashamed in the least.

The sun was setting on the horizon, and the wind was blowing from the East; the grass rippled and the leaves waved in the breeze. Loly turned her face to the sky and beamed at the sun. As the yellow orb warmed her face, she felt a stirring in her loins. Unable to help herself, she lowered herself onto the warm grass, lay on her back, inched her hand below her waist, and put her index and middle fingers inside the warmth between her legs. As her special area became wetter and wetter, she fell deeper and deeper into herself; the world disappeared, and it was her, and her alone.

As Loly moved closer to the brink, she heard a voice: "Sweetie, you look fierce." Loly opened her eyes, and there was Vladymyr, kneeling over her, his hand hovering over her nipple. "Would you like me to give it a pinchie-pinch?" he asked.

Her brain said "No" but her mouth said "Yes."

"As you wish, my KERBANGER." And then, as he caressed the moistness between her thighs, Vladymyr Targetpractice squeezed his sister's nipple as hard as he could.

Right then, right at that moment, right at the height of the pain, Loly felt the release that she craved each and every moment of each and every day. She emitted a wordless moan, and then . . .

Loly's eyes opened, and reality came crashing down upon her. She was not lying in the middle of a beautiful field getting a handjob from her brother, but rather lying in her bed, on the morning of the day she was to wed Ivan

Drago. For a brief moment, she could not decide which was more appealing: receiving hand pleasure from her effeminate brother, or marrying a half man/half horse. After mulling it over, she decided it was a tie, but if she got hitched, she would get a ton of great presents, so she rolled out of bed, slapped on her wedding dress (which consisted of a piece of string and two feathers), called to Magistrate Illinois that she should deliver her pre-wedding brunch, and padded to the dining room.

And what a brunch it was.

The pre-meal snack was a three-foot-long, two-foot-high piece of lemon bread, which was filled with raw chunks of boar, yak, venison, pheasant, and lizard. After slathering it in a butter concocted with the semen of a bull, she ate every single inch of the loaf, after which she licked the plate. Illinois then brought Loly the first course, a foot-high pile of scrambled platypus eggs seasoned with tree bark. Again, the future KERBANGER ate every bite and slurped every morsel from the plate. Then came the center-piece of the meal: three-dozen onions, finely chopped, sculpted into a sculpture of Ivan Drago's manhood. After staring at this work of art, Loly attacked it as if she had not seen onions or manhood in a million Summers. Dessert was the least memorable part of the meal, but impressive nonetheless: mudfruit drizzled with a condiment the Dorkis considered their greatest culinary contribution: mud. Again she cleared the plate, but this time, she did not lick it.

After pushing herself away from the table, Loly belched and called to the Magistrate, "Yo, Illinois, let's get this party started right! What's next?"

Illinois jogged into the room and said, "You will receive your gifts, KER-BANGER, after which you will proceed directly to the center of town and become Ivan Drago's betrothed."

Loly clapped her hands as if she were a child (which she was, albeit with the libido of three adults), and screeched, "Goody, goody, goody! Presents, presents, presents! Gimme, gimme, gimme!"

Magistrate Illinois then handed Loly gift after gift after gift, and nary a one of them was the least bit appealing, as they were all knickknacks made by Dorkis, fit for Dorkis. But the Targetpractice family, save for Vla-dymyr, was a polite bunch, so she told Illinois, "Send thank-you notes to everybody. But remember, these folks can't read, so don't spend too much time on them."

"As you wish, KERBANGER." Illinois curtsied. "But there is still one more gift." She then handed Loly a large, nondescript box marked FRAGILE.

Smiling, Loly said, "This can't be from a Dorki. They don't know what *fragile* means."

Illinois agreed, "I agree. They're idiots, on both the page and the small screen." And then the two of them laughed, and laughed, and laughed.

When they regained their composure, Loly opened the box, and, after digging through a pile of Styrofoam peanuts, pulled out a blue egg. And then a red one. And then a purple one. And then a green one. And then an orange one. And then a yellow one. And then a note, which she handed to her Magistrate.

Illinois cleared her throat, then read, "To the once and future KER-BANGER, I offer you these eggs. I do not know what kind of eggs they are, but I know they are important, so don't drop any of them. And let them incubate for at least 175 pages. And whatever you do, DO NOT UNDER ANY CIRCUMSTANCES BALANCE THEM ON YOUR SHOULDERS WHILE WALKING THROUGH A FIRE." Magistrate asked Loly, "Why would anybody walk through a fire with eggs balanced on their shoulders?"

Loly shrugged. "No idea. That's just about the silliest thing I've ever heard. Walking through a fire with eggs balanced on your shoulder . . . ridiculousness, sheer ridiculousness." She then picked up the blue egg and promptly dropped it.

Without noticing the fallen egg, Magistrate finished reading the note: "P.S. Don't drop the eggs. Especially the blue one."

Loly asked, "What's so special about the blue one? Why not the yellow one, or the green . . ." Before she finished the thought, she was overtaken by a stench worse than that of a Dorki sewage plant. As she ran from the room, Loly threw up in her mouth a little bit.

After she cleansed the taste of vomit from her tongue with some onion juice, Loly hustled to the *chuppah* at the center of town, where Ivan Drago, a Dorki reverend, and Vladymyr awaited her arrival. Before she went under the *chuppah*, Vladymyr pulled her aside and whispered, "Don't forget, when horsey-boy dies, I'm King."

Loly mumbled, "Or Queen."

"I heard that," Vladymyr huffed, then spun around and walked right into a Dorki's hindquarters. Purely on instinct, the Dorki bucked, then kicked Vladymyr in the midsection. He doubled over, sat on the ground, and winced. "Godsdamn it," he whined. "You got mud all over my suit."

Ivan Drago grunted at Loly, then beckoned her to the *chuppah*. He nodded at the reverend and said, "Ooga booga."

The reverend nodded back and agreed, "Ooga booga." He then turned to the throng of Dorkis and preached, "Booga booga boogity boo! Oonga doonga Ivan Drago bobbity bobbity bobbity Lolyta Targetpractice, Princess of Duckseventually zippity doo dah! Blahbitty blah blah, na na na na, hey hey, giggidy giggidy goo, zabida babida zabida KERBANGER!"

The crowd then let loose with an almost violent cheer, after which the reverend motioned that Loly and Ivan Drago should kiss. Ivan Drago kneeled down and put his face an inch or two in front of Loly's, seemingly nervous to make the first move. After an awkward minute, Loly grabbed Ivan Drago's long ponytail, pulled his head close, and mashed her lips against his. Ivan Drago moaned, and his horse manhood became engorged with whatever the hell it was that coursed through the body of a Dorki.

Loly and Ivan Drago broke the embrace, and then the crowd chanted in unison, "Oonga boonga KERBANGER! Oonga boonga KERBANGER! Oonga boonga KERBANGER!" Then they dumped bottles and bottles of Dorki wine over both of the Targetpractices.

The Targetpractices both licked the wine from their respective lips, after which they collapsed face-first in the mud.

The crowd went silent. Ivan Drago and the reverend stared at the fallen Targetpractices for a brief second, then the reverend nudged Vladymyr with his toe; he did not move. The reverend looked at Ivan Drago. Ivan Drago looked at the reverend. The reverend then took a breath and said, "So what do you think?"

Ivan bent over and held his hand just in front of Loly's mouth. "Perfect. Alive, but out cold." He turned to the crowd and said, "Okay, they'll be up in ten minutes, so let's light this candle. I'd like to call to order the fifteenth meeting of the Brotherhood of the Committee of the Bureau of Dorkis for a Marxist State. The first item on our agenda was the last item from last week, and that is making a decision on our slogan. Me, I think it should be something about the group philosophy rather than us as a horsepeople."

From the middle of the crowd, somebody yelled, "Why? All horsepeople are equal! And equality amongst the masses is the whole point!"

"I understand that, Ivan Bill," Ivan Drago placated, "but if all the horsepeople are equal, what's the point of mentioning them? That's a given, so by focusing on that, we're not advancing anything, but rather stating the obvious. If you'll recall, Ivan Dave put forth, 'History repeats itself, first as tragedy, second as farce, third as epic fantasy,' which I think sums up our philosophy quite well; we're all about learning from our mistakes and making the future a better place to be where everyone gets to star in a chapter told from their perspective, even if they die later on in the book. Now what was it that you countered with last week?"

"'All for one, and one for all,'" Ivan Bill said.

Ivan Drago shook his head. "How does that relate to Marxism? For that matter, how does that relate to *anything*?"

Ivan Bill explained, "It's a simple dissemination of Communist theory."

A female voice called out, "*Too* simple, as far as I'm concerned. And stupid."

Ivan Bill said, "How about we put it to a vote? Ivan Dave's Karl Marx ripoff versus my catchy little line?"

"It's not catchy," the female voice noted. "It's stupid. If we want to be simplistic, why don't we just use 'Power to the proletariat' or something."

Somebody yelled, "That's Lenin! We're Marx!"

Just then, Vladymyr let out a huge snore, and Ivan Drago said, "Ahhh, crap. They're getting up. Meeting adjourned! *Hasta la victoria siempre!*"

As one, the crowd yelled back, "Until victory always!"

Loly sat up several seconds later, blinked into Ivan Drago's face, and asked, "What happened?"

Her new husband said, "Ooga booga," then pinched her nipple.

Loly gave Ivan Drago a salacious grin and said, "How about we consummate this marriage?"

Ivan Drago pointed at his engorged horse manhood, pointed at the *chuppah,* and said, "Boogie oogie oogie?"

Surmising that he wanted to consummate right here and now, right in front of everybody—and that was a correct supposition on Loly's part, because consummating in front of everybody is one of the things that pop culture critics have cited as a particularly memorable (if not a tad fetishistic) plot point—she shrugged, removed her tiny wedding dress, spread apart her thighs, caressed her new husband's horse manhood, and said, "Sure, Ivan Drago, what the heck, let's boogie oogie oogie."

JUAN

J uan tiptoed into Allbran's bedroom and was shocked by the boy's condition. "My poor *hermano seudo*,"[17] he growled. "I shall destroy the *cabrón*[18] who hurt you! The man who put you in this bed shall pay with his life!"

Allbran's eyes popped open. "Oh, hey Juan," he smiled. *"Cómo está usted, jerkoff?"*[19]

Juan put his hand on Allbran's shoulder. "Tell me where it hurts, *semental pastels*."[20]

Stretching his limbs happily as if he'd just woken up from a deep, peaceful slumber (which he had), Allbran said, "Nowhere."

"Not here?" Juan asked, punching Allbran in the bicep.

"Well, *now* it does," Allbran said, rubbing the tender area.

Juan patted the boy's arm and whispered, "There, there, young soldier. You shall heal soon."

"I'm healed now," Allbran pointed out, then sat up and tried to get out of the bed. Before his feet could touch the floor, Juan punched him in the gut. Allbran doubled over and coughed, "Hey, cut it out!"

"You are quite infirm, Allbran," he said, then backhanded his brother across the cheek. "You must get your rest. Now go to sleep."

"But I'm not tired, and I won't be able to fall . . ."

---

17. Sorta-kinda brother.
18. Insert your own epithet. The more vulgar, the better.
19. How are you, jerkoff?
20. Stud cakes.

Before Allbran could finish his sentence, Juan coldcocked him in the temple with the butt end of his sword.

When Allbran was completely unconscious, Juan gently, lovingly caressed his cheek and whispered, "Rest, sweet prince. Recover. Get healthy. You'll be up and about in no time at all." He tiptoed backward toward the door, but before he could get out of the room, he crashed into someone or something. *"Mil perdones,"*[21] he said.

"Enough with this odd language of yours, jerkoff. I order you to speak a weird, bastardized brand of English. You're in Summerseve, for Gods' sake, where everybody speaks a weird, bastardized brand of English. No clue why. I mean, it's not like saying 'Gods' instead of 'God,' or spelling 'sir' *s-u-r* adds anything to the proceedings, you know?"

Juan spun around, and stood face-to-face with Lady Gateway Barker. They stared at each other for a moment, then Juan asked, "Why do you always talk to me in such a harsh manner, m'Lady? Why don't you like me?"

"Hmm," Gateway wondered, "gee, gosh, why don't I like you, let me think, oh, right: *My husband boned some slut and out came you.*" She took a deep breath, rubbed her temples, and apologized, "Apologies. That's no way for a Lady to speak. It's been a long day, what with Allbran in such pain . . ."

Young Barker's eyes popped open, and he exclaimed, "I'm really not in any pain, Mother." Again, Juan smacked him upside the head with his sword, and again, Allbran fell unconscious.

Glaring at her sleeping son, Gateway said, "Like I was saying before I was so *rudely* interrupted, it's been a long day, and I need to unwind." Pulling a pile of Godsweede from her purse, she asked the jerkoff, "Do you indulge?"

Smiling, Juan exclaimed, *"El infiernos a los que sí, perra!"*[22]

Lady Gateway said, "No clue what that means, but I'm going to go with, 'Let's smoke.'"

"Close enough."

Fifteen minutes later, Gateway and Juan were lying on the floor and

---

21. My bad.
22. Hells to the yeah, bitch!

staring at the ceiling, their heads touching. Gateway rambled, "Snakes are poor denizens of hell. They have come slithering through the tall weeds to face the puddles of opaque lizards. Trying to get to sunny Los Angeles, *boo-ya*. It's the awful peacoat making me look like a self-defeated self-murdering false thug."

Juan said, "No clue what that means, but you are *soplando mi mente*."[23] He paused, then added, "But if I may be honest, I'd rather you were *que sopla mi polla*."[24]

"No clue what that means." Gateway inhaled. "But it sure sounds pretty." After letting out an endless stream of smoke, she asked, "So what's this I hear about you pledging for the Fraternity of the Swatch?"

"Oh, *caca*,[25] I have to go say farewell to Malia!"

"Why Malia?" Gateway asked. "We're, like, sixty-three pages in to this thing, and as far as anybody knows, you barely have a relationship with her. We know you're tight with Allbran because you're visiting him in his sickbed . . ."

"I'm not sick," Allbran called out.

". . . and you shot arrows with Bobb, so we know you're pals with him," Gateway continued, "and we know that Head is your jerkoff father."

"What's your point?" Juan asked.

"My point is," Gateway said, "here you are going away to party at the Wall for who-knows-how-many seasons, and the one member of my family you go out of your way to say good-bye to is Malia? What's that about?"

Juan stood up and struggled to gain his balance. After he found solid footing, he rubbed his bloodshot eyes and explained, "I forgot what you just said."

Gateway sat up and scratched her head. "Wait, what were we talking about?" she asked.

"I don't remember," Juan said.

"Me neither."

"Couldn't have been that important." He cleared his throat, then said, "Okay, I'm off to join the Frat."

---

23. Blowing my mind.
24. Blowing my cock.
25. Poopy.

"If things get tough on the Wall, remember this, jerkoff: When you're in your normal, square city, and you're having a normal, square daydream, hang it up and see what the next daydream brings. Like the hoo-hah dude once told me, play your guitar, girl, play your guitar."

A single tear rolled down Juan's cheek. "No clue what that means, but that's beautiful, man." They stared meaningfully and wordlessly into each other's eyes, then he tiptoed backward toward the stairwell, but before he could get out of the room, he crashed into someone or something. *"Mil perdones, otra vez,"*[26] he said.

"Hey, watch where you're going, Shecky."

Juan spun around, and stood face-to-chest with Tritone Sinister. They stared at each other for a moment, then Juan asked, "Who's Shecky?"

"Never mind. So what's this I hear about you pledging for the Fraternity of the Swatch?"

"*Wow,*[27] word gets around fast."

"I keep my ear to the ground, baby. So listen, how're you getting to the Wall?"

"Sinjean Barker and I are riding together," Juan explained.

"Sinjean Barker?!" Tritone exclaimed. "He's so ugly, he makes blind kids cry. But I won't tell him that, because he's, you know, insane. He ever tell you that story about Hamburger Hill?"

"No."

"How about Operation Eagle Pull?"

"No."

"The Ho Chi Minh Order?"

"No."

"The Second Battle of Quang Tri?"

"No."

"The Tet Offensive? I *know* he told you about the Tet Offensive."

"He didn't."

"Yeah, well, you're better off. So at any rate, I'm tagging along with you, Sheckys."

"Why?"

---

26. My bad again.
27. Wow.

"Us jerkoffs have to stick together." Tritone smiled. "Plus I have to get out of Summerseve. This place is as exciting as watching paint dry on a piece of growing grass." After Juan remained expressionless, Tritone asked, "Not funny?"

"Not really," Juan answered.

Tritone mumbled, "Ahhh, lighten up, onion breath. They can't all be winners. Anyhow, see you at the city limits tomorrow. I'll be the tall one who looks like me." Then he strode away.

Juan tiptoed backward down the stairs, but before he got to the ground floor, he crashed into someone or something. *"Mil perdones, otra vez, otra vez,"*[28] he said.

"Hey, watch where you're going, handsome."

Juan spun around, and stood face-to-face with Malia Barker. They stared at each other for a moment, then Juan said, "I'm going to . . . ?"

Malia said, "Yeah, yeah, I know, you're going to join the Frat."

"How do you know?" the jerkoff asked.

"You've mentioned it about a million times in this chapter."

"So I have." He nodded, then pulled his sword from his belt and swung it over his shoulder, gouging a priceless painting in the process. "Before I leave, I have a gift for you."

Grinning, Malia said, "Nobody gives me gifts. They all go to Sasha, which is stupid, because she's such a pill." She gave him a hug, then said, "Juan Nieve, you're the best jerkoff brother a girl could have." Juan smiled, then held out his sword. Malia gulped, "I can't accept that."

Juan unscrewed the sword handle, then pulled a smaller sword from the bigger sword. He then unscrewed the handle of the smaller sword and pulled out an even smaller sword. He then unscrewed the handle of the smaller smaller sword and pulled out an even smaller sword. Offering the tiny weapon to Malia, he said, "Can you accept that?"

Malia took the gift from Juan, held it between her thumb and index finger, and waved it in the air. "It's wonderful. I'll call it Syringe."

---

28. My bad again again.

HEADCASE

King Bobbert Barfonme gazed sadly into his enormous mug of grog and said, "Did you ever meet Googlit Altavista?"

"I don't think so," Lord Headcase Barker declared. "Who's he? Or is it a she? You can never tell anybody's gender by the way they name people on this Godsforsaken continent."

"She's a she. She's the one who got away." Bobbert sighed. "The lovely Googlit Altavista. Kind. Warm. Intelligent. Gorgeous. No gag reflex. A keeper. But I let her go." He took a guzzle of grog, then said, "I met her at a joust. She liked me right away. I was skinnier then, you know . . ."

"I agree," Head agreed.

". . . and I had more hair, and I could get it up *whenever* I wanted, however many *times* I wanted."

Uncomfortable with the direction this conversation was heading, Head said, "Shouldn't we be on our way? Capaetal Ceity awaits." He pointed at the hundreds of men, women, children, and horses surrounding their campsite, and noted, "And I'm sure these people want to get home, do their Easterrabbitarian duties, and make sweet, sweet love to their relatives."

After another guzzle, Bobbert said, "Capaetal Ceity and these people can bite my bum." Raising his voice and shaking his fist, he yelled to his posse, *"You're all a bunch of ingrates!"* Then, to Head, he predicted, "I give it two weeks before you start hating everybody in the Godsdamn place. No, make that *one* week. No, make that one *day*. No, make that one *chapter*. No, make that one *page*. Now back to Googlit and her deeper than deep throat. She did this thing with her tongue that—"

"Alright," Head interrupted, "enough."

Bobbert said, "Fine. Be that way, you Godsdamn prude." He finished off the contents of his mug, then noted, "Me and you, Heady-Boy, we have something in common, something that you might not know about."

"What's that?" Head asked.

"Jerkoffs. I've one of my own."

"Thanks for sharing," Head said.

"Actually," Bobbert slurred, "I have twelve of my own."

Choking on his grog, Head choked, *"Twelve!"*

Bobbert shrugged. "Maybe more."

"Does Cerevix know?"

"Who cares?" Bobbert shrugged. "The bitch doesn't love me. Plus the bitch is as frigid as the Wall is cold. Plus, well, she's a bitch."

Head wanted to agree, but held his tongue.

"I have jerkoffs all over the place," Bobbert continued. "A jerkoff here, and a jerkoff there. Here a jerkoff, there a jerkoff, everywhere a jerkoff jerkoff."

Bobbert belched, and Head cringed at his friend's alcohol-tinged breath. Standing up, the new Foot advised, "Time to go. Are you okay to drive? Or do I have to take your reins?"

The King pulled himself up from his chair, then promptly fell on his backside, straight into the mud. "Nah, I'm good," he claimed.

Head and Bobbert's journey to Capaetal Ceity was long and boring, and not worth recounting here. If you feel shortchanged, read this paragraph 261 times, and that will replicate the length and monotony of their excursion.

When the Barfonme/Barker traveling party—which, for reasons that might or might not become apparent, included Sasha and Malia—*finally* arrived at their destination, they were greeted at the castle door by a short, pale, cherubic man, who lied, "It is a great honor to welcome home the King and his new Foot! Nothing pleases me more in the world than to gaze upon these two transcendent beings. So excited am I that, as we speak, I am erect."

Bobbert told Head, "He's not erect. He's a eunuch."

"I am *not* a eunuch," the short man insisted. Unbuckling his belt, he asked Head, "Would you like me to prove it?"

Rubbing his temples, Head sighed, "No, that's alright, I believe you."

Bobbert hopped off his horse and said, "Head, meet my Secretary of State, Lord Petey Varicose Bailbond. You may call him Tinyjohnson. He may be small, but he does the work of two men." Head and Tinyjohnson fist-bumped, then Bobbert asked Tinyjohnson if he missed anything while he was in Summerseve.

Tinyjohnson looked shiftily to the right, then to the left, and then mumbled, "There's news from Dork. Word on the street is that Lolyta Targetpractice got hitched to the King of the centaurs." After a couple more shifty glances, he whispered, "Word is, they made love *inside* the castle."

Bobbert rolled his eyes and refuted, "Nonsense. Everybody knows the Dorkis only do the do outside, in front of crowds." To Head, he said, "And don't knock it until you've tried it."

Head threw up in his mouth a little bit.

The King then asked Tinyjohnson, "Anything else?"

"Before you left, you asked me to prepare a good foreshadow for your return, so here goes: Barring some sort of battle of wits with a rival family member, Functionary Aaron's son Bobby Aaron will be ruling House Aaron before the Summer arrives."

"Excellent foreshadowing, Tinyjohnson, simply excellent." Bobbert then asked Head, "Hey Barky-Boy, when's Summer coming again?"

Head shrugged. "No idea. All I know is that Summer is coming."

"You sure about that?" Bobbert queried. "You're sure Summer is coming."

"Yes, Your Highness. Summer is coming."

"Let me get this straight. Summer is coming?"

"Yes. Summer is coming."

"To clarify: Summer is coming?"

"Yes. Summer is coming."

"Just so we're one hundred percent clear, Summer is coming?"

"Yes. Summer is coming."

"So what I'm gathering from you is that Summer is coming."

"Yes. Summer is coming."

"Great." King Bobbert smiled. "Summer is coming. Now that that's settled, let's go get our grog on."

GATEWAY

Gateway Barker stood on one side of her son Allbran's bed, with Maester Blaester on the other, both staring sadly at the sleeping boy. Gateway sighed, "There's no improvement, is there?"

Mirroring Lady Barker's sigh, Blaester explained, "Not even a little bit."

Allbran's eyes popped open, and he said, "Of course there's no improvement. Because there's nothing to improve. I'm feeling tip-top."

Nodding, Blaester said, "I'm certain you are, young man." He whispered to Gateway, "He's delirious."

"I heard that," Allbran exclaimed, "and I'm not delirious!"

Gateway whispered, "That's exactly what a delirious person would say."

"Hel-*lo*," Allbran said. "I'm right *here*. I can *hear* you."

Blaester patted Allbran on the arm and soothed, "There, there, young man. You'll be fine soon enough." And then he punched young Barker square in the nose.

Wiping the blood from his face, Allbran kvetched, "Hey, that hurt."

Gateway said, "I know you're in pain, my love. You'll be fine soon enough."

Allbran roared, *"Aargh!"* then pulled the covers over his head.

"That's right, sweet prince," Gateway said. "Sleep the sleep of healing. You'll be fine soon enough."

Allbran repeated, *"Aargh!"* then went silent.

Just then, Bobb Barker burst into the room and roared, "Lady Gateway Barker, come on down! You are the next contestant on . . ." And then he trailed off.

After a moment or two of awkward silence, Gateway asked, "I'm the next contestant on what?"

Bobb scratched his head and said, "I forget. So how's Allbran?"

From under his bedsheet, Allbran said, "Peachy keen!"

Gateway contradicted, "In massive pain."

"I'm certain he'll improve quickly," Bobb opined. "So Ma, now that Pa's off Footing it up in Cap Ceity, let's talk chain of command. Who's running this rodeo?"

Gateway said, "No idea."

"Well, I do," Bobb pointed out. "Firstborn male trumps the Lady of the House. All me, all the time."

"Is that correct?" Gateway asked. She had not read the endless House Barker Charter in many seasons—when you are *in* an insanely long book, it's well-nigh impossible to *read* an insanely long book—so it was possible Bobb was right.

"Sure," Bobb said. "What, you don't believe me? You think I'd make up some crazy rule just so I could be the leader? You think I'm a power-mad death merchant who wants to lead his House into battle strictly so he could taste blood?"

Allbran popped his head out from under the covers and said, "Yes," after which Maester Blaester elbowed the boy in the head, after which Allbran fell silent for the remainder of the chapter.

Bobb continued, "I'm the firstborn male, and it's my show now. No matter what that bigmouth Alyxandyr Hayg says, *I'm in charge.*"

Taken aback by her son's vehemence, Gateway took a step back and said, "Okay, okay, you're in charge, you're in charge. Jeez Louise." She then thought, *This is great. I won't have to do anything around this dump.*

Bobb screwed up his face and queried, "Wait, what do you mean you won't have to do anything? And you honestly think this castle is a dump?"

"Did I say that out loud?" After Bobb nodded, she grinned. "I was kidding! These are the jokes, folks!"

Bobb shook his head and said, "Leave the funny stuff to Tritone Sinister, Mom. Okay, then, I'm outta here. Maester Blaester, what say we figure out how, when, and where to blow some stuff up?"

"Yes, m'substitute Lord." Blaester bowed.

After the two men left, Gateway pulled some Godsweede from her cleavage, lit it up, took a soothing puff, and lowered herself to the floor. As she leaned against the wall, she decided it might be a good idea to plan how she would keep House Barker in order while Head was off getting on the good Foot, and Bobb was off being a power-mad death merchant, but then she got hungry and lost her train of thought.

A few puffs later, she heard a flock of cats meowing from across the castle . . . but that was far from uncommon, as auditory hallucinations were among Godsweede's side effects. But the meowing grew louder and realer, so she managed to get herself on her feet and stumbled down the hallway toward where the meowing seemed to originate: the library.

Gateway counted a dozen cats wandering around the small, dark library in a daze, a daze that most likely stemmed from the small pile of Godsweede that was smoldering next to the Fantasy Fiction section. She did not remember Godsweeding it up in the library, but she had a tendency to not remember much, so she was not particularly concerned.

After she stamped out the roach, Gateway returned to Allbran's room, where she found herself face to face with . . . herself. Smiling at her doppelgänger, she said, "Goodness, you are one beautiful woman."

The Lady smiled and said, "As are you, m'Lady. I apologize for my unannounced intrusion, but have wanted to meet you for a long time now, because I think we will be great friends, because aside from the fact that you and I look remarkably alike, I understand you worship at the altar of Nestamarley."

"I have been known to partake," Gateway admitted.

The Gateway lookalike pulled an onion-sized ball of Godsweede from out of nowhere and offered, "I offer this to you, m'Lady. A gift from one worshipper to another."

Gateway gawked at the ball of weede and said, "This is huge. No way I can bogart this all to myself. Care to join me?"

"No," the lookalike said, "this is all for you. It is my pleasure. And I should advise you that this is so pure that you can chew it."

"Then chew it I shall," Gateway exclaimed, before putting a large pinch between her cheek and gums.

One swallow later, the room disappeared, and Gateway Barker found herself floating in a red void. Her heart rate skyrocketed, she broke out in a drenching sweat, and she started panting. As she drifted through the scarlet nothingness, Gateway's entire body shook as if she were riding a hungry horse bucking for oats and onions. Then her entire body became cocooned by a bright, warming light, and she felt a sense of peace that was transcendent.

Gateway had no idea how long it was before she regained her faculties, but when she returned to some semblance of normal consciousness, her hand was bleeding and her near twin was crumpled in the corner, her face a mélange of blackness, blueness, and bloodness. She looked around the room and noticed a bloodied knife on Allbran's bed, then put two and two together, and even though she came up with five, she realized that the fake Gateway had tried to kill Allbran.

At that moment, Lady Gateway Barker decided it was crucial, no, essential, no, vital, no, imperative that she gather her troops and trek to Capaetal Ceity, because that's what all the royals in Summerseve did when somebody tried to kill a member of their family: Gather up a bunch of people and horses, and go from one place to another.

TRITONE

Tritone Sinister and Juan Nieve took their journey to the Wall, which was long and boring, and not worth recounting here. If you want to know what the trip was like, watch the moving picture *Eesy Ryder* on mute while listening to Garryson Keylor on Nationyl Publyk Radiyo.

SASHA

Oh. My. Gods. Dinky, you are, like, totally cute."

Sasha Barker's direpanda, Dinky, was far from the sharpest onion in the patch, but that didn't stop Sasha from loving the animal as if he were as smart as the great Easterrabbit scientist Steevyn Hawkyng. Sasha loved him, and petted him, and squeezed him, and called him George, which was quite confusing to Dinky, because even though he was not particularly bright, he did know his name.

The two of them were wandering along the muddy banks of the muddy Capaetal Ceity River, mud muddying up their feet and/or paws, neither with a care in the world . . . or that is what Sasha told herself. The truth was, she could not stop thinking about Goofrey Barfonme, and how valiant he was, and what a wonderful couple they would make, and how she was going to love him, and pet him, and squeeze him, and call him George. But she was not sure he would like that. For that matter, when it came to Goof, she was not sure of anything.

Sasha heard a voice cry, "Think fast!" then she felt a smack on the back of her head.

"Oh. My. Gods," Sasha simpered. "That, like, totally hurt."

Malia skipped up to Sasha—her direpanda, Stinky, was right behind her—and chuckled, "Wimp. That wasn't even as hard as I could throw."

"What*ever*," Sasha huffed, then stomped away. Dinky stayed put, however, and started nuzzling Stinky . . . and this nuzzling took place below Stinky's belt.

Still chuckling, Malia said, "Whoa, looks like our nation's philosophy of incest extends to the direpanda community."

Sasha stopped and asked, "Like, what's incest?" She turned around and was treated to the sight of Dinky pleasuring Stinky with his long direpanda tongue.

"*That,*" Malia explained, "is incest."

"*Ewwwwwwww,*" Sasha wailed. "That's, like, totally the grossest thing ever."

Malia explained, "If living creatures of any sort don't engage in that sort of behavior—direpandas, humans, whatever—their race will cease to exist. No foreplay means no procreation, and no procreation means no life."

Sasha scratched her head. "I don't understand."

"What don't you understand?" Malia asked.

"Any of it."

Malia scrunched up her face and asked, "Didn't Mother have the talk with you?"

"Maybe she did. I don't, like, remember."

Pointing at the ground, Malia ordered, "Down." Once the girls were seated comfortably in the mud, Malia said, "When two people love each other very, very much, they get certain feelings, feelings of excitement, and their private parts—the man's is called a penis, and the woman's is called a vagina—become sensitive to the touch . . . but in a good way." The younger Barker sister then went on to explain to the older Barker sister how, by making love, Lord Headcase and Lady Gateway could create another Barker sister, should they choose to do so.

After Malia finished her lecture, Sasha flicked some mud off her dress and declared, "Oh. My. Gods. That's, like, totally gross."

Shrugging, Malia said, "You may feel differently about that in a few years." The ground then began to rumble, and a horse emerged from the forest, a horse ridden by one Goofrey Barfonme. Noting Sasha's adoring gaze, Malia said, "Or you may feel differently about that in a few minutes."

Sasha waved at Goof, then extricated herself from the gooey mud. When Goof brought his horse to a stop, she said, "You look totally awesome, Goof. Like, *totally.*"

Goof gave Sasha an onion-eating grin, and agreed. "I agree." And then, silence.

"Do you think I look pretty, Goof?" she asked.

"What? Oh. Yeah. Sure. You look swell."

Sasha giggled, batted her eyes, and said, "Like, thanks. Come down here and talk to me. I have something to tell you." After Goof hopped off his horse, Sasha took his hand and pulled the reluctant pretender to the throne toward the riverbank. "So I heard something totally weird today."

"What's that?" Goof inquired.

"Okay, so when two people, like, totally love each other very, very much, they get, like, certain awesome feelings, awesome feelings of excitement, and their private parts become, like, totally sensitive to the touch, but in a radical way." The elder Barker sister then went on to explain to the dumber Barfonme offspring how, by making love, she and he could create a baby Barfonme, should they choose to do so.

After the talk was done, Goof gawked at Sasha and uttered, "That's repulsive."

Sasha looked at the growing lump in Goofrey's pink pantaloons and said, "I don't know. It might be rad." She took a step toward him, then kissed Goof on the cheek. He flinched, then pushed her away. The push was not hard, but Sasha's feet got stuck in the mud, so she lost her balance and fell into the river.

Malia, forgetting that only a handful of chapters ago it was noted that she and her sister were serious rivals, stepped right into Goof's face and growled, "She may be an idiot, and she may be spoiled, and she may be bitchy, and she may think she's a macaroni statue goddess, but she's my sister, and the only person who gets to shove her into the water is me." She then pulled her sword Syringe from behind her ear and said, "You have insulted my family, and we will now fight to the death. And you might want to pay attention, because there are a Godsdamn lot of fights to the death just around the corner. And around the corner from that. And around the corner from that." She then mumbled to herself, "Chryst, there're a lot of fights to the death around this dump. At some point, somebody has to say, enough is enough. Where's a good editor when you need one?"

Goof stammered, "Um, I don't think, um, that that's, um, such a good idea, because, um, because you're a girl, yeah, that's it, you're a little girl, and Barfonme men don't go to battle with swords against girls."

Malia got into a fighting stance and teased, "Are you sure it's not because you're scared?"

Puffing up his chest, Goof claimed, "Nothing scares me!"

Malia thrust her tiny sword into Goof's face and he gasped. "Sure, Goof," Malia sneered, "nothing scares you." She put her sword away, then added, "You have insulted my family, so we must battle. If swords aren't acceptable, you can choose your weapon."

Again puffing up his chest, Goof claimed, "You will never beat me in a battle of wits. *Never.*"

"Seriously?" Malia asked. "Me and you in a battle of wits?"

Goof nodded confidently and boasted, "Nobody has ever beaten me in a battle of wits. *Nobody.*"

Malia noted, "That's because everybody lets you win, dummy."

"I win my battles fair and square," Goof asserted, "as I will right now. I will even let you choose the topic."

"Okay. Baseball."

"What's baseball?" Goof asked.

"In 1967," Malia asked, "who won the American League Triple Crown?"

"The American what?"

"*Wrong!* Carl Yastrzemski, who batted .326 with 44 homers and 121 RBI."

"Wait a minute . . ."

Malia interrupted, "Next question: Name the only pitcher to throw a no-hitter on Opening Day."

"Opening what?"

"*Wrong!* Bob Feller, April 16, 1940. The Tribe beat the White Sox one–zip."

Goof sniffled and wiped something from his eye. "You're being really, really mean, Malia."

"Nut up, Barfonme. Next question, and this is an easy one: Who earned the nickname 'Mr. October'?"

"Um, I don't know, maybe Reggie Jackson?"

"Crap. Lucky guess." She peered at Goof's face. "Hey, are you crying?"

Goof wiped a tear from his cheek, then sniffled, "I hate you, Malia Barker! You suck! I hope you die! I'm gonna tell my mommy on you!" And then he ran toward the forest, bawling the entire way.

"Hey," Malia called, "you forgot your horse!" After Goof was out of view, she turned to her sister and said, "Well, I guess I didn't need to tell you about making babies, did I?"

Gazing adoringly at the forest, Sasha said, "Oh. My. Gods. Goofrey Barfonme is, like, the cutest boy *ever*. I'm going to totally make love to his penis."

Malia Barker threw up in her mouth a little bit.

HEADCASE

Gods, I'm hungry," Lord Headcase Barker complained from his position on the floor beside the throne, right beside the King's feet.

King Bobbert Barfonme topped off his mug of top-shelf grog and, staring at the thick, dark purple liquid, noted, "If you throw down a couple bottles of this stuff every day, your appetite won't seem like much of a problem. For that matter, *nothing* will seem like much of a problem."

Oblivion sounded appealing to Head, and he was tempted to go on a grog bender, because it turned out Bobbert had been right: Being the Foot was awful. Aside from having to keep the increasingly erratic King on track, it was one annoyance after another: If Queen Cerevix wasn't complaining about the horrible state of the castle's mudroom, it was Goofrey whining about how somebody stole his Leapstyr. If it wasn't Tinyjohnson trying to undermine what little authority Head had, it was some commoner complaining about the neighbor coveting their wife, their manservant, their maidservant, and their donkey, not to mention playing their music too loud. Taking all that into consideration, it was little wonder that Bobbert spent ninety percent of his life inebriated.

Another reason Head sympathized with his friend: the throne.

Head did not know the history behind the Capaetal Ceity King's throne, nor did he care to, because whoever devised that thing had to be a sadistic nutjob, and who has the time to read about sadistic nutjobs when there is mud to be slogged through, onions to be eaten, and main characters to be killed? The back of the throne was standard—black velvet covered with jewels, which, while certainly eye-catching, could not have felt good on the back—but there were no arms, and the seat was a white porcelain circle with a huge hole in the middle, and the chair itself was hollow. Whenever King Bobbert broke wind—which, while not as often as Head's son Allbran, was still a regular occurrence—the echo could be both heard and felt throughout the giant, high-ceilinged throne room. Sometimes Head heard other noises coming from the bottom of the throne, noises that he could not or would not identify, noises that made him happy he did not have to sit there. (The Queen's throne, it should be noted, was a bejeweled barstool. Cerevix had been trying to get the administration to allocate funds for a real chair for seasons, but she was always voted down, primarily because nobody on the Budget Committee liked her.)

Head told his friend, "Before I grog it up, I'd like to get something in my gut."

Bobbert nodded. "I understand. And get something in your gut we shall." Pointing across the room, he said, "But not until we deal with this."

Head followed Bobbert's finger and gazed at the entrance to the throne room, where he was greeted by the sight of his youngest daughter in the grip of four of Cerevix's cousins—he'd been introduced to all of the Sinisters upon his arrival at Capaetal Ceity, but they all looked exactly the same, almost as if they'd inbred for centuries—and Malia was squirming and screaming as if she were a toad who had eaten but not fully digested another toad, and the second toad was trying to jump up and down inside of the first toad's stomach.

"What's going on here?" Head asked. "Did you eat but not fully digest a toad?"

Queen Cerevix regally strolled into the throne room as if she were the Queen or something, followed by four blond Sinister cousins, and explained, "Your daughter, Lord Barker, appears to have made a fool of my son."

Bobbert slurred, "So what else is new?"

"I guess I know who's sleeping on the couch tonight," Cerevix snapped. "Again."

"Oh yeah? You and whose army?" Bobbert grumbled.

Cerevix gave her husband a confused look and said, "In any event, apparently your Malia threatened my Goof with a deadly weapon, then insulted him, then stole his horse. He doesn't deserve to be treated that way, on either the page or the small screen."

Head shook his head, then pointed out, "My Queen, Malia couldn't weigh more than, um, what's the unit of measure they use around here? Pounds? Grams? Stones? My stones?"

Bobbert said, "Let's say she's a skinny little tomboy and leave it at that."

"Fine," Head agreed, "she's a skinny little tomboy, and Goof is a strapping young man . . ."

"I don't know if *strapping* is the right word," Bobbert said. "I'd go with *nebbish*. You get a gander of those pantaloons he wears? Makes him look like a weenie."

"I guess I know who's sleeping on the couch *tomorrow* night," Cerevix snapped.

"Oh yeah? Well, put that in your pipe and smoke it," Bobbert grumbled.

Cerevix gave her husband a confused look, then said, "In any event, your daughter insulted my son, then she stole his horse."

King Bobbert snorted, then he chuckled, then he guffawed, then he tittered, then he giggled, and then he whooped. Then, laughing, he said, "Your son got beaten up by a *girl*?!"

"He's your son too," the Queen noted.

Shrugging, Bobbert said, "Maybe he is. Maybe he isn't. Maybe we'll get the real answer someday."

Off in the distance, Juan Nieve's direpanda Fourshadow could be heard growling.

"I guess I know who's sleeping on the couch the night after tomorrow," Cerevix snapped.

"Oh yeah? Well, I know you are, but what am I?" Bobbert grumbled.

Cerevix then said, "In any event, Lord Barker, how do you intend to punish your daughter?"

With his stomach grumbling, Head said, "I'll take care of it later. How about we order some Thai?"

Ignoring the Foot, the Queen exclaimed, "I have the perfect punishment: three years of hard incest!"

Bobbert rose from his seat, closed his throne's lid, and said, "Cerevix, we will not have Malia sleeping with Allbran, because the boy has one foot in the grave . . ."

Off in the distance, Allbran Barker could be heard yelling, "I'm feeling fine, thank you very much!"

". . . and incestuous behavior might kill him . . ."

Off in the distance, Allbran Barker could be heard yelling, "It wouldn't kill me, but it's really gross!"

". . . but I don't want this mess to carry on, so come up with a punishment we can all agree on, then go to your chambers and play with Jagweed or something."

"I concur," Queen Cerevix concurred. "Malia killed something important to Goof—his dignity—so we should kill something important to her . . . like maybe her direpanda."

Head's stomach again rumbled, and he thought, *Man, a direpanda-burger with grilled onions sounds mighty tasty,* but then he noticed the silent tears running down his daughter's cheeks, and said, "Cerevix, I will handle this."

Ignoring him, Cerevix turned to the quartet of blond Sinisters and shouted, "What do you say, team? Kill the direpanda?"

In unison, Team Sinister answered, "Kill the direpanda."

Cocking her ear, Cerevix called, "I can't hear you!"

"Kill the direpanda!"

"Let 'em hear you in Summerseve, my peeps!"

"KILL THE DIREPANDA!"

Cerevix turned to Head and smiled. "The masses have spoken."

"More like the *asses* have spoken," Bobbert mumbled, then glared at Cerevix and added, "I know, I know, I know, I'm on the couch."

To Head, Cerevix said, "So unless you want a bunch of Sinisters all up in your ass, I recommend you kill the direpanda."

Lord Headcase told his daughter, "Malia, I'm so sorry about this. But if I didn't make decisions based on a rigid, unbending adherence to a moral code that no one else bothers to follow and that only seems to harm my family while leaving the obvious villains unscathed, then I wouldn't be Headcase Barker. I just hope that this unrealistic obsession with moral rectitude doesn't come down on my head like an executioner's sword sometime in the future."

She shrugged. "You gotta do what you gotta do. Just make sure you don't kill Sasha's direpanda by mistake. After all, they look a lot alike. It would be easy to get them confused, and you might kill the wrong one. If you know what I mean."

"What do you mean?" Head asked.

"Hell," Bobbert said, "even I know what she means. And I'm a drunk."

"Hell," Cerevix said, "even I know what she means. And I'm a bitch."

"Hell," the Sinister cousins said in unison, "even we know what she means. And we're a bunch of inbred sociopaths."

Head walked over to Malia and asked, "Where is your sister?"

"I don't know," Malia answered, "nor do I know where Stinky is. But it just so happens that Dinky is right outside the back door."

Rubbing his beard pensively, Head stared contemplatively at the ceiling, then gazed thoughtfully at the floor, then glanced broodingly at the wall, then, heeding the will of his famished gut, said, "If I must kill the direpanda, then I must kill the direpanda." He pulled Slush from its case, then marched meditatively toward the throne room door as if there were boulders attached to his ankles. He stopped in the doorway, paused for a minute, two minutes, three minutes. Finally he took a hitching breath, turned around, choked back a sob, and then asked everybody, "Is everybody cool with medium rare burgers?"

GATEWAY

Lady Gateway Bully Barker and Maester Blaester stood behind the castle's closed front door. As Gateway peered into her shoulder bag, she asked Maester Blaester, "Could we go over the checklist again?"

"Of course, m'Lady. Knook e-reader?"

"Check," she checked.

"Tequila?"

"Check," she checked.

"Swimming attire, both two-piece and one-piece?"

"Check and check," she checked.

"Neutrogena Ultra Sheer Sunblock, SPF 94,167,211,467?"

"Check."

"Godsweede?"

"Check."

"Glass Godsweede delivery system?"

"Check."

"Advyl?"

"Check."

Blaester claimed, "Then I believe you are ready for your excursion."

Gateway queried, "Are the oddly named Knights waiting for me out front?"

"Of course, m'Lady: Sur Hornswaggle van der Putz, Sur Whiffenpoop Porkburger, Sur Dingotz Stugotz, Sur Ron Dee Ehm Cee, Sur Wylly Nylly, Sur Baron von Raschke, Sur Rufus T. Fyrefly, Sur Schmucko Cheesebreath, Sur Dyrk Dyggler, Sur Cankles Rottweiler, Sur Boris D'Spydr, Sur Bronski Motorboat, Sur Crayola Burntsienna, Sur Tushbutt Rumprear Fannyass,

Sur Heywood Jablome, Sur Banjo McChucklehead, Sur Donnybrook Fili-buster, Sur Mustache Bumbershoot, and, of course, Sur Taradiddle Slob-berknocker."

"What about Sur Hogwash Dipthong? I can't leave Summerseve with-out Sur Hogwash Dipthong."

"Sur Dipthong is running late, m'Lady. Shall I have him put to death when he arrives?"

"I would appreciate that," Gateway said, nodding, and added, "Well, then, the sun is probably sinking into the ocean, so I must begin my jour-ney." She pulled some smoldering Godsweede from her cleavage, took a puff, grabbed Blaester's face, mashed her lips against his, blew the smoky contents of her mouth into Blaester's lungs, then told him, "Get up, stand up, don't give up the fight," after which she flashed him the peace sign.

Maester Blaester merely gurgled.

Gateway opened the front door and, after one step, found herself face-first in the mud. As she struggled to a sitting position, she looked around to see what had caused her to fall; it turned out to be not a *what*, but rather a *who*, a short *who* with a high-pitched voice.

"Can I help you?" she queried, wiping the mud from her eyes.

The man stuck out his tiny hand and said, "Lord Petey Varicose Bail-bond. King Barfonme asked that I guide you back to Capaetal Ceity."

Standing up then shaking his hand, Gateway asked, "What do you mean *back* to Capaetal Ceity?"

"Well, I arrived here just this morning."

"When did you leave to come here?" Gateway wondered.

"Last evening."

"How did you get here?"

Lord Bailbond pointed at his tiny horse. "Him."

"And it took you only one day?"

He nodded. "Some say I do the work of two men."

"Impressive."

"Some say I can be in two places at once."

"Cool."

"Some say I'm a eunuch, but the fact of the matter is, I have a small member."

"Too much information."

"Understood," the tiny johnson'd non-eunuch agreed, then offered Lady Gateway his arm. "I know a simply *wonderful* whorehouse in Cap Ceity where I can stash you. The best in town. You'll fit right in. All the opium you can eat. Shall we?"

Gateway reached down, took his elbow, and smiled. "We shall."

As they mounted their respective horses, Tinyjohnson said, "Oh, I should probably mention that it was Tritone Sinister who put out the hit on your nearly dead boy."

From Allbran's room: *"Godsdamn it, I'm fine!"*

Ignoring her son, she asked, "How do you know it was Tritone?"

"It's a lengthy tale that I'll tell you during our lengthy journey. It's a ripping yarn, too, full of intrigue, violence, backstabbing, double-crossing, and messy sex. It's a pity that nobody other than you and I will get to hear it. Or read it."

Aside from the fact that all the oddly named Knights aside from Burntsienna were slaughtered during a random battle that had nothing to do with anything, Gateway and Tinyjohnson's journey to Capaetal Ceity was long and boring, and not worth recounting here. If this story were told on basic cable, we would jump to a commercial. But this isn't TV.

It's HBO.

HEADCASE

King Bobbert was out on some errand or another—if Headcase were to lay a wager, he would have bet it involved grog 90, much to the new Foot's chagrin, it was up to him to lead the weekly meeting of House Barfonme's High Council. As Head looked around the table—a table covered with plates and plates of the best onions Capaetal Ceity had to offer—he wondered how and why Bobbert chose his advisers, because to Head's eye, it was one Godsdamn motley crew.

Clad in a multicolored silk robe and a feathered hat, Tinyjohnson was positioned on Lord Barker's left, while directly to Head's right sat a man by the name of Bix Byderbek, a man who was shorter than Tinyjohnson and fatter than Bobbert. There were four people on the opposite side of the table: A bald, bucktoothed man named Wangle Strydant; a youngster named Hawkwynd Bagelthorp, who was as skinny as Byderbek was fat; a one-armed, one-legged gent named Cofffeee Teeormee; and an angry-looking deaf-mute who went only by the name Skype.

Head pounded the table with his fist—hard enough that it caused six onions to fall onto the floor, which caused Skype to look even angrier—then emitted, "Alright, this meeting is called to order. His Highness neglected to give me notes before he left town, so would anybody like to start?"

Tinyjohnson raised his tiny hand and offered, "I have a suggestion, Foot." After a lengthy pause, he explained, "This is difficult for me to say."

Desirous to make a pillow out of the onions and take a nap, Head grumbled, "Best to just say it, eunuch."

"I'm not a eunuch, Foot."

Staring at the feathered hat, Head drawled, "Riiiiiight, of course you're not. Now speak your piece."

"Well, good Foot Barker, it is the Council's opinion that you need to rethink your wardrobe."

Glancing at his brown burlap blouse, his gray burlap vest, and his tan burlap pants, Head asked, "What's wrong with what I'm wearing?"

"Look around this table," Tinyjohnson demanded. "We have certain standards here."

Head took a gander at his cohorts' respective outfits: Byderbek was wearing a tight white shirt with a long, skinny piece of material tied around his neck; Strydant had on an outfit similar to Head's, the primary difference being that his burlap was thick and colorful, rather than thin and drab; Bagelthorp wore only a vest, which, in Head's mind, was a mistake, as his ribs were as prominent as a snake who uncoiled himself in the stomach of a pregnant woman; Teeormee took Bagelthorp's stylistic choice a bit further, choosing to wear no shirt at all; and Skype was covered shoulder-to-toe with what appeared to be dried mud.

Giving Tinyjohnson a defiant look, Head offered, "I don't know, I feel like I'm doing okay here."

Tinyjohnson shook his head and disagreed, "I disagree. When you represent House Barfonme, you have to represent it with class and grace."

Pointing at Skype, Head pointed out, "But that one's wearing mud."

"It's the classiest, most graceful mud in all of Capaetal Ceity," Tinyjohnson noted.

"What about Bagelthorp?" Head asked. "Couldn't he put on a shirt or something? His ribs are . . . distracting."

"Bite your tongue." Tinyjohnson winced. "Hawkwynd has spent years cultivating that look, *years*."

Head rubbed his temples and sighed, "Fine. I'll get some new clothes."

Tinyjohnson beamed and clapped, then said, "Oh, goody! You and I shall go shopping posthaste. We'll get you looking like a good Foot in no time."

"Fantastic," Headcase monotoned. "Hey, I've been wondering: How did this major metropolis end up with such a motley governing body? Are you all Lords of some particular land?"

"I am Lord of all that I wear," Strydant said. "But not all that much otherwise."

"Well, how did you get these positions?" Head asked, scratching his namesake. "It's almost as if you were picked for your dramatic differences in style and culture."

Tinyjohnson claimed, "We were elected, you might say."

"By the people? Since when did we become a democracy?"

"No, no, no, there's no democracy here. We were each chosen by the author . . ."

"The *what*?"

"Er, I mean, many Summers ago, King Bobbbbbbbbb Barfonme thought a diverse council would appeal to multiple demographics." He then whispered, "Phew, that's thinking on your feet."

Everybody heard his whisper. But everybody ignored it. Because everybody wanted this meeting—and this chapter—over and done with.

Head asked, "Is there anything, um, important to discuss? Something about, oh, I don't know, ways to make Capaetal Ceity a better place to live?"

Teeormee raised his hand and said, "Did anybody mention to you that we're broke?"

Head blinked. "Broke?" he asked.

"Yep," Teeormee confirmed. "Broke. Busted. Empty. Drained. Penniless. Impoverished. Destitute. We got nothing. Nada. Zero. Zilch. Bupkus—"

"Okay," Head interrupted, "I get it. There isn't any money."

"Not a Godsdamn cent. Naught. Goose egg. Zip. Zippo. Zipper. Zipperino."

After he stopped, Head asked, "You done?"

Teeormee scratched his head, then asked, "Did I say impoverished?"

Head nodded.

"Then yeah, I'm done."

"Fantastic," Headcase monotoned. "Anybody have any ideas how we can dig ourselves out of this mess?"

"Burn it all down!" Bagelthorp exclaimed. "Burn down the whole Godsdamn city. We're insured up to the hilt."

Tinyjohnson spun on Bagelthorp and roared, "Hawkwynd, get it through your thick skull that insurance does not exist, thus we are not insured!"

Bagelthorp mumbled, "Tell that to my Stayte Farmm agent."

Ignoring him, Head asked, "Any other thoughts?" After nobody responded, he said, "I have an idea. We can borrow."

"From who?" Strydant queried.

"From another country," Head explained. "From a country that is benevolent, and kind, and wealthy, and willing to not ream us with an outrageous interest rate: Chyna."

Everybody at the table groaned, then Byderbek said, "We already owe them four million whatevers."

Head screwed up his face and wondered, "What do you mean, *whatevers?*"

"Cap Ceity's monetary units have never been made clear," Tinyjohnson explained.

"How about for the sake of this discussion, we call them dollars, like we do in Summerseve?" Head offered.

"I don't know," Bagelthorp said. "Pesos sounds better."

Teeormee offered, "I vote for lira."

"How about euros?" Byderbek asked.

Strydant suggested, "Dingleberries. I like dingleberries."

"I'm sure you do," Head said, "but the decision rests with the Foot, and the Foot says dollars. The Foot also says we're borrowing more whatevers, er, dollars from Chyna. We'll pay them back when we can . . ." After a pause, he added, *"maybe!"*

At that, the entire Council broke down in laughter.

Wiping the tears from his eyes, Head said, "Ahhh, that was a good one. Sometimes I crack myself up." He stood up, clapped once, and said, "On that note, gentlemen, meeting adjourned."

After everybody other than Head and Tinyjohnson filed out of the room, the self-professed non-eunuch turned to the Foot and chanted, "I have a surprise for you, Lord Barker. What's your stance on prostitutes?"

"Well," he responded, "I probably don't like them as much as Bobbert, but they're okay with me. Why?"

"You want the short version or the long version?"

"The short version, I beg you," he begged, "for the love of Gods, the short version! At this rate, we'll be looking at 751 pages in hardback, and 900-plus in mass market."

Tinyjohnson offered, "Lady Gateway needs to speak with you, and she wanted to remain incognito, so I stashed her away at a whorehouse."

Grinning, Head exclaimed, "Genius! There hasn't been nearly enough non-incestuous sex in these proceedings. Take me to the hookers, Tinyjohnson! Take me now!"

The moment Head and Tinyjohnson set foot in the whorehouse, they were assaulted by a stench composed of male ejaculate, female ejaculate, male sweat, female sweat, money, Rush by Gucci, M by Mariah, Tommy Girl, Fantasy by Britney, opium, and onions. As Lord Barker gagged, Tinyjohnson took a deep breath and said, "Ah, nothing gets me turned on like the scent of a semi-legal iniquity den."

Head glanced suspiciously at Tinyjohnson's beltline, and mumbled, "There's nothing down there to turn on."

Tinyjohnson, who either did not hear or ignored Head, said, "I believe Lady Gateway is in the opium den," then pointed to the closed door across from the entrance.

Head sighed, "Of course she is," then, followed by Tinyjohnson, he trudged across the floor, ignoring the fifteen women who caressed his manhood along the way.

The opium den's only occupant, Lady Gateway Barker, was curled up on a white vinyl beanbag chair, her face buried in a pile of pulverized poppy seeds. She rolled over onto her back, then, without getting up, roared, "Heady Heady Heady!" Then she put the powder on the floor and spread open both her arms and her legs.

Headcase Barker liked opium-fueled sex as much as the next Lord, but he had Footing to do, so he took Gateway's hands, pulled her to her feet, and suggested, "Let's get you to the castle."

She jerked away and snapped, "No! No no no no no! I'm staying here. Forget this Lady business. I want to have sex for money, and smoke all the dope I want." Then she plopped back down onto the beanbag.

"Darling," Head cajoled, "we have this discussion once a year. You are not, repeat, *not* going to become a whore."

"You used to be cool, Heady," Gateway pouted.

Tinyjohnson piped up, "Both of you, shut up and listen: Tritone Sinister was behind the plot to kill Allbran."

Lady Gateway Barker stared at Lord Headcase Barker. Lord Headcase

Barker stared back at Lady Gateway Barker. Lord Petey Varicose Bailbond stared at Lord Headcase Barker and Lady Gateway Barker. Lord Headcase Barker and Lady Gateway Barker stared at Lord Petey Varicose Bailbond. After several more minutes of back-and-forth staring, Gateway said, "Screw this. I'm totally becoming a whore."

JUAN

Faster, Nieve, you jerkoff! And get those knees up! Your form is horrible!" After Juan did not respond, the man in the sloppy, mud-covered suit yelled, "Do you hear me, plebe? March faster, march taller, march stronger! *March, march, march!*"

"*Sí, gilipollas*[29] Cooke," Juan answered.

"For the millionth time, what the hell does *gilipollas* mean?"

"For the millionth time, read the footnote!"

"For the millionth time, what the hell is a footnote?"

"For the millionth time, *chingar a su madre!*"[30]

"For the millionth time, what does *chingar a su madre* mean?"

"For the millionth time, read the footnote!"

Broheim Alistair Cooke glared at Juan and roared, "Alright, Nieve, drop your sword and drink a shot!"

Juan unclenched his naked butt cheeks, and the sword that had been jammed up his posterior fell to the muddy ground with a squish. His Frat Broheim Bluto threw him a green bottle and said, "Bottoms up, jerkoff."

"Indeed," Juan sighed, then removed the cork from the bottle and took a single guzzle. As he grimaced, a fire raged in his belly, his head spun, and his face became nearly as green as the bottle.

He heard an evil laugh that could only belong to one man: Broheim Otter. "Yo, Nieve, why don't you just boot and get it over with?"

---

29. Asshole.

30. Fuck your mother. (Normally that would be one of the most offensive insults known to mankind, but in Easterrabbit—the home of fucking one's mother—it's practically a compliment.)

Determined to hold down his gorge, Juan said, "Yo, Otter, *yo cago en la leche de tu puta madre!*"[31]

Otter laughed, then started to chant: "Boot! Boot! Boot! Boot!" The other pledges—Bluto, Flounder, Pinto, and D-Day—picked up Otter's mantra, and pretty soon, Juan had no choice but to hurl. Seeing the contents of his stomach mix with the wet mud set him off again, and he retched until he could retch no more. Once his gut was empty, his fellow pledges gave him a heartfelt round of applause.

Broheim Cooke said, "That was wonderful, Nieve, but now you have to put the sword back into your poopshoot and march back to base camp."

"Okay, *ese.*"

"I'm not going to ask what *ese* means," Broheim Cooke noted, "because I don't think there's a footnote attached, and if there's not a footnote, it's either not that important, or it can be gleaned from context, or it's something so obvious that it needs no explanation."

Juan did not answer, lost in thoughts of how much he hated the Fraternity of the Swatch. He came here not just to defend his continent, but also to find some semblance of acceptance, as he was not getting much in Summerseve. Instead, the Swatchmen seemed to enjoy creating conflict even when there was none, as if to put off going over the Wall and battling the Others. Perhaps it built suspense, but it also meant that Juan's chapters were not as important as Headcase's (Juan knew this for a fact, because he had cheated and read them); Head's chapters dealt with questions of murder and conspiracy, while Juan's dealt with puking. And here, by the Wall, his so-called brothers treated him worse than anybody in his pseudo-family ever had. Lady Gateway was not always nice to him, but at least she never got a bunch of her friends together to serenade him with chants of "Jerk*off,* jerk*off,* jerk*off,* jerk*off!*"

They allowed Juan to remove his sword from his hindquarters when he returned to his tent, but they would not let him sit down, nor would they let him put on his clothes. "Nieve, Pinto," Broheim Cooke called, "front and center." The two Fratboys hustled to the middle of the campground, where they stood at attention, side by side. "Gentlemen," Cooke said, "it is time for you two to battle."

---

31. I shit in your whore mother's milk. (That's a good one, isn't it?)

Unsurprisingly, Otter started a chant of "Battle, battle, battle, battle!"

Pinto asked, "What kind of battle, Broheim Cooke?" He eyed Juan nervously, as Juan was by far the best swordfighter amongst the pledges.

"No swords this time, Broheim Pinto." He pulled two items from behind his back and offered, "Gentlemen, choose your weapons."

Juan gawked at the contents of Cooke's hands. "Are you serious? Pillows? *Ay, chihuahua.*"[32]

"Taking out an opponent with a sword is child's play," Cooke claimed. "To take out an opponent with a pillow, you have to be a true craftsman." He threw the pillows at the two boys—Juan caught his easily, while Pinto's fell into the mud—and explained, "The rules are simple: Last one standing wins. Start on three. One . . . two . . ."

Before Broheim Cooke finished his count, Pinto smacked Juan upside his head. There was no pain—Pinto was the smallest of the pledges—but something snapped in Juan's brain. The weeks of physical abuse, mind games, and booting caught up to him, and he felt stronger and more focused than he had in his entire life.

Juan easily ducked Pinto's next salvo, then circled his pillow over his head three times and brought it down upon Pinto's temple. Pinto staggered, but managed to remain upright. Before he was able to raise his pillow for attack, however, Juan smacked him on the opposite temple, then followed up that shot with a blow to the jaw. This time, Pinto did fall over, rump first. He looked up at the sky, clearly dazed.

"Come on, Pinto," D-Day called, "send this jerkoff over the Wall!"

Juan picked up a handful of mud and flung it at D-Day's midsection. While his throw was remarkably fast, his aim was slightly off, so rather than hitting D-Day in the solar plexus, the mudball nailed him in his groin. After D-Day turned ghost white and passed out, the remaining pledges shut their mouths.

Pinto looked at Broheim Cooke, lifted his right arm into the air, and said, "I'm done."

"That's right you are, Pinto," Juan gritted, after which he spiked his pillow onto the ground and stomped away from the tents. Nobody called after him.

---

32. *Oy vey.*

The closer he got to the Wall, the angrier he became. Needing to burn off some energy, he took three running steps, then tripped over a man who was sitting in the mud, legs crossed. Jumping up, Juan said, "I'm sorry. I didn't see you."

"That's the *second* time anybody's ever said that about me." The man looked at Juan's naked body, pointed at the appendage dangling between his legs, and said, "Wow, that thing's so small you could turn it sideways and it'd disappear."

Juan sat up and greeted him. "Good afternoon, Tritone."

"You gotta quit tripping over me, Shecky. You might hurt yourself. Or, more importantly, you might hurt me. But I'm not seeing this issue going away, because from what I can tell, you're so klutzy that you could trip over a cordless phone."

"A cordless *what*?" Juan asked.

"You're so klutzy that you couldn't make your way out of a paper bag if it was open on both ends."

"A *what* bag?"

"You're so klutzy that shit thinks you smell bad." Tritone paused, then mumbled to himself, "Wait, that doesn't make sense."

Juan stood up and said, *"Joder este ruido, me voy de aquí. Paz a cabo, hijo de puta."*[33]

Tritone smiled. "I don't know what language you're speaking, but I'll say this: It sure is beautiful. Nothing that sounds so lovely could be insulting."

"Sí, comediante. Nothing in my language could be insulting."

As he returned to the camp, Juan realized that he did not want to be a Swatchman, nor did he want to be a Barker. All he wanted was to be left the hell alone. When he made it back to his tent, he grabbed a shirt and some pants, but before he could get dressed, Broheim Cooke took him by his elbow and dragged him behind a tree.

Juan angrily pulled his arm away and asked, "What do you want, *ese*?"

Cooke handed Juan a pile of envelopes and said, "You got some raven-grams, jerkoff." As Juan snatched the notes from Cooke, the head Broheim said, "You're lucky they even made it. What with all the Internet cafés be-

---

33. Fuck this noise, I'm outta here. Peace out, muthafucka.

tween here and Summerseve, most ravens e-mail their messages, and the Wall doesn't offer wireless, so no e-mails for us."

Juan tore open the first note: *Dear Jerkoff,* it said, *I regret to inform you that due to his fall from the castle roof, your pseudo-brother Allbran Barker is crippled for life. Please include him in your prayers. Sincerely, Lord Headcase Barker.*

Blinking back tears, Juan tore open the second note: *Dear Juan,* it said, *I just wanted to let you know that I'm feeling great, and no matter what Maester Blaester says, I'm going horse riding with Bobb tomorrow. Kill some of the Others for me!!! Love, Allbran.*

His heart filled with joy, Juan tore open the third note: *Dear Jerkoff,* it said, *Allbran is in horrible, horrible pain. If you were any kind of brother, you would be here to support him. But instead, you chose country over family. I hope you are happy with yourself, you selfish jerkoff. XOX, Lady Gateway.*

With steam coming out of his ears, Juan tore open the third note: *Dear Juan,* it said, *Everybody is driving me crazy, and I want out. If you come and get me, we can run to the Wall and I can pledge for the Fraternity of the Swatch. And yes, I said "run," because I* can *run, no matter what anybody says. Love, Allbran.*

His heart filled with joy, Juan tore open the fourth note: *Dear Brother,* it said, *Allbran's hurt. It sucks, but we'll be okay, because I'm in charge. Best, Bobb.*

Rolling his eyes, Juan tore open the fifth note: *Dear Juan,* it said, *I'm fine. Love, Allbran.*

The next note read, *Dear Juan, Allbran's dead. Yours, Lord Barker.*

Next: *No I'm not. Love, Allbran.*

Next: *Yes he is. Maester Blaester.*

Next: *I hate you, Blaester. Allbran.*

Next: *Quit farting, Allbran. You stink. Best, Bobb.*

Thirty-six letters later, it was clear that Allbran might or might not be healthy, Bobb might or might not be in charge, Gateway might or might not be crazy, and Head might or might not be in or out of the loop. Trudging back to his tent, he thought, *Maybe the Fraternity of the Swatch isn't that bad after all.*

MALIA

The small, hairless man clad in the skintight one-piece outfit clapped his hands three times and snapped, "How many times do I have to tell you: We're starting with a double lutz, then transitioning into a triple salchow! I'm happy to stay here all day until you quit doing that Godsdamn axel!"

Malia Barker picked herself up from the small patch of ice in the middle of the muddy field behind the Barfonme castle and complained, "All these stupid jumps look exactly the same."

Cereal Foreskin, Malia's new ice skating instructor, said, "Well, missy, they are most definitely *not* the same." Cereal then went on to explain the difference between lutzes, salchows, axels, toe loops, and flips, a confusing and ultimately useless explanation that took almost three hours. Halfway through the lecture, Malia was seriously contemplating removing her ice skates and slitting Cereal's throat, and then her own.

After Cereal's interminable sermon came to its conclusion, Malia pointed out, "Cereal Foreskin, you can explain this stuff until you're blue in the face—which you are—but it doesn't make a damn bit of difference, because Summer is coming, and when Summer comes, all the ice will be gone." She gestured to the tiny circle of frozen-ish mud she was balancing upon and noted, "It's not like we have all that much to work with right now."

Sighing, Cereal agreed, "You're right, Malia. But House Barfonme signed me to a long-term contract during the Winter, and if I stop teaching, I stop getting paid, and that simply won't do. So you get on that ice and do that lutz/salchow combo right now, or I'll, well, I'll murder you."

A white-hot bolt of anger shot through Malia and she pulled Syringe out from behind her ear and sneered, "You're not the boss of me, Cereal Foreskin!"

Cereal raised his hands in the air and simpered, "Whoa there, missy, that's quite a weapon you have. Mind if I take a look?"

"You don't fool me, Cereal Foreskin! I'm not giving you my weapon."

"Malia, before we continue this delightful discussion, I have a quick question: Why do you insist on calling me by my full name each and every sentence?"

"Because, Cereal Foreskin, Cereal Foreskin is the best name in this entire book, and since you're only in two scenes, it needs to be repeated as often as possible. Got it, Cereal Foreskin?"

He nodded. "Got it. Now that that's cleared up, can I show you something?"

"As long as it's not a lutz."

"It is most definitely not a lutz," he noted, and then reached behind an ear and pulled out a sword that could have been Syringe's little sister.

Malia gasped. "Cereal Foreskin, that sword could be Syringe's little sister!"

"So I gather," he said, and then added, "How about we get rid of these ice skates and I teach you something that you might be able to use in a few chapters."

"Cereal Foreskin." Malia beamed. "That's the most brilliant idea I've heard in weeks. You're the best, Cereal Foreskin."

"That's my name, don't wear it out." He grinned.

"Too late, Cereal Foreskin." Malia then took a near-perfect fencing stance, pointed Syringe at Cereal, then commanded, "School me, Cereal Foreskin. School me but *good*."

TRITONE

For the fifth time that morning, Tritone Sinister stepped in a warm pile of vomit. "Godsdamn it," he mumbled to himself, "these Swatch morons are dumber than . . . dumber than . . . dumber than . . ." He was so honked off about the vomit situation that he could not even come up with a quality "dumber than . . ." insult.

Another thing that appalled the giant about the Frat boys: they were lightweights. Three drinks, and those chumps were *out*. Tritone, on the other hand, could drink seven boxes of the most potent grog in Easterrabbit, and still ride a horse like nobody's business.

Tritone walked back to base camp—slowly and carefully, so as not to tromp through another heap of regurgitated onions—but before he got back to his tent, he ran into Broheim Alistair Cooke. Cooke smiled. "Ah, Mr. Sinister, I hope your stay with us continues to be a happy one."

"This place blows. The people who run it are so dumb, they'd get run over by a parked horse," Tritone claimed.

"That's A-1 material, Tritone, just great," Cooke claimed. "So listen, how long do you plan to stay with us? Because we're heading North. Remember, Summer is coming."

"Ah. Right. Summer is coming. Haven't heard that one in two chapters. I'm cutting out tonight. But before I split, Cooke, I've got a question for you: Who's the best booter in this dump?"

Cooke shyly said, "I've been told I can boot pretty well."

"If that's the case, Shecky, then you are most definitely *not* the poster child for *those who can't do, teach,* because your boys can't *do.*"

With an offended look on his face, Cooke said, "Do you think you can do better? Do you think you can out-boot me?"

"Broheim, I could out-boot you with one intestine tied behind my back."

Cooke removed his shirt and roared, "Tritone Sinister has challenged me to a booting duel!" Then he raised his head to the sky and made a remarkably loud gagging noise, after which all the Swatch pledges came running, except for Juan Nieve, who came trudging. "Bluto," he called, "recite the rules of a booting challenge."

"The first rule of a booting challenge," Bluto said, "is that you do not talk about a booting challenge!"

"Correct!" Cooke roared.

"The second rule of a booting challenge," Bluto continued, "is that *you do not talk about a booting challenge!*"

"Correct!" Cooke roared.

"The third rule of a booting challenge," Bluto continued, "is that if someone says *stop,* the contest is over!"

"Correct!"

"The fourth rule of a booting challenge is that there are only two guys to a boot! The fifth rule is that there's one boot at a time! The sixth rule is no shirt, no shoes, no boot! The seventh rule is that all boots go on as long as they have to! The eighth rule is that if this is your first night, you *must* boot."

"Swell," Tritone grunted. "On your mark, get set, go."

"Wait, I'm not ready," Cooke whined.

"Tough titties," Tritone said, then pulled a box of grog from his sack, downed it in three gulps, and projectile booted on Broheim Cooke's head.

Cooke mumbled, "Stop," and thus, according to rule three, the contest was over.

Disgusted, Tritone grumbled, "Lightweights," then took Juan by the elbow and told the jerkoff, "You and me, we have to talk."

Juan jerked his elbow away and complained, "I don't want to talk to you, giant. I'm tired of hearing how stupid I am. Also, I'm not fat, so you can stop with that, too."

Tritone pinched Juan's stomach and said, "I don't know, Shecky. It looks like you're packing on the pounds. If you don't watch it, you'll have to marry three girls just to get a full-body hug. Which is actually what I wanted to talk about."

"I'm not the marrying kind, Tritone," Juan said.

"Apparently, you're not the boinking kind, either."

Juan blushed. "In case you haven't noticed, there's nobody to *hacer lo desagradable*[34] with around here."

"*Hacer lo* what?"

"I don't mess around with dudes."

"Yeah, me neither. I think my old pal Vladymyr Targetpractice has that mess-around-with-dudes thing covered. I want to talk because in case you ever have the opportunity to mess around with a girl, I want you to be prepared."

"Tritone," Juan said, "I don't need—"

"When two people love each other very, very much," Tritone interrupted, "they get certain feelings, feelings of excitement, and their private parts—the man's is called a penis, and the woman's is called a vagina—become sensitive to the touch . . . but in a good way."

"Tritone, I . . ."

"Listen, you need this lesson, my friend, because I've seen your junk, and that thing is so small that you have to jump when you pee just so you can get the piss over your nuts."

"Tritone . . ."

"Your dick is like a landmine: small, hidden, and explodes on contact."

"Tri . . ."

"Your dick is so small that bacteria laughs at it."

"Oh yeah? Well your head is so soft that if I hit it with the butt end of my sword, it would hurt."

"That's not a zinger, Juan," Tritone said.

"Here's the punch line," Juan said, then hit Tritone Sinister with the butt end of his sword. As Tritone crumbled to the muddy ground in a heap, Juan yelled, "Thank you very much, everybody! Tip your waitress, and try the veal with onions, and please always remember, and please never forget, wherever you go, there you are! Good night!"

As Juan walked away, Tritone grumbled, "That small-dicked jerkoff stole my exit line."

---

34. Do the nasty.

ALLBRAN

Dickoff, the youngest Barker child, was despised by his siblings—and justifiably so, as he was a little snot who did nothing to move the story forward—so he had become an expert at amusing himself, primarily with mud. Nobody in Summerseve baked a better mudpie, or built a better mudman, or threw a better mudball than Dickoff Barker.

Normally, Allbran wanted nothing to do with Dickoff and his muddy shenanigans, but he had been locked in his bedroom for the last two weeks—Maester Blaester said he would heal faster if he was confined day and night—and he was so bored that making a mud sculpture did not sound so bad.

As was his wont, Dickoff was playing in the mud pile directly below Allbran's bedroom window. While Allbran watched his little brother longingly, he unconsciously leaned farther and farther out the window; the farther away Dickoff walked away from the castle, the farther out Allbran leaned. When Dickoff wandered out of sight, Allbran took a deep sigh, then released a deeper fart that launched him into the air and through the window.

Allbran fell three stories, then crashed to the ground without making a sound. He lay still for several minutes, taking inventory of his injuries, of which there were none. He extricated himself from the mud, then looked around to see who had noticed the fall. Since most of our characters were either in Capaetal Ceity or journeying from one place to another, nobody saw or heard Allbran's tumble. He jogged over to the castle and scaled the wall without the benefit of a rope, and was back in his bed in three minutes, Maester Blaester none the wiser.

After he removed his muddy clothes, he crawled into bed and, for the first time in forever, thought about Old Bag, his nanny who has yet to be mentioned *before* this chapter, and will never be mentioned again *after* this chapter.

What with the gigantic green wart on the tip of her nose, her wrinkled skin, and her three saggy breasts, Old Bag was still the ugliest person All-bran had ever seen in his life. Her eyes were rheumy, her breath was hideous, and where Allbran's gas expulsions were charming, Old Bag's were appalling.

As Allbran drifted off, one of the many fables Old Bag subjected him to popped into his head: the story of the three Others.

According to Old Bag, half of the Others behind the Wall were kind and benevolent, while the other Others were violent brutes with no conscience whatsoever. One day many Summers ago, a kind Other named Mork Myndy decided to convert three of the other Others to a life of giving. The first Other Mork approached was named Filthy McNasty.

"Filthy," Mork said, "I believe that you would be more fulfilled if you stopped tearing off the limbs of the other Others."

Filthy regarded Mork skeptically, then nodded and said, "I believe you are correct, but I will stop tearing off limbs only if you can convince our middle brother to do so too."

His heart singing, Mork skipped over to the home of Filthy's brother, Dirty. "Dirty," Mork said, "I believe that you would be more fulfilled if you stopped tearing off the limbs of the other Others."

Dirty scratched his chin, and told Mork, "You might be right. Talk to our youngest brother, and if he's on board, then so am I."

Floating on a cloud, Mork skipped over to the home of the youngest McNasty, Grungy. "Grungy," he said, "I believe that you would be more fulfilled if you stopped tearing off the limbs of the other Others."

Grungy dug a finger in his ear and said, "I would tell you I think that's a good idea, Mork, but honestly, I don't." And then he tore off Mork's left arm. Blood jetted from both Mork's dismembered limb and the gaping hole near his shoulder, painting the walls of Grungy McNasty's house, as well as Grungy himself. Grungy then stuck his fist into the shoulder hole and felt around as if he was on a treasure hunt . . . which, as it turned out, he was. He snapped off a chunky piece of Mork's collarbone, gave it a thoughtful look, then popped it into his mouth. It took him several minutes to fully chew it, during which time Mork bled out. Grungy then called for his brothers, and when they arrived at the house, they feasted upon Mork's body as if it were their last meal . . . which, as it turned out, it was, because, as it so happened, Mork's blood type was AB negative, a blood type that was an anathema to the McNastys' gastrointestinal systems. Once Mork's blood hit Filthy, Dirty, and Grungy's intestinal tracts, their stomachs all exploded, yellow bile flew from their mouths, and they died horrible, painful deaths. The moral of the story, Old Bag explained, was this: *Don't fuck with the Others.*

For weeks after hearing that tale, Allbran had nightmares of dismembered arms and exploding stomachs. Eventually Headcase and Gateway got wind of Old Bag's awful bedtime stories, so she was summarily fired. But that did not put an end to Allbran's nightmares.

Remembering the story's awful climax—and flashing back on the ensuing nightmares—Allbran flew out of bed and jumped out the window, landing in Dickoff's mud pile with a sickening squish. He lay still for several minutes, taking inventory of his injuries, of which there were none. He extricated himself from the mud, then looked around to see who had noticed the fall. Since, as noted, most of our characters were either in Capaetal Ceity or journeying from one place to another, nobody saw or heard Allbran's tumble . . . but Allbran saw and heard one of the characters: Bobb.

His older brother was stomping across the front yard, talking to himself. Allbran strained to discern what Bobb was saying, and he did not like what he heard, not one bit.

"House Barker has no leader," Bobb blustered. "Father's getting old, and Mother's an idiot. If we're attacked, his Lordship would give the enemies a lecture about how they should be nice to one another, and Mother would invite them in for Godsweede and cake. Me, I'd put together an unstoppable army and slaughter them. I'd slaughter them all! *Bwah hah hah hah hah hah hahhhhhhhhhh!*"

Once Bobb was out of earshot and eyeshot, Allbran cut the loudest, smelliest cheese he had ever cut; it was so powerful that it lifted him off the ground, and up the three stories to his bedroom. He wiped off the mud from his nude body, crawled into bed, and decided that solitary confinement was not so bad after all.

LOLYTA

Curled up in her enormous mud-bed, under her 600-thread-count Easterrabbitian cotton sheets, Loly Targetpractice smiled and thought, *It's good to be the KERBANGER.*

The past few months had been the best of her life: Her every need was catered to, she was treated with respect by each and every person in Dork (except Vladymyr, naturally), and it turned out that Ivan Drago (and his enormous horse schlong) was damn good under a horse blanket. All in all, a magical existence.

Except for the dreams.

Each and every night, seemingly minutes after she closed her eyes and drifted off to sleep, Loly found herself in the middle of a giant field filled with eggs of all colors and sizes, many of which were alive, many of which tried to attack her. She ducked and dodged, but the egg assault was so intense that there was nothing she could do to fully protect herself, so she inevitably got nailed. Most of the eggs were filled with what she figured most eggs were filled with—gooey whites and gooier yolks—but some of them carried hatchlings, and those creatures were hideous: tiny, yellow, and covered with soft feathers. These awful beings tried to communicate with her, but she was unable to understand their language, which seemed to consist of two words: *quack* and *awk*.

When Loly told Magistrate Illinois about the dreams, Magistrate gave her a strange look and explained, "KERBANGER, it sounds like you're dreaming of ducks. And you're obsessed with ducks. You're the Princess of Duckseventually, for Gods' sake."

"Those aren't ducks, Chicago. Ducks are huge, bigger than you could ever imagine, and they're green, and they have scales, and a long tail covered with thorny things, and they breathe fire. *Duh.*"

"My KERBANGER, you're talking about dragons," Illinois explained.

"No, I'm definitely talking about ducks. Dragons look like horses, except they have black and white stripes."

"Those are zebras, my KERBANGER."

"No, zebras are short," Loly claimed, "and are black with white tummies, and they waddle, and even though they have wings, they can't fly."

"Those are penguins, my KERBANGER."

Loly flung open her bedroom door and called, *"Vladymyr!"*

Her brother was there in the blink of a dragon's eye. "Yes, sister dear?"

"Tell Magistrate Illinois what dragons look like."

"Horses, except with black and white stripes," Vladymyr explained.

Illinois rolled her eyes and stomped out of the room, mumbling, "House Targetpractice and their Godsdamn home schooling."

Loly called to Illinois, "Before this is all said and done, I bet you a duck'll play a big role in this story!" She turned to Vladymyr and asked, "Ducks will play a big role in this story, won't they? I mean, we've been going on and on about them, and it has to lead *somewhere.*"

Before Vladymyr could answer, a Dorki galloped into the bedroom and said, "Congo bongo, bongo congo, riding lesson."

Vladymyr gave Loly a shocked look, then asked her in a whisper, "Did he just say *riding lesson*?"

She whispered back, "Yeah. They seem to be picking up the language."

"Weird. That was quick," he noted.

The KERBANGER shrugged. "Whatever. Let's go ride."

The Targetpractices both enjoyed their lessons for the same reason: Rather than ride on horses, they rode on Dorkis, and to Loly and Vladymyr, straddling a male Dorki's back was far more satisfying than straddling a horse's back. (Vladymyr wasn't impressed with his first Dorki, a female called Ivan Barbara, so he whined until they gave him a male named Ivan Kevin.) Loly had become quite attached to her lesson Dorki, Ivan George, and taking into account the way he moaned when she straddled him, she thought that he liked her too.

It was their fifth lesson, and Loly was already an expert at riding a

Dorki; truth be told, she did not need any more lessons, but she did not want to stop. Vladymyr, on the other hand, seemed confused, almost as if he were trying to find himself.

After they both mounted their centaurs, Ivan George said, "Oingo boingo, let's go go go go."

Under his breath, Vladymyr asked Loly, "Did he just say, 'let's go go go go'?"

"Who cares?" she asked.

Vladymyr claimed, "It's weird that they went from being subhuman morons to decent speakers in only a few chapters."

Ivan Kevin growled, "Bippety boppety boo, I can totally hear you."

Pointing at the Dorki, he hissed to Loly, *"See?!"*

As she scratched Ivan George behind the ear, she told Vladymyr, "As your KERBANGER, I command you to shut up." To Ivan George, she exclaimed, "Oingo boingo, let's go go go go!"

After their lesson—which, as usual, they both enjoyed a bit too much—they jumped off their Dorkis and walked slowly back to the castle. Loly did not have much to say, as she was focused on the tingling in her loins. Vladymyr, who seemed to have trouble walking, was equally quiet. Right before they entered the castle, Loly noticed her brother was adjusting something below his beltline, his expression a combination of pleasure and pain. Staring at his beltline, Loly asked, "Everything okay, brother dear?"

He pulled his hand away from below his waist and began to furiously scratch his head. "Everything's fine," he claimed. "Why would you think it wasn't? I'm great. As a matter of fact, I'm perfect. No, I'm *fierce*!"

Loly stared at her brother for an awkward moment, then asked, "Is there something you'd like to tell me?"

"What? Tell you? What do you mean? Tell you what? Nothing to tell here. I'm fierce."

"I'm sure you are," she said. After another uncomfortable pause, she blustered, "I'm just going to come right out and say it: Do you like boys?"

He pshawed, "No way! You *know* I like girls. For that matter, I *love* girls. I'm all about the tang. I mean, look how often I pinch your nipples."

"And I do love that," Loly admitted, "but I sometimes feel like you're doing it to, I don't know, compensate or something."

Vladymyr's face turned beet red, and he screeched, "You shut up, little

Miss Duckseventually! You shut up right now! Girls are the best! Nothing's better than what goes on between their legs, *nothing*! If there was a girl here right now, I'd dive on in."

Loly pointed out, "I'm here. And as they say all over Easterrabbit, incest is best."

Vladymyr stammered, "But . . . but . . . but . . . you're *married*!"

Shrugging, Loly said, "I'm cool with it if you are."

They stared at one another for a couple of beats, then Vladymyr stomped off, chanting, "All about the tang, all about the tang, all about the tang . . ."

Loly called, "Come out of the closet, brother dear!" When he didn't respond, she whispered to herself, "Come out of the closet," then slowly and thoughtfully walked back to her bedchamber.

HEADCASE

Headcase sat in the muddy bank of the muddy Capaetal Ceity River, staring at the placid water as if it were a snake coiling then uncoiling, unconcerned that the new feather-covered outfit Tinyjohnson had procured for him was growing filthier by the second. Tinyjohnson, however, seemed less than pleased.

"Your Footness," the non-eunuch whined, unsuccessfully attempting to keep the whininess out of his voice, "those silken trousers were not made for sitting in a muddy riverbank and staring at placid water as if it were a snake coiling then uncoiling."

"I appreciate your concern," Head lied, "but there are more pressing matters on my mind. I have birthed an idea."

Tinyjohnson said, "Birthed an idea? That sounds disgusting."

"I'm certain anything having to do with birthing sounds disgusting to you, eunuch."

Indignant, Tinyjohnson declared, "I am *not* a eunuch!" He motioned as if to pull down his trousers, then asked, "Would you care to see the proof?"

Head picked up two fistfuls of mud and rubbed them into his eyes, then begged, "Again, no, no, for the love of Gods, no. For the sake of argument, I will stipulate that you are not a eunuch, and will never mention it again. This isn't to say that somebody else won't mention it a few chapters down the road, but there you have it."

"Thank you," Tinyjohnson sighed. After a pause, he added, "I can show it to you anyhow. Just for fun."

After putting more mud over his eyes, Head reiterated, "Thank you, but no. Now I called you down here to discuss how we can get Capaetal Ceity out of this financial mess. I have decided we shall have a festyval."

"You mean a festival?" Tinyjohnson asked.

"No," Head reiterated, "I mean a festyval. With a *y*. I shall call it the Woodstok Festyval of Frolicking, Fryvolity, and Fyghting. It will be three days of war and screaming. The fee shall be ten dollars per day, and the population of Cap Ceity is two hundred thousand, so if every citizen attends the festyval each day, that will net us six million dollars, which will give us more than enough money to repay our loans from Chyna. Not that we *will* repay them, but that's neither here nor there."

Tinyjohnson stated, "I greatly doubt that everybody in the Ceity will attend."

"Oh, they will, Tinyjohnson."

"How do you know?"

"Simple: Those who miss the festyval will be beheaded."

Beaming, Tinyjohnson exclaimed, "Now *that* is how you Foot!"

JUAN

s Juan Nieve cleaned the mud from his shoes, he mumbled, "*Barro maldito,*[35] *barro maldito,*[36] *barro maldito,*[37] then glanced at the Wall, noting the puddles forming at its base. "I can't imagine what will happen to that thing now that Summer is coming," he grumbled.

From behind him, a voice asked, "Is Summer indeed coming?"

Without turning around, Juan agreed, "Yes. *El verano se acerca.*"[38]

"Summer is coming?" the voice asked.

"*El verano se acerca,*"[39] Juan agreed.

"Summer is coming?" the voice asked.

"*El verano se acerca,*"[40] Juan agreed, then he turned around and found himself face-to-stomach with a boy who could generously be described as husky, but would more realistically be described as repulsively obese. "Can I help you, *el gordo*?"[41] Juan asked.

The fat boy said, "Don't call me fat boy."

Juan gave the fat boy a long look, then whispered, "You understand my language. You are the only person in all of Easterrabbit who does." With a lump in his throat, he said, "I feel a lump in my throat."

---

35. Godsdamn mud.
36. Godsdamn mud.
37. Godsdamn mud.
38. Summer is coming.
39. Summer is coming.
40. Summer is coming.
41. Fat boy.

Rubbing his jiggly gut, the fat boy said, "And I feel a lump in my stomach."

They stared into each other's eyes for a long moment, then ran into an embrace, the boy falling on top of Juan. The jerkoff coughed, "*Gxgglmrldtwop.*"[42]

The boy rolled off of Juan, then apologized, "I apologize. Bad habit." He then offered Juan his hand and said, "Snackwell Fartly, rotund one from the city of Heavensmurgatroyd."

While shaking Snackwell's porky hand, Juan pulled himself up and said, "Juan Nieve, jerkoff from the city of Summerseve." After a beat, Juan pointed out, "Don't take this the wrong way—you seem like a great guy and all—but it's kind of odd that you just rolled up here, out of nowhere. Doesn't make sense that some strange fat kid would just *show up*. It's like you're there to remind us of the importance of staying healthy, or maybe you're a metaphor for alienation. Or maybe comic relief. Whatever you're doing here, it's random, and it had better lead somewhere, because the last thing this story needs is another character who's there just to fill space." Pointing at Snackwell's jiggly tummy, Juan added, "But I will say this: if there's one thing I bet you're good at, it's filling space."

A brilliant grin overtook Snackwell's face, a smile so beatific that for a brief moment, it was almost as if his corpulence was not an issue . . . the key word being *almost,* because Snackwell's corpulence would *always* be an issue. "Juan Nieve, you and I will be great friends. You're a jerkoff, and I'm a fatass. We're two peas in a pod."

"Well, Snackwell, that would have to be an awfully big pod!" Juan joked, and then the boys laughed, and laughed, and laughed. After the chuckles died, Juan asked, "So, fatass, if you're not a metaphor, what brings you to the Wall?"

"Well, jerkoff, I want to start Rush Year today! I want to be a member of the Fraternity of the Swatch!"

Shaking his head, Juan said, "No, you don't."

"Yes, I do!" Snackwell cried. "I want to defend the border! I want to

---

42. Gxgglmrldtwop.

have adventures! I want to be a metaphor! I want to be a simile! I want to be an allegory! I want to battle the Others . . ."

From the distance, a voice cried, *"We're not the Others! We're the Awesomes, asshole!"*

". . . and most importantly, I want to be part of a brotherhood."

A voice from behind called, "You would be a wonderful addition to the family."

The two outcasts turned around, and Juan sneered, "Hello, Otter."

"Hi, there, jerkoff," Otter sneered back. "Who's the fatass?" Snackwell offered Otter his hand and an introduction, to which Otter—ignoring the proffered hand—pointed out, "You're the fattest person I've ever seen. I bet you can boot like there's no tomorrow."

Snackwell scratched his head, then asked, "Boot?"

"Yeah, boot. You know, barf. Hurl. Heave. Honk. Ralph. Gack. Wolf. Urp. Spew. Chunk. Earl. Yak."

After a bit of silence, Juan asked, "Are you done?"

"Oh, Gods no," Otter scoffed. "Launch lunch. Blow foam. Yawn chunks. Clean house. Thunder chunder. Toss a tiger. Flash your hash. Mark the mud. Laugh at the lawn. Park the pea soup. Growl at the gravel. Lob some liquid hand grenades. Sing the ballad of the grog." Pointing at Snackwell, he added, "I *know* that you know what I'm talking about, big boy."

Snackwell stammered, "I . . . I . . . I think it might not be a good idea to go down that road. Because . . . because . . . because once I start down that road, there's no telling when I'll stop."

Otter beamed, "Broheim, you sound like a natural boot-meister." Then he raised his head to the sky and made a remarkably loud gagging noise, after which all the Swatch pledges came running. "Yes, Broheim Otter," they said in unison.

"Fellow pledges, meet Snackwell Fartly. You can call him Snack."

"No, you can't," Snack protested.

"Yes, we can," Otter disputed. "Broheim Snack is apparently one of the finest booters in all of Easterrabbit, and he's going to give us a demonstration."

"No, I'm not," Snack protested.

"Yes, you are," Otter disputed.

Juan said, "Just get it over with, Snack. If you want to be one of them, you'll have to do it eventually."

Snack stammered, "My . . . my . . . my stomach is empty, because I, um, what do you call it, hooted . . ."

"Booted," Pinto corrected.

"Right. I booted on my way over." Patting his stomach, he added, "Nothing there."

"Not for long," D-Day grinned, then tossed Snack an enormous box of grog. "Polish off half of that, and you'll be booting until Summer."

Snack sighed, "I don't like grog."

"Great," Flounder said, "you'll boot that much faster."

Naturally, Otter then began a chant, which the Frat boys immediately picked up: *"Drink! Boot! Drink! Boot! Drink! Boot!"*

Finally, Snack succumbed. "Okay," he said, "over the lips and past the gums, look out stomach, here it comes." In one endless guzzle, he dumped the entire box of grog down his gullet. The Swatchmen gasped in amazement—even Juan was impressed—and were, for a change, speechless.

Eventually, Otter whispered with awe, "That was genius, Snack. I can't wait to see the boot. Now let it go. You know you want to."

His forehead dotted with sweat, Snack gurgled, "I *do* want to." Then he took a deep breath, then another, then another, then leaned back as far as he possibly could—which, truth be told, was not that far—opened his mouth, and delivered a belch that uprooted three trees and knocked Otter et al. onto their backsides.

Otter sat up and felt the front of his shirt. "It's dry," he said. "Where's the boot?"

Snack stared at his shoes, clearly embarrassed. "I can't boot," he admitted. "Never have, and probably never will."

Otter said, "Well you clearly don't have what it takes to be a Swatchman. I recommend you leave the area immediately. If you don't, you shall suffer dire consequences." And then Otter et al. stomped away.

Watching them go, Snack asked Juan, "What do they mean by dire consequences?" He paused, then said, "Wait, let me guess: they'll boot on me."

"*Sí.* They'll boot on you."

Snack hung his head, then whispered, "The fellowship I was seeking is not here." He glanced at the Wall and said, "Maybe the Others will have me."

"No, we won't! And we're not the Others! We're the Awesomes, asshole!"

"Well, that answers that question," Snack sighed. "I shall be on my way."

He took two steps, then, out of nowhere, Broheim Cooke appeared. "Where're you going, fatass?"

"Away," Snack groaned.

"Nah, hang around. I think you might provide some comic relief down the line." To Juan, he said, "Listen, jerkoff, your pal Sinjean Barker has disappeared."

"Gosh," Juan mused, "I haven't thought about him in, what, ten chapters, maybe fifteen. Any idea where he might be?"

From behind a tree, they heard an *Ahem.*

"What was that?" Cooke asked.

Juan and Snack both shrugged, then heard again, except louder: *"Ahem!"*

"What the hell was that?" Cooke asked again, and again, Juan and Snack shrugged.

The *ahem* turned into a cough . . . a cough that sounded remarkably like the cougher, rather than coughing *"Hack, hack, hack,"* was saying *"Sin, Sin, Sin."*

Snack turned to Juan and asked, "Does it sound to you like he's saying *'Sin, Sin, Sin'* rather than *'Hack, hack, hack'*?"

"No," Cooke disagreed, "it definitely doesn't."

"Yes," the cougher cried, "it definitely does." And then, from behind the tree, out emerged Sinjean Barker.

Juan's face broke into a goofy grin. "Uncle Sin, for the last twenty-six seconds, I thought you were gone, and those were the worst twenty-six seconds of my life!"

Sinjean asked, "Do you want to know the worst twenty-six seconds of my life, jerkoff?"

"Not really," Juan said.

Ignoring Juan, Sin said, "It was Sixty-eight. I was in Da Nang, assdeep in a stinking rice paddy, Charlie to the left, Charlie to the right, Charlie in front, Charlie in back. My buddy Horse had caught some shrapnel in his gut, and that magnificent bastard was bleeding out at my feet. As he told me to tell Lucy and the girls that he loved them, it hit me: if Horse could bite it, I could bite it. I mean, I was out of ammo, out of acid, out of water, and just about out of time, and for twenty-six seconds, I was certain that I was dead, certain that House Barker would have to go on without the Sin Man. But then the choppers came, and they took me right to Summerseve." He paused, then said, "I'm not ashamed to say I kissed the mud when I landed."

From over the Wall, somebody yelled, *"It's not nice to refer to the Viet Cong as Charlie, asshole!"* And then Sinjean Barker was vaporized by an AGM-87 Focus guided missile.

Juan, Cooke, and Snack stared somberly at the pile of ash that was once Sinjean Barker. Finally, Cooke said, "No offense, jerkoff, but I am not going to miss that big psycho. Not one bit."

Under his breath, Juan whispered, "Me neither," then he clapped Snackwell Fartly on the shoulder and said, "Come on, *culo enorme*,[43] I'm not sending you out into the world all by yourself, Broheim-less. Let's teach you how to boot."

Snack gave Juan a grateful grin and whispered reverently, "Nothing would make me happier, you gigantic jerkoff. Nothing at all."

---

43. Huge ass.

HEADCASE

According to the Encyclopedya Easterrabbitica, House Barfonme was the second worst House in terms of illiteracy—just behind House Targetpractice, naturally—in part because Capaetal Ceity's schools were only open during the Summer—which never came—and in part because the town's lone bookstore was located at the foot of an active volcano, in a mall that also housed the area's only apothecary.

As Lord Headcase Barker trudged to said store, he read, and reread, and reread Lady Gateway Bully Barker's ravengram:

> I know you're all wrapped up in your lame-brained festyval, but don't forget that Tritone Sinister tried to kill our kid, and you need to find out why. Hugs, Gateway.
>
> P.S. I decided not to become a prostitute.
>
> P.P.S. You have to keep watching the girls by yourself, because I'm not coming back to Capaetal Ceity, but rather going to visit my sister for reasons that are not quite clear yet. Make sure Malia eats her veggies.
>
> P.P.P.S. Your little friend Tinyjohnson is traveling with me. I think he's a eunuch.
>
> P.P.P.P.S. Think of me when you touch yourself.

Head wanted nothing more than to think of his wife when he touched himself, but in the little time for self-touching, he could not concentrate. His brain kept going to the Sinister situation, because when it came to why House Sinister was at battle with House Barker, there were dozens of plot holes, and it was driving him to distraction. In true Head-like fashion, he decided to do some research, so he could fill those blanks right on in, thus the trip to the bookshop.

The floor of Baredor's Books was coated with a thin layer of volcanic ash, but Head thought that just added to the shop's charm. When Head sauntered up to the counter, the shop's proprietor, Blubbernerd Millipede, fell to his knees and, through a haze of ash, said, "My Lord, the King's Foot, how may this humble bookseller aid you on this fine day?"

"First," Head said, fanning the ash from his face, "I command you to stand up." After Millipede rose, Head continued, "Second, I need a history book."

"What kind of history book?"

Shrugging, Head admitted, "No idea. What happened in Easterrabbit's past is a bit confusing. I mean, the years aren't logically numbered, the Summers and Winters come and go with no rhyme or reason, and the maps of this place make zero sense. But I'll worry about that later; my main goal right now is to find out why all the Houses hate each other so Godsdamn much."

Millipede raised his index finger, claimed, "I have just the thing," then skittered off to the stacks. A couple of minutes later, he returned with an oversized book, which he handed to Head, then said, "This might be just what you're looking for."

Head peered at the cover: *The Lineages and Histories and Stories and Secrets of the Lots and Lots of Kingdoms, with Caricatures and Distorted Renderings of Many High Lords and Noble Ladies and Their Children and Their Pets and Their Slaves and Their Silverware and Their Horses and Their Sigils and Their Breakfasts and Their Lunches and Their Dinners and Their Onions* by Grand Maester Baeter.

After giving the two-thousand-plus-page book a quick thumb-through, Head said, "I don't know, Blubbernerd, it looks interesting, but I don't think it's the one."

"I understand, my Footship. I believe I have the perfect title," he claimed, then again skittered off. A couple of minutes later, he returned with an even more oversized book, which he handed to Head, then said, "I believe this will be more to your liking."

Head peered at the cover: *The Chronicles and Records and Sagas of the*

World as We Know It and the Individuals and Figures and Peoples Who Created the Infrastructures and the Organizations and the Societies and the Unions That Will Be Endured and Enjoyed by Each and Every Sentient Man and Woman and Child and Dragon Throughout the Land and the Terra Firma and the Soil and the Terrain and the Historical Histories That Emerged from the Meetings and the Gatherings and the Assemblies That Led to the Creation of the Infrastructures and the Organizations and the Societies by Grand Maester Broocelee.

"I'm not sure, Blubbernerd." Head shrugged after giving the 3,000-plus-page book a fast peek. "This might be a little too broad."

"Ah, you want something specific. I understand, my Footship. I believe I have the perfect title." A couple of minutes later, he returned with a miniature book—a pamphlet, really—which he handed to Head, then said, "I believe *this* will be more to your liking."

Head peered at the cover: *Why All the Houses Hate Each Other So Godsdamn Much* by Grand Maester Flaysh.

"Perfect!" Head exclaimed. "I'll take it!"

On the walk back home, Head read the book from cover to cover, and it clarified exactly nothing. The thought of reading either *The Lineages and Histories and Stories and Secrets of the Lots and Lots of Kingdoms, with Caricatures and Distorted Renderings of Many High Lords and Noble Ladies and Their Children and Their Pets and Their Slaves and Their Silverware and Their Horses and Their Sigils and Their Breakfasts and Their Lunches and Their Dinners and Their Onions* or *The Chronicles and Records and Sagas of the World as We Know It and the Individuals and Figures and Peoples Who Created the Infrastructures and the Organizations and the Societies and the Unions That Will Be Endured and Enjoyed by Each and Every Sentient Man and Woman and Child and Dragon Throughout the Land and the Terra Firma and the Soil and the Terrain and the Historical Histories That Emerged from the Meetings and the Gatherings and the Assemblies That Led to the Creation of the Infrastructures and the Organizations and the Societies* from cover to cover made him queasy—who in their right minds would want to read over five thousand pages about Easterrabbit?—so he figured he would go back to work and let the Barker/Sinister thing play itself out on its own.

Back at the castle, Tinyjohnson was awaiting Head at the front door.

Grabbing Head's elbow, the non-eunuch breathed, "Come quick, Foot. I have pressing news."

"You *always* have pressing news, Tinyjohnson."

"Indeed. We have an appointment."

"Where? With who?"

"At the apothecary. With the apothecary."

"I just came from there," he kvetched. "You couldn't have called me on my cell?"

Tinyjohnson explained, "There's no reception by the volcano. And good luck getting a raven to go down there on short notice."

"Why do we need to see the apothecary at the apothecary?"

"Apparently he has some news about Lord Functionary Aaron."

"Functionary? Really? Just like that?"

"What do you mean, *just like that*?" Tinyjohnson asked.

"I mean, what's with all these callbacks?"

"Callbacks?"

Head said, "Well, we hadn't heard anything about Sin Barker in who-knows-how-long, then he shows up out of nowhere and gets blown up. And nobody's said a word about Functionary Aaron in *forever,* and now we're going to talk about him with the apothecary? What's next? Are Airhead and Jarhead coming back?"

In the distance, Juan's direpanda, Fourshadow, roared.

The apothecary was named Warblethroat Millipede, Blubbernerd's brother, and where Blubbernerd was subservient and modest, Warblethroat was flamboyant and pretentious. "Friends," Warblethroat intoned when Head and Tinyjohnson entered his shop, "Barkers, Barfonmes, country-men, lend me your ears, for I follow you to serve my turn upon you."

"Thank you, Warblethroat," Head thanked. "My short friend here tells me you have something to share with us."

"That is correct, my Footship. Some cupids kill with arrows, and some with traps. Oft expectation fails, and most oft there is a happy dagger, and nothing can come of nothing."

Lord Barker gave the kind apothecary a strange look and admitted, "You aren't making sense, kind apothecary."

"Apologies, my Footship. Let me clarify, for there is a method in the madness. All that glitters is not gold during the Summer of our discontent.

A King of infinite space bids a long farewell to all my greatness. Oh, villain, villain, smiling damn villain!"

"Still lost," Head admitted.

"Apologies, my Footship. Let me *further* clarify: The man that hath a tongue I say is no man. Oh, what men dare do! Or remedies oft in ourselves do lie. So when shall we three meet again?"

"Listen," Head explained, "the only reason we're here is that we were led to believe you have some news of Lord Aaron."

Warblethroat sniffled, then, with his voice down an octave, and his posh accent gone, he said, "Oh, yeah, right, that. Okay, so a few months back, some dude comes in and makes me make some poison that can make another dude laugh himself to death."

As Head was speechless, Tinyjohnson asked, "Do you know who it was?"

"Nah, but he looked like the kind of dude who'd totally bone his twin sister."

"Well," Head told Tinyjohnson as they left the shop ostensibly to search for the culprit, "that narrows it down to only half the population of Easterrabbit."

GATEWAY

Five days after an attack on her traveling party that we felt wasn't worth mentioning—because how many attacks does one book need, really?—Lady Gateway Bully Barker was still in shock, so much so that she still had not said a multi-worded sentence to Tinyjohnson or the sole oddly named Knight who had survived the battle, Sur Crayola Burntsienna. But Burntsienna was a gregarious, persistent traveling partner who insisted on reliving the incident again and again and again.

"They took them all in one fell swoop, m'Lady," he panted for the bazillionth time, "*One fell swoop!* Sur Porkburger put up valiant fight, he did, as did Sur Fannyass, but even with Sur Slobberknocker and Sur Jablome at their sides, they could not withstand the waves and waves of little gray men and those shiny weapons of theirs."

"Grunt," Gateway grunted.

Burntsienna continued, "And when they took Sur Dyggler, Sur McChucklehead, and Sur Motorboat into that . . . that . . . that . . . what did you call it?"

"Airship," Gateway grunted.

"Right, right, right, that *airship*, well, that was a sight to behold. It was almost as if my fellow Knights had lost their free will, almost as if they were floating above the ground. I believe if I hadn't been hiding behind a tree, I'd be up there with them right now."

"Grunt," Gateway grunted.

"And when the airship left the ground, it made that funny noise." Burntsienna attempted to replicate said funny noise—his version of it sounded like *bliblibliblib,* when in reality, the airship sounded like *blublublublublub*—

then he came to a sudden halt. Wiping his eye, he asked Gateway, "M'Lady, did you feel that?"

"What?" Gateway grunted.

Burntsienna opined, "I believe a drop of rain has fallen into my eye."

Tinyjohnson agreed, "I believe one has fallen on my testicles. Because I *do* have testicles, you know."

Gateway turned her head to the sky, and sure enough, a dropling of sun-dappled water dropling'd onto her nose. She whispered with wonder, "Summer is here."

Burntsienna agreed with equal wonder, "Summer is here."

"Summer is here," Gateway repeated.

"Summer is here," Burntsienna repeated.

"Summer is here."

"Summer is here."

"Summer is here."

"Summer is here."

Their mantra continued for twenty-odd minutes. Burntsienna paused, looked around, and said, wonderingly, "Speaking of seasons, doesn't it seem odd to you that, despite the length of our cold and hot spells, our flora and fauna seem more suited to thrive in a temperate climate? Not that I'm criticizing whichever of our Gods created this place or anything. I mean, I know there are a lot of things to think about when creating an entire world, like the variations on traditional spelling of names, places, and animals. But you'd think that the Gods would have taken the effect of long Summers and Winters on the plants into a little more consideration. Priorities, and all that."

The sunshower began in semi-earnest. At once bored and not bored, Lady Gateway brushed ten drops from her eyebrows and noted, "This is no weather to be traveling in." She pointed straight forward and said, "Look, Burntsienna! A motel! And in the middle of the forest, yet." She sighed contentedly, then mused, "It's almost as if it appeared out of nowhere."

After two knocks on the motel's front entrance, the door was opened by a slender woman with long blond hair and a beatific smile. "Do you have a reservation?" she asked.

"How would we make a reservation?" Gateway responded. "We didn't even know you existed until two minutes ago. It's almost as if you appeared out of nowhere."

The woman poked her head farther out the door, looked around as if to make certain nobody was listening, then whispered, "We did. Don't ask questions." Then, in a normal tone, she offered Gateway her hand and said, "Marsha Braedy, proprietor of the Renyssance Inn. Please come in."

The lobby was warm and welcoming, decorated in warm and welcoming colors, the kind of colors that made the Renyssance Inn feel warm and welcoming. A young man sat in front of the fire, strumming a guitar, and warbling a tune:

> I hope I could offer Sister Roberta her mild thrill
> Then I'd stick Roberta in a cage at the top of a hill
> Then ride to the onion patch in my Cadillac Coupe de Ville
> Roberta could eat onions and take a crazy pill

Gateway thought that the song's lyrics, while semi-interesting, were nonsensical to the point of annoyance, but the most off-putting aspect of the troubadour's performance was his voice. It was a gravelly voice, a whiny voice, an out-of-tune voice, a voice that, had it not been attached to semi-interesting lyrics, would have been dismissed altogether.

Upon seeing the inn's new guests, the troubadour stopped singing and said, "Ah, wonderful, an audience!" He gently placed his guitar on the floor, stood, and added, "Permit me to introduce myself." Offering his hand to Gateway, he said, "Bobdillon."

She accepted his hand offer and said, "Lady Gateway Barker."

Smiling, he went down on one knee and said, "M'Lady, it is an honor to meet you. Did you enjoy my music?"

Gateway shrugged and said, "Meh."

"Would you prefer another song? I've written approximately four hundred fifty-eight of them."

"Thank you, but I'm quite exhausted, and . . ."

Bobdillon snatched up his guitar, cried, "One, two, three, four!" and then launched into the following:

> Looks like they'll onion me when I'm trottin' down the street
> They'll probably onion me when I'm tryin' to stay on my feet
> They might also onion me when I'm hoppin' on the ceiling

They'll onion me when I'm boppin' and free wheelin'
But I could not be so by myself, because I have ten bunions
That'll probably get worse unless my woman gets me ten onions

After fifty-one more verses without a chorus, Bobdillon grinned and asked, "Was that one more to your liking, m'Lady?"

Gateway shrugged and said, "Meh."

Bobdillon reached into the hole of his guitar, pulled out a palm-sized bag and some small rectangular papers, then queried, "Would this be more to your liking, m'Lady?"

Smiling, Gateway exclaimed, "Princess on the steeple, and all the pretty people!" And then Gateway, Bobdillon, Burntsienna, Tinyjohnson, and Marsha Braedy proceeded to get baked.

Some period of time later—and it is impossible to discern the exact amount of time that passed, because Bobdillon's Godsweede was, as he put it, "bomb chronic" that made the hours evaporate—there was a knock at the front door. Marsha Braedy yelled, "Go away! No vacancy!" At which her smoking partners laughed and laughed and laughed.

"Give me a break, Shecky, there ain't a single horse in the parking lot, and this is a one-horse town. This place is such a dump that it makes Duskendale look like Maidenpool."

At that, Gateway et al. laughed, and laughed, and laughed, then Marsha Braedy said, "Ah, great stuff, stranger. I think we can squeeze you in." When she opened the door, she found herself face-to-belt with a gawky giant.

"Good afternoon, my good Lady," the giant said. "Tritone Sinister: If you give up the bucks, I'll give up the fu . . . Oh. Lady Gateway. Surprise, surprise. Of all the gin joints, eh?"

After trying and failing to stand up, Gateway giggled, "Tritone. Fly-tone. High-tone. My moan. Tie groan. I'm blown." She patted her tummy, then asked, "Yo, Pie-phone, you got any Cool Ranch Doritos on you? Or maybe a ham and cheese Hot Pocket?"

"Sorry, Gateway, I left my junk food in my other burlap suit. How's tricks?"

"Tricks are good," she said, then scratched her head and noted, "Hold on, I'm supposed to be mad at you for something."

"Who, *me*? Nobody gets mad at me. I'm the one Sinister people like." Puffing up his chest, he claimed, "Some even say I'm the best character in both the book *and* the first season of the show. So suck on *that*, Sean Bean."

After finally staggering to her feet, Gateway said, "Well, I'm supposed to be mad at you, so I'm totally taking you prisoner."

Tritone shrugged. "If it gets things moving along, that works for me." He then clapped his hands once, made a trio of impressive armpit farts, and said, "You got any grub around this dump? I'm so hungry, I could eat Sasha Barker's direpanda."

SASHA

O h. My. Gods. There're, like, so many people here. It's, like, oh,
my, Gods."

"Well put, Sasha." Sistyr Glynda Roesy Raegan Melvyn
smiled. "I couldn't have said it better myself."

"Totally," Sasha Barker agreed. "Like, how many people are there, do
you think?"

"*Everybody* is here, Sasha. Remember, your father's decree: 'If you miss
the Woodstok Festyval of Frolicking, Fryvolity, and Fyghting, you shall
die. And do not ingest the brown acid.'"

"Totally," Sasha Barker agreed. Pointing to a section of well-dressed men
and women sitting in the first three rows, she asked, "Like, who're those
people?"

Sistyr G.R.R.M. explained, "Why, Capaetal Ceity's hoi polloi,
of course. That's Lord Analwarts Candlestick and his wife, Lady
Ringworm. And that's Lord Worthington Smithington Knockknock
and his wife, Lady Abscess. And that's Lord Afrocentric Schadenfreude
and his wife, Lady Hakunamatata. And that's Lord Showtyme Scis-
sorlegs and his wife, Lady Genericbrand. And that's Lord Sherlock
Hemlock Hoofnmouth and his wife, Lady Pinocchio Pistachio. And
that's Lord Billybeen Rocknjock and his wife, Lady Antybellym. And
finally, that's Lord Nosepicker Wallamaloo and his wife, Lady Belly-
flop."

Sasha then pointed to a pair of multi-armed men standing on the edge
of the battlefield, far away from the dozens of Knights doing downward
dogs in the center of the ring. "Who're those guys? They're, like, totally
grotty to the max."

Sistyr Melvyn sneered, "Those are the Leghorn brothers. Sandstorm is the one with three arms. Grandstand has four."

Sasha squealed, *"Ewwwwwwwww!"*

The Knights soon dispersed, after which a fat man with a fatter beard strolled out to the center of the ring and lifted his arms in the air. "Good afternoon, Cap Ceity!" he yelled. "I'm Wavimus Gravimus, and welcome to the Festyval of Frolicking, Fryvolity, and Fyghting. What we have in mind today is onions in bed for four hundred thousand!"

Somebody from the crowd roared, "Screw these obscure Woodstok references, chunky-style! Let's see some blood!"

Unfazed, Wavimus Gravimus asked, "You want some blood?!"

As one, the audience roared, "Gods, yes!"

"I can't hear you!"

"Gods, yes!"

"Scream so they can hear you in Summerseve!"

"GODS, YES!"

"That's what I'm *talkin'* about!" Wavimus Gravimus grinned. "Alrighty then, our first event is a battle royale. The rules are simple: there are no rules, and the last man standing wins." He pointed at the two dozen Knights standing off to the side and said, "Gentlemen, start your engines."

The weaker participants were either mortally wounded or knocked unconscious within seconds, their blood covering the muddy field of battle. Five minutes after the battle started, there were eight men left standing: the Leghorn brothers and six men whose names and physical descriptions are not the least bit important.

Sandstorm and Grandstand stood on one side of the field, and the other six on the other. The Leghorns gave each other the briefest of looks, after which Sandstorm pulled a tiny twig from his glove and slowly advanced on the nameless Knights. All six of them chortled, chuckled, and guffawed, but before they could further titter, snicker, or snigger, Sandstorm stabbed two of them in their respective left eyes, stabs that were so firm and true that both men died instantly.

As Sandstorm backed away from the remaining four Knights, Grandstand advanced, brandishing a somewhat bigger twig. Realizing that the Leghorns knew their way around sticks, the four Knights brandished their own weapons, gigantic swords that were each the size of three men standing on top of one another while standing on stilts. Grandstand rolled his eyes at the oversized swords, then sidestepped each of the blades, and waved his stick around and around and around. One minute later, all four Knights were taking permanent mud naps.

Grandstand ran to the middle of the ring, then cried, "Fight's over, people! It's a tie! Leghorns rule! Deal with it!" after which the brothers ran out of the stadium to a chorus of boos. Before they left the arena, they turned around and gave the audience the septuple bird, and went on their merry way.

Sasha turned to Sistyr G.R.R.M. and said with awe, "Oh. My. Gods. That was, like, *radical.*"

"Well put, Sasha. I couldn't have said it better myself."

Just then, Sasha felt a tap on her shoulder: Goofrey Barfonme. Goof cocked an eyebrow, gave Sasha an up-and-down look, and leered, "Hey, baby. You look fine today, just fine. You could kill somebody on that rack, if you know what I mean."

"Like, I don't know what that means." Turning to the Sistyr, Sasha asked, "What does that mean?"

Sistyr G.R.R.M. mumbled, "It means young Goofrey has been taking how-to-pick-up-girls lessons from his Uncle Jagweed."

"Totally awesome!" Sasha exclaimed, then she stood up, took Goof's elbow, kissed him on the cheek, and purred, "Let's, like, totally get out of here and totally make out."

Blushing, Goof stuttered, "I, er, I, er, I, er . . ."

"We should totally, like, go back to the castle and, like, hang out in your bedroom," Sasha said. "Malia totally told me about penises and vaginas and stuff."

Goof gulped, then croaked, "Homminuh, homminuh, homminuh."

"I'll take that as, like, a yes." Sasha smiled, and off they went.

When they arrived back at the castle, they came upon the Leghorn brothers, who were parked at a large square table in the center of the living room, staring intently at . . . *something.* Sasha scampered over to their table and squealed, "Oh. My. Gods. You guys were, like, tubular at the Festyval. The best there, f'r sure." They silently glared at Sasha, then turned back to the table. She tapped Sandstorm on the bicep and asked, "Like, what're you doing?"

Without looking up, he pointed at a rectangular board covered with tiny pieces of some sort. "That's Risk," Sandstorm explained. He then pointed at a sloppy pile of playing cards and grunted, "And that's War." Then he gestured to a flat box that blinked bright colors and made all kinds of funny noises, then rumbled, "And that's Myst."

"That's, like, totally, totally, totally cool," she burbled. "Can I play?"

"These aren't games," Sandstorm snarled.

"Yes, they are," Grandstand corrected.

Sandstorm glared at his brother and said, "Nice job, idiot. Now we either have to let her play, or kill her."

"We can't kill her. She's a plot point."

"Can we at least hurt her? Maybe chop off a toe or two?"

"Not sure. Possibly. I need to check with G.R.R.M."

"You mean Sistyr Glynda Roesy Raegan Melvyn?"

"No, the *other* G.R.R.M."

"What *other* G.R.R.M.?"

"The one with the pretentious white beard."

"Oh. Right. Him. I hear he doesn't answer his fan mail."

"He'll answer a ravengram."

"How do you know?"

"Ravengrams were his idea in the first place."

Goof took Sasha's hand and told the Leghorns, "We were just leaving, guys." After Goof dragged her up to his bedchambers, he said, "You don't want to play their silly games. I have something else you can play with, something better." He then dropped his trousers and murmured, "I believe you were saying something about penises."

Sasha stared at the small bluish appendage dangling beneath Goofrey's waist, and felt her gorge rise. "That's, like, totally gross," she yelped. "I so don't want to touch that. I mean it's, like, all small and mushy. I thought it was supposed to be big and hard."

Goof complained, "I'm tired, Sasha. I can't work on command." Then he blushed, pulled up his pants, and added, "But you'd better get used to touching it no matter how big or small it is or isn't."

Sasha squealed, *"Ewwwwww."*

"If you don't shape up," Goof threatened, "you might not get to be my wife."

Off in the distance, Juan Nieve's direpanda, Fourshadow, could be heard growling.

TRITONE

T ritone Sinister, Lady Gateway, Bobdillon the troubadour, Sur Crayola Burntsienna, and Tinyjohnson journeyed to visit Gateway's sister, Lysergic Bully Aaron of House Aaron, in the town of Vailcolorado. Further details will not be offered, because, frankly, said details are not particularly interesting.

HEADCASE

You can't suck in your stomach any more than that?"

King Bobbert Barfonme took as deep of a breath as he could; his stomach moved nary an inch. After a whooshing exhale, he panted, "I'm doing the best I can, Barky-Boy."

"Well," Lord Headcase Barker sighed, staring skeptically at Bobbert's gut and the lower half of his armor, "I think we're going to have to try a different size."

Bobbert disgustedly struggled out of the metal pants and snapped, "You must've picked out the wrong size by mistake, or this suit was mislabeled or something. No surprise, because that armor room is a disaster. I mean, this *can't* be an extra large. Gods knows I don't need extra-extra-large. I've been an extra-large for five Summers now."

Head murmured, "Yeah, but that was about ten million onions and twenty million pints of grog ago."

"Can it," Bobbert hissed. "We're talking a pound or two. It's not like I've become the corpulent embodiment of all the waste and excesses of my reign. It's not like my own lack of self-control is an obvious literary symbol for my poor governance of this Godsdamn kingdom. Now go get me some iron that fits. And look closely at the label this time. Extra-large, not large, and pick something from the Henry VIII line—they run large. Got it?"

"Got it," Head mumbled.

On his way to the armor room, Head ran into Lord Petey Varicose Bailbond, knocking the little man onto his backside. "I thought you were traveling with Gateway," Headcase noted as he helped Tinyjohnson up.

"I am," Tinyjohnson said.

"You are? But you're here," Head pointed out.

"I mean, I *was* there. But I'm now here. I'm most definitely not there. Obviously."

"Sometimes," Head mused, "it's almost like you're two characters combined into one."

Tinyjohnson scoffed, "That's ridiculous."

"It seems like you're in two places at once."

"No way."

"You're supposed to be traveling with Gateway, and yet you're here with me."

"I'm not. I'm not there, I mean. I mean, I'm not there now. Now this line of questioning ends, because I have pressing news."

"Always with the pressing news," Head mused.

"You must pass this on to Bobbert," Tinyjohnson confided. "If he jousts today, he will die."

Headcase continued to the armor room, with Tinyjohnson nipping at his heels. "Nobody will hurt him," Head pointed out. "He's the King."

"My sources are good," Tinyjohnson insisted.

"Just like your sources who told you about the apothecary having something important to add to the story?"

Tinyjohnson threw up his hands and said, "Fine, disregard my warning, but don't come crying to me when you and the King get murdered, and Goof takes the throne."

"Right, like that'll ever happen."

Ten minutes later, Head returned to Bobbert's bedroom empty-handed. "There weren't any extra-larges," he lied, "so I guess you're off the hook."

The King looked visibly relieved. "Can I tell you a secret, Barky?"

"Sure."

Bobbert whispered, "I'm as hungover as a snake who coiled then uncoiled."

"As a snake who *what*?"

"I know, it's a great metaphor, right? Point is, I'd get killed if I jousted today."

"That's the word on the street," Head said under his breath. Then, at full volume, he said, "Let's go to the Festyval."

Bobbert the King and Head the Foot made it to the arena in time for the closing events, a series of one-on-one tussles, and the first battle promised to be a good one: the Not-Kingslayer versus the three-armed man.

Clad in an exceptionally shiny armor suit with a suspicious bulge below the waist, Jagweed Sinister strutted to the center of the ring, sword pointed to the sky. In contrast, Sandstorm Leghorn stood on the perimeter, looking like he was waiting for a bus, which, considering there were not any buses in Capaetal Ceity, would have made his wait a considerable one.

After Wavimus Gravimus told Jagweed and Sandstorm to start their engines, Jagweed cried, *"Cowabunga!"* and charged Sandstorm. Sandstorm neatly sidestepped the sloppy attack, bopped Jagweed in the back of his head with the butt end of his steel, and the fight was over. It was difficult to tell whether the audience was booing Jagweed's miserable performance, or Sandstorm's general obnoxiousness.

Once the medics carted Jagweed off the field of battle, Wavimus Gravimus took to the middle of the ring and cried, "To my left, may I introduce Grandstand Leghorn!" After the crowd voiced their disapproval—and after Grandstand lifted four middle fingers to said disapproving crowd— Wavimus Gravimus screamed, "And to my right, a late entry hailing from our very own Capaetal Ceity, give it up for the Knight of Knutsack, Sur N&N!"

What with his short platinum hair, steely blue eyes, and foul mouth, Sur N&N touched something in the crowd. He pointed at Grandstand and said, "You fuckity fucking fuck fuck, you can fuck my fuck fuckity fucking fuck fuck." Yes, N&N's cursing was gratuitous, and yes, his preening and primping seemed contrived—it was almost as if he were trying to somehow darken his pale skin—but the Festyval attendees nonetheless ate it up.

After the opponents donned their headgear, Grandstand advanced on Sur N&N. The Knight of Knutsack advanced on Grandstand. They moved closer to each other at an impossibly slow pace, irking both the crowd and the reader to no end. Finally, finally, finally, they met at the center of the ring, and, in traditional Leghorn fashion, Grandstand took out Sur N&N with a single blow. Angered that they had not gotten their money's worth, the entire crowd stormed the ring. Swords were drawn, mud was flung, and popcorn was thrown.

In the King's box, Bobbert, who was covered in a layer of mud and two layers of popcorn, glared at Head and growled, "Foot, is this how you envisioned this playing out?"

Wiping the muddy popcorn (or popcorny mud) from his friend's eyes, Head shrugged. "I told everybody they'd get three days of war and screaming, and they got three days of war and screaming." Gesturing at the increasingly intense riot in the battlefield, Head continued, "I also told them not to take the brown acid."

MALIA

As was the case with many of the characters in Easterrabbit, Cereal Foreskin had disappeared without a trace, and Malia Barker was greatly saddened by her teacher's departure, even though he had not taught her anything she could not have figured out herself, but he did have the best name in the entire book, thus the great sadness.

In tribute to her vanished mentor, Malia, ice skates in hand, squished her way down to the muddy banks of the muddy Capaetal Ceity River. Once by the water, she donned her skates and wobbled along the big babbling brook, in search of a patch of ice she would never find. Fed up with falling face-first into the gushy mush, she sat down and removed her bulky footwear, then laid her head down in the mud and closed her eyes.

Just as she was about to drift off and fall into a deep sleep in which she would have endured a nightmare of ravens, onions, men named Robert (or some derivation thereof), and thousand-plus-page books that lack satisfying endings, she heard two voices coming from the forest, one belonging to a man, and one belonging to either a woman, or a man with a high voice . . . the kind of voice one might expect to come from the mouth of a eunuch.

"We must plot and plan," the man hissed.

"And plan and plot," the woman/possible eunuch agreed.

"Because there is a lot of planning and plotting to do if we are going to have *everybody* murdered," the man chuckled evilly.

The woman/possible eunuch said, "I don't know. Maybe we ought to rethink this. Having *everybody* murdered will take more planning and plotting than we have the time and means for. Sure, we *could* plan and plot for, I don't know, fifteen more chapters, but there gets to be a point when enough is enough. Should we consider doing all our planning and plotting right now, then actually, you know, *doing something*?"

"Okay, okay, I see what you're saying," the man concurred. "So it would be quicker and more efficient to have *almost* everybody murdered."

"Exactly." Malia then heard a briefcase open, followed by the ruffling of some papers. "Alright, I did up a spreadsheet. We'll whack him, and him, and her. We'll let this guy, and that guy, and that girl live. What do you think about this one?"

"I don't even know him," the man admitted.

The woman/possible eunuch said, "Oh. I thought you put him on the list."

"Nope. Wasn't me." After a pause, he asked, "What about this other guy here?"

"Oh, he's *totally* getting whacked."

When Malia sat up, the squish of mud could be heard miles away. At the noise, the man asked, "What was that?"

"Ah, it's probably just one of the Foot's kids waking up after her nap, a nap that followed an unsuccessful attempt to find a place by the river to skate, a place where she could pay homage to her ice-skating-slash-sword-fighting teacher—you know, the one with the hilarious name. It's probably nothing to worry about. I mean, it's not like she'll go running to the Capaetal Ceity Outdoor Mall to track down the Foot and tell him about all our plotting and planning."

Malia then flung her skates into the river and ran to the Capaetal Ceity Outdoor Mall in order to track down the Foot and tell him all about the man and the woman/possible eunuch's plotting and planning.

Ten minutes later, Head asked Malia, "They said they're going to murder *everybody*?" as he pulled some caked mud from his daughter's ears.

"*Almost* everybody," Malia corrected.

"Did they name names?"

"They said they're going to whack him, and him, and her, and this other guy."

"Did they mention me?" Head asked.

"Well, no."

"Your mother, your sister, or your brothers?"

"Um, no."

"The King, or any of the Barfonmes?"

"Er, no."

Head patted Malia's head, then claimed, "So we have nothing to worry about."

"Then I don't understand what they're doing," Malia whined. "I mean, what's the point of murdering somebody if they're not somebody important like you?"

"There *is* no point, Malia. That's my point."

"So you think you won't be murdered," Malia asked.

"I don't think I won't be murdered. I *know* I won't be murdered."

"You're sure?" Malia asked.

"One hundred percent sure. No way, no how, no sir, nobody is murdering Lord Headcase Barker!"

HEADCASE

Somebody's going to murder you, Lord Headcase Barker," Tinyjohnson claimed.

"No way, no how, no sir, nobody is murdering Lord Headcase Barker."

"I don't know, Foot," Tinyjohnson asserted, "the buzz on the street is undeniable. Lot of planning and plotting. Not to mention plotting and planning. Word is they're going to murder almost everybody."

From his odorous, burbling throne, King Bobbert Barfonme growled, "Both of you, stop this madness right now. *Nobody's* murdering *anybody*. Except me." Head and Tinyjohnson gawked at Bobbert, to which the King responded, "Oh, don't give me that *Bobbert's a drunken buffoon* look. I'm not going to murder her myself. One of those Leghorn freaks will do it for five or six . . ." He trailed off, then asked Head, "What do you call that monetary unit again?"

"Dollars."

"Right. One of those idiots will do it for five or six dollars."

Head queried, "And just who is this *she* you're planning to have murdered?"

Bobbert leered and said, "That hot young piece of ass the Dorki is dorking."

"Lolyta Targetpractice?" Head asked. "She's never done anything to anybody. I mean, from what I've heard, she's a little bit obsessed with those eggs of hers, but so what? Why her?"

Bobbert reached to a small box next to his throne and riffled through a pile of magazines until he came to a small book. He showed it to Head and Tinyjohnson, then asked, "Either of you ever read this?"

They peered at the cover: *Why All the Houses Hate Each Other So Godsdamn Much* by Grand Maester Flaysh. "As a matter of fact, I have," Head stated. "And it clarified exactly nothing."

"In general, you're right," the King agreed, "but on page six, it says that House Barfonme has hated House Targetpractice for five hundred fifteen seasons, so who am I to buck tradition?"

"Genius, Your Highness," Lord Petey Varicose Bailbond grinned. "Killing Lolyta Targetpractice would be a brilliant political move. That will get you reelected for certain."

"We're a monarchy, Tinyjohnson," Bobbert pointed out.

"I know, Your Highness, but if you *were* a democracy, you'd win by a landslide."

"I appreciate that, Tinyjohnson, but as long as we . . ."

Head interrupted, "Are you two dummies listening to yourselves? You want to kill a girl just because your father's father's father's father's father had some beef with her father's father's father's father's father's father's father? That's ridiculous, Bobbert, even for you."

Tinyjohnson nodded. "The Foot has a point, Your Highness. It might start a war, and I suspect within a few chapters, we are going to have a couple of other wars on our hands."

Bobbert roared, "Headcase, remember, I'm the King, and what I say goes!"

"Ooh, that's a compelling argument for killing Lolyta," Tinyjohnson said. "*Very* compelling."

"Bobbert," Head noted, "Woodstok got us back on our financial feet, and we can start repaying Chyna . . ."

"*Or not!*" Bobbert and Tinyjohnson cried in unison.

"Correct, or not. But a war will bleed us dry."

"Good point," Tinyjohnson said. "Bobbert, my advice would be to *not* murder Lolyta Targetpractice."

"But it'll be *fun*," Bobbert whined.

"Good point," Tinyjohnson said. "Bobbert, my advice would be to *definitely* murder Lolyta Targetpractice."

Head noted, "The Dorki Army will come after you and your family with everything they've got."

Bobbert asked, "Wait, let me get this straight: You're saying that if I have Lolyta Targetpractice whacked, all those psycho horse-people will try and whack both Cerevix and Goof?" He paused, then added, "As appealing as that may sound, I'm still moving ahead with my plan: Pulverize KERBANGER Lolyta and those Godsdamn eggs!"

"Brilliant idea, Your Highness," Tinyjohnson said.

"You're an idiot, Bobbert," Head sighed. "A drunken, impulsive idiot."

"He's right, Your Highness," Tinyjohnson said. "You *are* an idiot."

"No, *you're* the idiot!" Bobbert roared at the Foot.

To Head, Tinyjohnson asserted, "He's right, Your Footness. You, too, are an idiot."

Bobbert reached into his pocket and pulled out an onion. "*Allium cepa* in your grill, Foot!" And then he hurled the *allium cepa* at Head's head.

As Head pulled onion spew from his beard, Tinyjohnson simpered, "Brilliant throw, Your Highness."

Head glared silently at his old friend, then ran out of the throne room, returning a minute later with a bag of onions almost big enough to feed Snackwell Fartly. He unsheathed Slush, coolly picked the biggest onion from the bag, stuck it on the end of his blade, then flung the sword at King Bobbert's midsection. It missed wide right and kept on going until it stuck in the wall.

"Brilliant throw, Your Footness," Tinyjohnson professed.

Bobbert leapt off the throne, reached into the onion bag, pulled out as many as he could hold in both arms, then ran to the opposite side of the room. "Onions at fifty paces, Barky-Boy!" he cried, then tossed one of the vegetables at Headcase, missing by several feet.

"Brilliant throw, Your Highness." Tinyjohnson grinned.

At once, Head and Bobbert roared, *"Shut up!"* They pelted the possible eunuch with ten onions each, knocking him unconscious.

The two old friends then stared silently at one another, panting and sweating, sweating and panting. Finally, King Bobbert broke the silence: "Maybe you should go back to Summerseve."

Shrugging his head coyly, shuffling his feet, and avoiding eye contact with Bobbert, he said, "Maybe I should."

"Okay, then," Bobbert answered. "Then go."

"Fine. I'll go." He was motionless.

"Fine. Go."

"Fine. I'll go." He remained motionless.

"Good. I'll be glad when you're gone."

"Yeah, me too. So I'm going." Still he remained motionless.

"Then go."

"Fine. I'll go."

"Good. Go."

"I'm going."

"Great. So go."

By the time this back-and-forth banter wound up some four hours later, they both forgot what they were angry about . . . but that did not stop Lord Headcase Barker from resigning his Footship, packing his bags, and preparing for a journey back to Summerseve.

LOLYTA

KERBANGER Lolyta Targetpractice was perched on her bejeweled throne, Magistrate Illinois on her left and Vladymyr Targetpractice on her right. Loly squirmed uncomfortably because the entire throne was bejeweled, seat included, and her buttocks were exceptionally sensitive from last night's paddling session with Ivan Drago. (After initially being nervous about the act of making love with each other, Loly and Ivan Drago had become quite open and comfortable with each other and, despite the language barrier, had managed to make each other aware of their respective needs and desires. It turned out that Ivan Drago liked paddling, and Loly liked being paddled. It was as if they were a match made by the Gods, a salacious match that would translate well to both the page and the small screen.)

Standing beside the throne, Vladymyr glared at Loly and complained, "I haven't seen much of you. Seems like you've been awfully wrapped up in your work."

"That's KERBANGER to you, subject," she said. "And KERBANGING is a busy profession. As much as I enjoy them, I don't have time for your feeble nipple tweaks and bitchy tirades."

He glared at her, then whispered menacingly, "You know, if you keep speaking to me in this manner, you shall wake the ducks. And trust me, you do *not* want to wake the ducks, because if you wake the ducks—"

Loly interrupted, "Again with waking the ducks. On the page: waking the ducks. On the small screen: waking the ducks. Listen, brother dear, you can try as hard as you want, but you're not going to inject any catchphrases into this whole mess. It isn't that kind of project. Besides, we're on premium cable, and catchphrases are totally CBS."

"If you wake the ducks," he repeated, "all hell will break loose. If you wake the ducks, KERBANGER, the sun will fall from the sky, and the moon will explode into a million bits. If you wake the ducks, KERBANGER, the mud will turn to diamonds, and diamonds will turn to mud. If you wake the ducks, KERBANGER, the . . ."

"Hey, Vladymyr."

"Yes?"

"Kneel when you're in the presence of your KERBANGER."

Vladymyr glared at Loly, then gritted, "First of all, I'm your older brother, and I will not kneel before you. And second of all, these are new pants, and since all the floors in this castle are filthy, my knees never touch the ground."

Magistrate Illinois mumbled, "That's not what I heard."

"I heard that," Vladymyr said.

"You were meant to," Illinois noted. At that, Illinois and Loly tittered. At that, Vladymyr stomped his foot, grunted something that sounded like "Uch," then minced out of the room.

After he was out of earshot, Illinois intoned, "Would you like an update on the Dorki political situation, my KERBANGER?"

"Not really." Loly frowned.

Ignoring her, Illinois took a Word document from her pocket and reported, "Ivan J'Marcus is twelve points ahead of Ivan Derek in the polls for District Four. It behooves us that Ivan J'Marcus emerge victorious, because he's running on the platform of 'Ooga booga boo boo boo,' whereas Ivan Derek's 'Inga binga bing bing bing' approach will have dire consequences for us."

With a blank look, Loly asked Illinois, "Um, what?"

Illinois continued, "Things are a bit more heated in District Ten, where Ivan Margaret is neck and neck with Ivan Steve. That could be a problem because Dork is simply not ready for a female representative. We're trying to dig up some dirt on Ivan Margaret. No luck so far, but we haven't exhausted our resources. I'll spare you the details for reasons of plausible deniability."

Aside from the fact that she was both clueless and apathetic about the upcoming elections, Loly was unable to focus on Illinois's rundown because she could not stop dreaming of Ivan Drago, his magnificent human chest, and his even more magnificent horse junk. Last night's paddling was the culmination of a week of experimenting that left Loly at once sated and hungry. Just as Illinois was about to explain why Ivan Francois was going to triumph in his battle with Ivan Gerard, the KERBANGER asked, "Illinois, do you know where Ivan Drago is?"

"Don't you want to hear the rest of the polling?"

"Gods no. This KERBANGER wants a piece of her man, and what this KERBANGER wants, this KERBANGER gets."

Magistrate Illinois muttered, "Power tripper."

"I heard that," Loly said.

"You were meant to," Illinois noted. "Anyhow, last I heard, your man was in the center of town."

Loly stood up, reached under her skirt, pulled off her panties, handed them to Illinois, and noted, "You know what to do with these, Magistrate."

Wrinkling her nose, Illinois took Loly's unmentionables between her thumb and forefinger, holding them away from her nose as if they were a snake coiling then uncoiling, then stomped away without a word.

Ivan Drago was indeed in the center of town, lying on his side, slathering himself with Neutrogena Ultra Sheer Sunblock SPF 94,167,211,467, whinnying contentedly. Loly slinked over to him and said, "You need any help with that, big boy?"

Smiling, Ivan Drago gave his bride a onceover, then neighed, "Wowzie wowzie woo woo woo!"

"That's what I thought," Loly purred, grabbing his equine tumescence.

While she tugged at his fifth leg, Ivan Drago moaned, "Ooga booga use both hands, and try some lubrication."

As that was the most coherent sentence she had heard come from Ivan Drago's lips, Loly stopped, and asked, "Wait, what did you say?"

Ivan Drago coughed. "Um, crap, I mean rippedy zip, zippedy rip. Oonga. Mmmmmm."

"Oh," Loly said, then continued her tugging. As Ivan Drago's breath quickened, a crowd formed around the couple, which, as she was more aroused than she had been in all of her thirteen years, she barely noticed. However, when the audience launched into a chant of what sounded like *Faster, faster, faster,* she paused . . . but, undaunted, continued mere seconds later, going faster, faster, faster.

Ivan Drago took Loly's hands from his member, tenderly removed her clothes, and mounted her. After a while, their screams grew in volume, eventually mingling with those of the crowd. When the couple reached their climaxes, their cries could be heard in the hills, and the viewers' applause could be heard in the mountains.

After they disentangled from each other, the crowd dispersed; Ivan Drago galloped over to a nearby water trough, and Loly wobbled back to the castle, her body happily sore inside and out.

Vladymyr was waiting for Loly at the front door. Glaring at his sister, he sneered, "Just got an interesting ravengram, sister dear. Apparently you and Ivan Drago had yourselves a nice little pants-free party in the center of town. Real classy, sis. You're sure doing the Targetpractice name proud."

"Hey, that's the way it's done around here." She smiled. "And when in Dork, do as the Dorkis. Besides, what happens in Dork stays in Dork."

"Does he pinch your nipples like I do?" Vladymyr griped.

Loly patted her brother's right cheek and said, "Nobody pinches my nipples like you do, darling. Thank Gods."

He flicked her hand away and claimed, "Nobody pinches underage nipple as well as I do, *nobody*! I'm more masculine than Ivan Drago will ever be!"

Patting his other cheek, Loly soothed, "Of course you are, Vladymyr. Of course you are. He's only half the man you are. Now if you'll excuse me, I'm going to sit on my eggs for a while. I think they might be ready to hatch."

Off in the distance, Juan Nieve's direpanda, Fourshadow, could be heard growling.

GATEWAY

When they were mere minutes away from House Aaron, Lady Gateway Barker peered at Tinyjohnson and said, "I thought you were in Cap Ceity."

"I am," Tinyjohnson said.

"You are? But you're here," Gateway pointed out.

"I mean, I *was* there. But I'm now here. I'm most definitely not there. Obviously."

"Sometimes," Gateway mused, "it's almost like you're two characters combined into one."

Tinyjohnson scoffed, "That's ridiculous."

"It seems like you're in two places at once."

"No way."

"You're supposed to be advising the King, and yet you're here with me."

"I'm not. I'm not there, I mean. I mean, I'm not there now. Now this line of questioning ends, because we have arrived at our destination . . . *finally.*"

Two steps onto the grounds of the castle, Gateway crashed into a man clad in a one-piece blue burlap jumpsuit. "Can I help you, ma'am?" he asked as he pulled himself up from the ground and tried to wipe the mud from his backside.

"Lady Gateway Bully Barker here to see Lady Lysergic Bully Aaron."

The guard gave Gateway a snooty onceover, then said, "Strip."

"Excuse me?"

"All of you, strip."

At that, Tinyjohnson put his hands over his crotch and sprinted away, screaming, *"I am not a eunuch! I am not a eunuch! I am not a eunuch!"*

Ignoring Tinyjohnson's sudden exit, Gateway asked the burlap-wearer, "Why? I've been here dozens of times, and not once have I been asked to remove my clothes."

"We're tightening up security," the guard said. "We need to make sure you're not armed."

Pointing at her sword, Gateway pointed out, "We're *all* armed."

"I don't mean armed with weapons, ma'am. I mean armed with liquids."

"Um, what?"

"If combined in a certain manner, liquids can be deadly, even water. Our security partners conducted extensive explosives testing last summer and determined that liquids, aerosols, and gels, in limited quantities, are safe to bring into the castle, the key phrase being *limited quantities*. You may fill either a three-ounce bottle, or one quart-sized clear plastic zip-top bag. Medications, baby formula and food, and breast milk are allowed in reasonable quantities, and are not required to be in the zip-top bag. Officers may need to open these items to conduct additional screening. Now strip, please."

After a moment or two of silence, Bobdillon asked, "What's plastic?" after which the guard pulled out a knife and slit the troubadour's throat. Immediately, Gateway, Tritone Sinister, and Crayola Burntsienna tore off their respective clothes.

The guard picked up a handful of leaves from the muddy ground, wrapped them around his hand, then told Gateway et al., "Okay, kiddies, bend over and spread 'em."

He stuck his right index finger up Burntsienna's rectum, and his left index finger up Tritone's. When Burntsienna yelped, Tritone told the guard, "I think he's honked off that you didn't buy him dinner first."

The guard sneered, "Both of you are clean. Get dressed and proceed." To Gateway, he murmured, "Let's see what you've got hiding up there, sister." He poked his index finger in up to the first joint, then the second, then the third. Right before he was about to attempt a fist, he grinned, said, "Jackpot," then yanked out a small bag of Godsweede. "Busted! Confiscated! Get dressed and proceed."

"But Godsweede isn't illegal," Gateway remarked.

"No, it isn't, but it's *really* hard to get any good stuff around here. The Vailcolorado soil is a disaster, and every single plant we grow comes out all skunky." He opened the bag and took a whiff, then winced. "Godsdamn it, Lady Gateway, how long has this thing been up your backside?"

She scratched her head, then guessed, "Two years. Maybe three."

He dropped the back of weede onto the ground and used his foot to cover it with mud. "Proceed to the throne room. Lady Lysergic is expecting you."

As they walked toward the castle, Gateway grumbled, "That was still smokable, jerkoff."

The House Aaron throne room was enormous, even bigger than the Barfonmes'. When Gateway, Tritone, and Burntsienna entered, Lysergic ran to her sister, arms spread. During a long, strong hug, Lysergic said, "Gateway, Gateway, Gateway, you look smashing!"

"You too, big sister," Gateway said. "Again, my condolences for Functionary. I can't imagine your pain. He was the only person in Easterrabbit who could hit a curveball."

"Curveball?"

"Remember, we had to take out all those awesome baseball jokes based on Fuctionary's last name?"

"Right, right, right. Forgot about that. Losing those jokes was almost as painful as losing my husband." She paused, then added, "I received your ravengram. It was quite touching, and for that, I thank you." She pulled herself from her sister's embrace. "But I should point out that Cerevix Barfonme sent flowers. And we don't even like each other."

Gateway stated, "Don't you think a ravengram is more personal? I actually took the time to sit down and write something. Anybody can go to a florist."

"A ravengram is free, sister dear," Lysergic declared. "Flowers aren't. And let's face it; you spend your money on . . . other things."

"What are you saying?" Gateway asked.

Lysergic's face turned pink, then red, then crimson. *"What I'm saying,"* she roared, *"is that you're a Godsdamn weedehead who'd rather have sex without protection so she can spit out another kid, which gives her yet another excuse to not visit her sister and her nephew!"*

"If your castle wasn't located on the top of a mountain that's on top of another mountain, maybe I'd come around more often! But it takes so Godsdamn

*long to get here that we had to consolidate the Godsdamn journey into a single
Godsdamn paragraph!"*

"*Selfish bitch!*"

"*Elitist twat!*"

"*Arrogant wench!*"

"*Ugly snob!*"

Before Lysergic could call Gateway a putrid whore, Gateway wrapped
her hands around her sister's neck and squeezed, immediately after which
Lysergic wrapped *her* hands around *her* sister's neck.

Tritone whispered to Burntsienna, "Jesus Chryst, these psycho hose
beasts make my siblings look functional."

A screech was heard from the other side of the throne room. Lysergic
stepped down on Gateway's foot, and, after Gateway let go of Lysergic's
neck, she called, "Honey, come say hi to your auntie!"

Clad in only a tiny codpiece, Lysergic's son Little Lord Bobbby Aaron
called, "You mean Auntie Shit Face?"

Lysergic shrugged, then said, "Kids. I have no idea where they pick up
this stuff. I'm sure yours are the exact same way."

"Not so much." She kneeled down, held out her hands, and said, "Come
to Auntie, Bobbby!"

Bobbby sauntered toward Gateway, but before he made it over to his
aunt, he came to a stop in front of Tritone and whispered, "You're so tall!"

"Oh yeah, Shecky? Well, you're so short that you could walk under
a snake while wearing a top hat."

"Oh yeah? Well . . . well . . . well, how's the weather up there?"

Tritone hocked a loogie on Bobbby's head and said, "It's raining.
Zzzzzzing!"

Wiping the spittle from his head, Bobbby turned to Lysergic and asked,
"Can we cut the giant into little, teeny, tiny pieces, then throw them off
the mountain so we can watch them fly?"

Lysergic agreed, "I think that's an excellent idea, son. Maybe we can do
that to some other people, too." Staring at Gateway, she asked, "Would
you like to see your aunt fly, honey?"

HEADCASE

Tinyjohnson offered to accompany Head back to Summers-eve, but the ex-Foot was sick of the sight of the possible eu-nuch, so he traveled home all by himself. Before he took to the road, he ravengrammed Maester Blaester, telling him to send a posse to retrieve the girls, explaining that he needed some "me time," and what better time for "me time" than a lengthy journey from one House to another?

When Head crossed the border out of Capaetal Ceity, he heard a cry from ahead: "Lord Barker, I request the honor of a battle!"

Head cried back, "Since when is a battle an honor?"

"You're right! That was weird! It sounded better in my head! Let me try again: Lord Barker, you have wronged my family! Thanks to an anony-mous ravengram, I have learned that Lady Barker is holding my brother prisoner for reasons that were not made clear, so to avenge Tritone's incar-ceration, I request the pleasure of murdering you!" He paused, then added, "And yes, I know Tritone's an idiot, but he's family, so whatever."

Head sighed, "Seriously?"

"Seriously. The Not-Kingslayer never jokes. I mean, look at me: I have a blond mane that looks great on the tube, and muscles on top of muscles, and a jawline that won't stop. I get more mentions on blogs than any of the secondary characters, except for maybe that Vladymyr jerk, but whatever. Point is, I don't *need* to joke."

"Okay, Jagweed, show yourself." On one hand, Head was irked that his "me time" was being usurped by a snot like Jagweed Sinister, but on the other, he knew he could beat the tar out of the incestuous fop without breaking a sweat.

Perched on top of a white stallion that Head thought was far too beautiful for the likes of a sister-screwing moron, Jagweed called, "Here I am, Lord Barker. Now hop off your steed and draw your steel. As I am a gentleman, you may have first thrust."

Head called, "Isn't that what you told Cerevix last night?"

His face reddening, Jagweed jumped off his horse and gritted, "That, Lord Barker, was your first thrust."

Head dismounted, then reached for his sword and came up with nothing. *Godsdamn it,* he thought, *it's still stuck in the wall of Bobbert's throne room.* "Listen, Jagweed, I left my steel in my other burlap pants. I'd love to kill you in a painful, painful fashion, so can I take a rain check?"

"Request denied, Lord Barker. The battle has been declared. But as I am a gentleman, I will not engage in a battle in which the combatants do not have the same weapon." He placed his sword on the muddy ground and asked, "Any ideas?"

Head looked around, then offered, "Sticks?"

Jagweed noted, "Nah. Too Tolkienesque."

"Tree branches?"

"Too hard to reach."

"Mud?"

"Too humdrum."

"Snowballs?"

"Too late in the season."

Just then, he heard a wet splat that sounded as if it originated behind his horse. He grinned, then said, "Equine droppings?"

Jagweed grinned right on back. "Perfect. Go on my count: *One . . . two . . .*" Before he could say three, Headcase Barker sprinted toward his horse. "Come on, Lord Barker," the Not-Kingslayer whined, "you weren't supposed to go until *three.* That's not fair. Just because you're a Lord doesn't mean you get to . . ."

Jagweed was unable to complete the sentence because Head threw a massive ball of manure that landed directly in Sinister's open mouth. Jagweed spit the crap onto the ground, then retrieved it, molded it into a tight ball, and tossed it at Head's head. After a neat duck and roll, Head took another handful of poo from behind his horse and sidearmed it at Jagweed's knee, hoping the incest-er would fall onto the ground mouth-first and drown in mud. With surprising quickness and skill, Jagweed slid to his left and avoided the ca-ca. Noticing that his horse hadn't excreted since the battle began, Jagweed reached his hand up the steed's anus and extricated several handfuls of turds.

Head ran behind his animal, knelt down, and began fashioning large pellets from the feces. Jagweed, however, had the same idea, and when Head peered around his horse, he was pelted with ten well-aimed guano slugs. *I'm old,* Head thought. *Two Summers ago, this battle would have been over, and Jagweed would be so full of shit that the whites of his eyes would have been brown.* But now Head had to rely on his wits and experience.

After surveying the field of battle (such as it was), Head concluded that his best option would be a quick frontal attack—hit him hard, and hit him fast. He picked up his dung balls, took a deep breath, and, with a wordless scream, jumped out from behind his horse and charged the Not-Kingslayer.

Before Lord Headcase Barker took his fifth step toward Jagweed Sinister, a pain and stench worse than anything he'd ever experienced overtook him, and the world went black. The next he awoke, he was in a small, dark room, lying in a bed, a needle stuck in his arm, and a pile of white powder on his pillow. Before he fell into oblivion, a single thought drifted through Head's overtaxed brain: *Summer is coming.*

ALLBRAN

My balance is fine, Bobb. I don't need any of this stuff," Allbran carped.

Bobb Barker was fastening Allbran's makeshift leg brace to the horse's saddle. "Yes, you do," he growled, "because if you fall off of this thing and further injure yourself, Mother would never let me hear the end of it. I can hear her now: *If you can't take care of your brother, how could you expect to take care of House Barker, blah blah blah.*"

"There's no way I can *further* injure myself, Bobb, because I'm not injured in the first place," Allbran explained with a high-pitched fart.

"If you're going to *ride* on this horse," Bobb sneered, "you're going to be *glued* to this horse. If you don't like it, well, I'm sure Dickoff would love to work on his dressage."

Allbran growled, "I hate you, Bobb." Then he called, "Hinky, come!" Allbran's direpanda—who had grown considerably in the last dozen or so chapters—loped over to the horse, his tongue hanging pinkly from his mouth. Pointing at Bobb, Allbran added, "Hinky, attack!"

Bobb then called, "Blinky, come!" And then Bobb's direpanda, who we have yet to meet, ran over and head-butted Hinky into tomorrow. Fortunately, tomorrow came early, so Hinky shoved Blinky across the lawn, where he lost his balance and fell into a mud puddle. Hinky seemed to laugh, which angered Blinky, but before he could again attack, he appeared to join his direpanda brother in a chuckle. The two direpandas then put their arms around each other and wandered off to the East.

Allbran and Bobb stared at each other, then Bobb sputtered, "Okay, since I'm in charge here, I make the decisions, and my decision is to track down those Godsdamn bears."

"Good to see you're prepared to make those tough choices, Bobb," Allbran said.

"Hey, no lip out of you, kid. My next decision is that we separate. You go North, I go South."

Allbran pointed out, "But Hinky and Blinky went East."

"Shut up, gimp!" Bobb roared. *"I'm in charge, and I'm a Godsdamn tactical genius, and I say you go North, and that's all there is to it!"* He then smacked Allbran's horse on its hindquarters, and the beast took off to the North, then, once it sensed Bobb was not paying attention, turned to the East.

Allbran scratched the horse behind its ear and grinned. "Atta boy. That's a good horse."

The horse mumbled, "Your brother's a douche. And try not to fart on my back, please."

"What?" Allbran screamed.

"I mean, *neigh, neigh, neigh!*"

Several miles later, seven horses and their respective riders emerged from behind a cluster of trees, their animals in a triangular formation. The lead rider pointed at Allbran and roared, *"Who art thou?! And why art thou trespassing upon mine forest?! Trespassers die!"*

"I art Allbran Barker of the House Barker! Who art thou? And why art we speaking like this?"

One of the riders in the second row said to the leader, "Now that's a damn good question, Brian. I thought we decided that Shakespearean crap was out."

Brian said, "You hath made that decision. I hath not agreed."

Another rider pointed out, "We voted, Brian. You lost. Deal with it."

Yet another rider claimed, "This is why we still don't have a name. Nobody can make a decision, and when a decision is actually made, nobody abides by it."

"I declare the name hath been decided," Brian declared, "and that name is the Sharks!"

Yet another rider insisted, "No, Brian, we're not the Sharks. Three of us voted for Sharks, and three of us voted for Jets, and Warren abstained."

Warren, the smallest of the riders, said, "Get off my back. They're both good."

Brian commanded, "Maketh a decision, Warren. Thou art holding up our jacket order."

"Thou art being an wiener," Warren pointed out.

Just then, Hinky and Blinky trotted over, covered in mud, tongues hanging out. Brian stared wide-eyed at the animals and asked Allbran, "Art those direpandas?"

"Yep, they sure art."

"Methinks that direpandas are extinct."

"Nope, they sure aren't."

"Methinks the Sharks should kill young Barker, then vacate the premises. And quickly." To Allbran, he explained, "We art deathly allergic to direpandas. Yes, we know that up until several chapters ago, direpandas were extinct, so it might seem odd that we know we're allergic, but it's probably best if you don't ask too many questions, because frankly, Easterrabbit is in danger of overstaying its welcome. At some point, the story has to end . . . especially when there are so many rambling monologues. Like this one."

Allbran asked, "Will you not kill me if I call them off?"

"You hath control over the beasts?" Brian asked.

"Sure," Allbran lied.

"Then we shall let you live. Tell thine beasts to depart!"

"You got it." He called, "Hinky! Blinky! Take a hike!"

At the sound of the familiar voice, Hinky and Blinky hopped toward Allbran, stopping on their way over to give a loving lick to each and every one of the Sharks/Jets. The second the direpanda saliva touched the riders' bodies, their skin melted, then they fell off their horses, and died a painful, ugly, foamy death. Hinky and Blinky high-fived each other, then hopped off to wherever it is that adolescent direpandas hop off to.

Allbran was so distracted by the bubbling corpses that he did not notice his brother's arrival. "What the hell, Allbran!" Bobb exclaimed. "I leave you alone for two minutes and you run into this? Seriously, Mom's going to freak. What happened?" After Allbran related the story of Hinky and Blinky's killer spit, Bobb pointed at the dead bodies and mused, "Holy Gods, I've heard about these guys. These were some bad, bad men." He scratched his chin, then thought aloud, "If I can have these ass-clowns on my resume . . ." and trailed off.

"What do you mean," Allbran asked, "'on my resume'?"

"Quiet, kid," Bobb commanded, then jumped off his horse, unsheathed his sword, and stabbed each and every one of the dead men until his weapon was covered with their blood.

The two brothers silently stared at the bodies for a couple of minutes, then Allbran asked, "So, um, what was that all about?"

"As far as you know, I killed those gangsters fair and square. And if you say anything differently, well, if you think you're in pain now, well, *phew*!"

"Bobb," Allbran complained, "I'm not in pain."

"Yes, you are!"

"No, I'm not."

"Yes, you are!"

"Nope. Not even a little bit."

"Yes, you are, and I'm in charge, and my word is law, and you were hurt worse than anybody's ever been hurt, and I'm going to protect you from more hurt!"

"Okay, okay, okay, fine, I'm hurt. Ouch. Ow. Such pain, such pain."

Bobb smiled. "There, there, Allbran. I'll protect you. Because I'm in charge."

"Of course you are, Bobb," Allbran agreed, "of course you are," then directed his horse back to the castle, secretly thrilled that he was only going to appear in two more chapters.

JUAN

Broheim Otter, I hate to complain, but might it be too hot for a campfire?"

Otter glared at Snackwell Fartly and sneered, "Maybe if you weren't carrying around so much tonnage, you wouldn't be *schvitzing* like a Frenchman."

"*What-ing* like a *what*?" Juan Nieve asked. Before Otter could answer, Juan added, "It's *muy caliente*[44] out here, Otter. Admit it."

"But it's also dark," opined Pinto. "And I don't know about you guys, but I prefer to have some light when we're this close to the Wall."

Bluto pointed out, "I hate to admit it, boys, but the jerkoff here might have a point. The Wall's puddling up like crazy, and we're making things hotter."

D-Day gestured to Snack and offered, "If you're worried about the Wall melting, we could always use fatso-comic-relief-metaphor-boy over here to plug up the holes."

Juan butted in, "Gentlemen, is this what a Frat's about? Pointing out your Broheims' faults, and making fun of their questionable parentage? Is that why you're all here? Is that what you left your families for? To tease and complain? *Repugnante*,[45] simply *repugnante*."[46]

"It's okay, Juan," Snack sighed. "I'm used to it. Back at home, everybody would . . ."

"Guys," Otter interrupted, "I'm bored as hell, it's *still* muddy, the Wall

---

44. A bit toasty.
45. Disgusting.
46. Disgusting. (Just wanted to make sure you're paying attention.)

is *still* melting, Snack's *still* fat, Juan's *still* a jerkoff, and nothing's happening. How about we wrap it up here and see what Tritone's up to?"

Juan smiled. "Otter, that's the first intelligent thing I've ever heard come out of your mouth. *Estimados lectores, por favor disfrute el siguiente capítulo, un capítulo que incluye, entre otras cosas, una conversación fascinante entre Tritone y Lysergic.*"[47]

---

47. Translate it yourself. I mean, do I have to do *all* the work around here?

TRITONE

From the floor of his jail cell, Tritone Sinister called to the guard, "Hey, tall, dark, and ugly, when am I getting out of here? This place smells so bad it'd make a skunk gag."

The guard sauntered over and demanded, "Wait, you're calling me ugly? *You?!* This coming from a guy who's so skinny that he uses dental floss as toilet paper?"

"Whoa, great spritz! You and me, we're two peas in a pod. Granted, if we're hanging out together in a pod, people would have trouble telling your face apart from my ass. *Zzzzzzing!*"

Chuckling, the guard explained, "Nice one, stretch. Listen, if it were up to me, you could leave right now, but Lady Lysergic wants you to confess to your crimes."

"Crimes? Brother, the only crime I've committed is joke plagiarism." He paused, then asked, "Wait, did I say that out loud? I meant *parody*. Joke *parody*."

"Well," the guard elucidated, "that's not what the Lady says. She thinks you killed Functionary."

"Fantastic," Tritone grumbled, annoyed that this was the second time he had been framed in the book, and curious as to which of his idiot relatives killed Lord Functionary Aaron. *It was probably Jagweed and Cerevix,* he thought. *You can never overestimate the stupidity of one blonde person, but if you multiply that times two, you're looking at a level of idiocy that could . . . well . . . that could have them ruling Easterrabbit. Aaaaaaand there's your motive.* "So let me get this straight, Shecky," Tritone continued. "If I confess to some crimes, they'll let me out of this dump?" After the guard nodded, he continued, "Okay, pal, you tell that crazy Aaron broad I'm going to confess like nobody's ever confessed. I'm gonna confess my ass off to the point that I'll need a new ass."

Ten minutes later, Tritone was in the Aaron throne room, standing in front of Lysergic Bully Aaron, Gateway Bully Barker, and Sur Crayola Burntsienna. "Well, well, well." The giant smiled. "If it isn't the law firm of Dewey, Cheatham, and Howe." After the three gave him a blank stare, he mumbled, "Tough crowd. Anyhow, word is if I confess to some stuff, I can go blow this pop stand."

"That is correct, giant," Lysergic explained. "You are accused of the successful murder of Lord Functionary Aaron, and the botched murder of Allbran Barker. Do you confess to your crimes?"

"Honey, I've got plenty of crimes to confess to. First confession—and this was a *true* crime—I produced *Journey Through the Secret Life of Plants*."

"What?" Lady Aaron asked.

"The worst crime of Stevie Wonder's career. I also confess to producing every Nickelback album. Chryst, I should be executed for those things alone."

"I don't understand."

"Yeah, me neither. Seriously, how that band has a record deal, I have no idea. I also confess to producing Peter Criss's solo album, everything by Creed, the Black Eyed Peas' later stuff, most of that boy-band crap, Liz Phair's self-titled set, Lil Wayne's *Rebirth*—man, that thing was an abortion—this Nine Inch Nails remix album that I forget the name of, Madonna's *Who's That Girl*, and Lady Gaga's *Born This Way*." He paused, then added, "Wow, it's great to get that off my chest." He clapped once, then grinned. "So. Where's my ride?"

Lysergic growled, "Confess to killing Functionary."

"Couldn't have killed him if I tried. That guy wields a bat like no other, plus, good luck trying to get a slider by him."

Lysergic frowned, "What do you mean, *wields a bat*? And what's a slider?"

"It's one of those Godsdamn lost baseball jokes. Don't worry about it."

"Believe me, I won't. Now confess to trying to kill Allbran."

"Didn't do that, either, but I had to be accused, or else this whole house of cards would've come crashing down, and you'd be looking at a short story, rather than a series of cash-cow novels. And when I say cash-cow, I ain't talkin' no bull. *Ch-ching!*"

Over Burntsienna's chuckles, Lysergic roared, "You whacked Functionary, you tried to whack Allbran, and now you will pay with your freedom!" She turned to the door and called, "Guard, take Mr. Sinister back to his cell."

Tritone held up his hands and said, "Hey there, ho there, whoa there, Shecky. No trial?"

"We have no evidence," Lysergic explained. "Thus we have no trial, thus you're sentenced to life in prison."

Lady Gateway piped up, "Sister dear, that's not the way we do things in House Barker. We don't chop off anybody's head until we're good and certain they deserve it. And if there's no evidence, we let them battle their way out."

"Battle?" Lysergic asked.

"If they can beat up Headcase, they can go."

"How's that working out?"

Smiling, Gateway said, "Head's undefeated. Eighty-two up, eighty-two down."

Lysergic nodded. "That's fair, and I suspect that's the way Functionary would've wanted it. Fine, let the stick figure go down swinging." She turned to Tritone and said, "So, murderer, I will allow you to fight for your life. For that matter, I'll even let you choose your weapon."

Tritone smirked. "Any weapon?" he asked.

"Any weapon," Lysergic agreed. After a pause, she added, "But no mud or onion fights. We've already had plenty of those."

"Fine," Tritone said, "I choose my tongue."

In unison, Gateway and Lysergic screamed, "Your *tongue?!*"

Nodding, Tritone confirmed, "Indeed. My tongue. I want to engage House Aaron's finest in an insult battle."

In unison, Gateway and Lysergic screamed, "An *insult battle?!*"

"But not *just* an insult battle," Tritone continued.

In unison, Gateway and Lysergic screamed, "Not *just* an insult battle?!"

"No. A 'yo momma' insult battle. Modern colloquialisms and contemporary references allowed."

In unison, Gateway and Lysergic screamed, "*Noooooooooooooooo!*"

HEADCASE

*T*he mud was gone.

Head fell to his knees onto the green, green grass behind the castle and stared up into the blue, blue sky. He touched the lawn, reveling in its feel, its scent, its color, and its cleanness. As he was about to lie on his stomach and put his face in the luscious grass, he felt a tap on his shoulder. Without turning around, he intoned, "Yes?"

"Good morning, Lord Barker," the voice said. It was a deep, guttural voice, yet somehow had a tinge of effeminateness. "How are you on this lovely morning?"

Head answered, "I'm wonderful." Then he looked over his shoulder to find out whose question he was answering.

It was a horse. But not any horse: a white horse with golden eyes, and, oddest of all, a horn protruding from its forehead. "Who are you?" Head wondered. "And why are you able to speak?"

"I'm a unicorn," the animal explained, "and I speak because it has been spoken that I speak."

"Who spoke that you can speak?"

"It's not a who, Lord Barker," the unicorn noted, "but rather a what."

"Well, then," Head said, "what spoke that you can speak?"

"It's not a what, Lord Barker," the unicorn noted, "but rather a who."

"But you just said it was a who, not a what."

The animal shrugged. "What can I tell you, Barky-Boy. Unicorns are flighty."

Just then, someone did something to Head's leg, something more painful than anything he'd ever experienced. He looked at the limb and, noticing nothing out of the ordinary, asked the unicorn, "Did you see anything weird?"

But the unicorn was gone, which was odd, because he heard its voice repeating, "Barky-Boy . . . Barky-Boy . . . Barky-Boy . . ."

". . . Barky-Boy. Hey, Barky-Boy. Knock-knock, pal. Wakey, wakey, wakey. Helloooooo . . ."

Lord Headcase Barker opened his eyes and got a gander of Bobbert Barfonme's smiling face. "Ah." The King smiled. "There he is, back from the dead."

Rubbing his eyes, Head asked, "Where am I? And what happened?"

"Doesn't matter." Bobbert pointed at the pile of white powder on the table next to Head's bed, then asked, "You going to do something with this?"

"What is it?"

"Powdered onion," the King sneered. "Come on, buddy, don't play dumb. It's heroyne."

Head had heard about heroyne, but had never seen any up close, let alone indulged. "Why is there heroyne here?" he asked.

"You might want to take a peek at your leg."

Head lifted up the bedsheet, and, when he saw (and smelled) what had happened to his left leg, almost vomited: his leg was brown, and lumpy, and reeked of waste. "What happened? How did that get . . ." And then he remembered the excrement battle with Jagweed. Covering himself up, Head sighed, "To quote my oldest daughter, *that is seriously grotty to the max.* It looks brutal. I'm surprised it doesn't hurt."

"Barky-Boy, you have enough heroyne in your system to take down a Dorki. I'm surprised you can even move." He paused, then added, "But you're feeling okay?"

"I suppose."

"And you don't need any painkiller?"

"I guess not."

"So you think I could get a taste?"

"A taste of what?"

Pointing at the powder, Bobbert elaborated, "A taste of your *H.* Your scag. Your smack. Your scat. Your junk. Your whoopee dust. Your rootie tootie kazootie. That's the best shit House Barfonme has to offer, and I never even get a snort."

Head agreed, "Go for it."

Bobbert said, "Thanks, pal. Say hello to my little friend." He picked up a two-handed scoop of the powder, rubbed it all over his face, took a deep inhale, and moaned, "Barky-Boy, it's like kissing Gods." He picked up another heap, took another snort, and slurred, "My wife's on her way over. No matter what she says, it's *not* okay for you to touch her boobies." He then climbed into Head's bed, rested his head on his friend's chest, and passed out.

Several minutes later, as promised, Queen Cerevix Barfonme entered the room and sat on the edge of Head's bed. Pointing at her husband, she advised, "I'd roll him over if I were you. He drools."

Head gently pushed Bobbert off his chest, then asked, "Has anybody given you any idea of how long it'll be until I can go back to Summerseve?"

"That's up to you, Headcase. You can leave the second you're able to walk, but you have some things to answer to. You have committed some crimes. Some serious crimes. Crimes that could lead to your execution."

"What are you talking about?" Head intoned. "I'm the only truly moral adult in this whole Godsdamn book."

"That's not what I hear," Cerevix said. "I hear you're a criminal, and if you confess to your crimes, you can go back to your jerkwater burgh." Cerevix stood up, pointed an accusatory finger at his face, and accused, "Confess, Lord Barker!"

"Confess what?"

"Confess that you produced *Journey Through the Secret Life of Plants*!"

"What?" Head asked.

"And confess to producing every Nickelback album, and Peter Criss's solo album, and everything by Creed, and the Black Eyed Peas' later stuff, and most of that boy-band crap, and Liz Phair's self-titled set, and Lil Wayne's *Rebirth*, and that awful Nine Inch Nails remix album, and Madonna's *Who's That Girl*, and Lady Gaga's *Born This Way*!" After a pause, Cerevix added, "Oh yeah, you might want to also confess to kidnapping my stupid taller brother, and attempting to murder my sexy twin brother."

Head said, "Okay, maybe, just *maybe* I produced Liz Phair, but I *definitely* didn't kidnap Tritone, and Jagweed attacked me first."

Cerevix caressed Head's cheek, then said, "Oh, you poor, poor fool. You don't know what's *really* going on in Easterrabbit, do you?"

"Honestly, Cerevix," Head complained, "what with all the shifting perspectives and rambling plotlines, I don't think *anybody* knows what's going on in Easterrabbit."

She kissed him on the forehead and explained, "What's going on is you're about to be punished for crimes you might or might not have committed. Sorry, handsome." Then she smacked Bobbert on the top of his head and growled, "Wake up, chunks! Time to sentence Headcase."

Bobbert popped up, burbled, "Who? What? When? Where? Oh, right, that. Barky-Boy, you're sentenced to be King for a day." He rolled out of bed, fell to the ground, added, "I'm hitting the links. Gotta work on my putting," then crawled out of the room.

After the King was out of sight, Queen Cerevix told Head, "Meet you in the throne room in an hour. We have a town hall meeting. You'll love that." She turned to go, but before she left the room, asked, "Hey, now that you're King, do you want to touch my boobies? Bobbert said it was okay . . ."

GATEWAY

Lady Gateway Barker turned to her sister, Lady Lysergic Aaron, and asked, "Are you sure your people can handle this? I think there are better ways to go about . . ."

"Why do you always question me, sister dear?" Lysergic asked. "You think when something wasn't *your* idea, it's a *lousy* idea. You know, you aren't always the smartest person in the room, Gateway."

"Well, sister dear, when you and I are the only people in the room, I *am* the smartest person in the room."

"Smarmy know-it-all!"

"Uptight virgin!"

"Weedehead degenerate!"

"Hairy-legged spinster!"

Tritone Sinister interrupted, "Ladies, those are some fantastic insults. Write them down for me, and I'll pay you a nickel for whichever ones I use in my act. So let's get this ball rolling. Who do I insult first?"

Lysergic grinned evilly. "Oh, you won't be insulting us, Sinister." She put two fingers in her mouth, gave a shrill whistle, then called, *"Knights!"*

A dozen armor-clad men clattered into the room in lockstep, coming to a halt in a perfect line to the left of the throne. In unison, they yelled, "Squad Four, reporting for duty, m'Lady!"

Tritone gave the Knights an appraising look, then noted, "Pretty awkward that you all showed up to work wearing the same outfit."

"Silence, Sinister!" Lysergic cried. "Now let the contest begin! Sinister, as the guest of House Aaron, you may launch the first salvo." Pointing at the first Knights, she commanded, "Sur Repetitious Runningjoke, step forward!"

Tritone pointed at Sur Runningjoke and said, "Hey, Shecky, yo momma's like a squirrel: she can't keep the nuts out of her mouth." Runningjoke clutched his heart and fell to the ground.

Staring at her downed Knight, Lysergic said, "Lucky shot. Sur Warblenose Chickenbroth, you're next."

Tritone pointed at Sur Chickenbroth and said, "Yo momma's so fat, she has more Chins than a Chynese phone book." After Chickenbroth gagged and collapsed, Tritone strutted up to the third Knight in line and said, "Yo momma's so fat that her bathtub has stretch marks." To the next: "Yo momma's so old that when Gods said, 'Let there be light,' she hit the switch." To the next: "Yo momma's like a hockey team: She changes her pads every three periods." To the next: "Yo momma's like an ice cream cone: everybody gets a lick." To the next: "Yo momma's so poor that when burglars break into her house, they *leave* money." To the next: "Yo momma's so ugly that when she entered an ugly contest, they told her, 'Sorry, no professionals.'" To the next: "Yo momma's a carpenter's dream: flat as a board, and easy to nail." To the next: "Yo momma's so dumb that she put lipstick on her head so she could make up her mind." To the next: "Yo momma's so fat that she fell in love and broke it." And to the last: "Yo momma's so . . ." But before Tritone could finish, the last Knight screamed and sprinted out of the room.

As Lysergic and Gateway stared at the fallen, weeping, moaning Knights, Tritone said, "Okay, that was fun. I'm outta here." Motioning to Sur Crayola Burntsienna, he asked, "You want to stay here with these chuckleheads, or you want to come have some fun?"

Burntsienna saluted Gateway and Lysergic, and said, "M'Ladies, it's been a pleasure," and then he followed Tritone Sinister out of the throne room and toward the front door.

After they were long gone, Gateway said to Lysergic, "So did that work out the way you planned it?"

"Ah, pipe down, you insufferable primate."

"You putrid simpleton!"

"Imbecilic pinhead!"

"Pompous phony!"

"Ego-tripping snot!"

TRITONE

Tritone Sinister stared at the cave. "We should go in. Maybe there's something we can kill and cook. I'm so hungry, I could eat a buttered monkey."

"No way," Sur Crayola Burntsienna chattered. "I ain't going in there."

"Are you admitting you're a dirty coward?" Tritone asked.

"No, a clean one!"

"You know what you are, Burntsienna? You're a swine."

"Oh yeah? Well, you're a pig."

"Pig is the same as swine."

"Alright," Burntsienna retorted, "you're a ham!"

Rolling his eyes, Tritone ordered, "Come on, we're storming the place."

"You can storm. I'll stay here and drizzle."

Despite himself, Tritone chuckled, then said, "Ah, Burntsienna, we're quite the pair, aren't we? Me, the outcast from a royal family, you a deserter from a family nobody's heard of. We're so mismatched that we belong together."

Burntsienna clapped Tritone on his butt—he could not reach his back—and said, "You're right, Tritone. If I have to take the road to Summerseve, I'm glad I'm taking it with you."

Tritone smiled. "Ah, yes, the road to Summerseve."

Burntsienna smiled back and said, "Yes. The road to Summerseve."

Tritone reached up into a tree, pulled out two top hats and two canes, threw one of each to Burntsienna, and shouted, "One! Two! One, two, three, four!" And then they began to sing:

Road to Summerseve

Music and lyrics by Tritone Sinister (Sinister Sounds/ASCAP)

We're off on the road to Summerseve
Squishing through the mud like a dog
One of us is tall, and the other one is short
The short one looks a little like a frog

Well, we're off on the road to Summerseve
Onions are the only things we eat
There are weird and scary animals everywhere we turn
And don't get us started about the heat

Well, we're off on the road to Summerseve
We're not sure why we're going there at all
To start a war? To stage a coup? To try and game a throne?
No matter what, we're still having a ball!

After the applause died down, Tritone and Burntsienna found themselves sitting in the mud, huddled up by a campfire. Burntsienna said, "I hate to complain, but might it be too hot for a campfire?"

"Those idiot Swatch guys went through that too-hot-for-a-campfire crap already," Tritone pointed out. Then, apropos of nothing, Tritone asked, "Hey, did I ever tell you how I popped my first cherry?"

"How you *what*?"

"Picked my first lock? Tore off my first piece? Trimmed my first teacup?"

"Still not getting it," Burntsienna complained.

Sighing, Tritone explained, "My first sexual experience."

Grimacing, Burntsienna mumbled, "I'm not really interested in . . ."

Tritone bulled ahead: "It was magical, Burntsienna, just magical. Sure, it was in a whorehouse, but it was the finest whorehouse in all of Easterrabbit. And sure, my brother and sister were in the corner watching, but they were really quiet. Plus it was really dark, and I couldn't see anyhow."

"Sounds lovely."

"It was. It really, really was." Tritone was then hit with a massive wave of tiredness, so he laid down in the mud and fell into a deep sleep.

The whorehouse's scent was scintillating, a combination of male ejaculate, female ejaculate, male sweat, female sweat, money, Rush by Gucci, M by Mariah, Tommy Girl, Fantasy by Britney, opium, and onions. It was a scent that Tritone Sinister would never forget.

Jagweed held him by his left elbow, Cerevix by his right. Jagweed explained, "It's all paid for, Tri. All you have to do is get it up and stick it in."

Cerevix panted, "That's right. Get it up and stick it in."

Tritone asked his sister, "Are you okay? You're sweating."

Wiping her forehead, Cerevix claimed, "It's not sweat. It's, um, it's lemonade."

Before he could follow up on his sister's ridiculous answer, he locked eyes with the most beautiful woman he had ever seen, a dark-skinned brunette with pouty lips. He leaned toward Jagweed and whispered, "Can I have her?"

Jagweed said, "No, we have somebody else picked out." He pointed across the room to a woman leaning in a doorway: "Her."

"Her?" Tritone asked, giving the tall blond girl a onceover. "I don't know, Jag, she looks a lot like Cerevix. That's just weird."

"Word is she's the best one," Cerevix noted, "and only the best will do for our baby brother!"

"Beggars can't be choosers, I guess," he said, and then strolled into the room, his twin siblings close behind. "Hey, guys, a little privacy?"

Jagweed explained, "Listen, Tri, we've both had sex before, and you might need some advice."

"And Jag has moves," Cerevix claimed. "You should totally listen to him."

Shrugging, Jagweed said, "Aw, you're being nice, sis."

Tritone sighed, "Okay, fine, you can watch, but keep it quiet."

"Not a word," Jagweed agreed.

When all four were in the room, the prostitute blew out the candle and told Tritone, "Take off your clothes, and we'll start." While he was getting naked, he heard somebody else remove their garb, but it barely registered, as he was so trembling with anticipation. The girl took his hand, led him to the bed, and brought him to places he had never been either before or since, places like Nome, Alaska, and Fort Lauderdale.

After Tritone recovered, he asked to go again, but the woman whispered they only paid for one pop, and it was time for them to go. He threw on his clothes, and the three Sinisters walked out of the cathouse arm-in-arm-in-arm, one happy family.

Nine months later, Cerevix Sinister Barfonme gave birth to her only son, Goofrey Barfonme.

Tritone's eyes popped open, and a hopeful mantra drifted through his head: It was just a dream . . . I didn't sleep with my sister . . . I'm not my nephew's father . . . It was just a dream . . . I didn't sleep with my sister . . . I'm not my nephew's father . . .

"Did you say something?"

Tritone spun around, and there was Burntsienna, giving him a strange look. He claimed, "Just clearing my throat, Shecky. Let's get out of here. This patch of woods is so ugly that . . . that . . . that . . ." And for the second time in the book, Tritone was so disconcerted that he could not finish the joke.

LOLYTA

Lolyta Targetpractice was not enjoying her pregnancy, not one bit. Sure, her skin glowed, and sure, it was nice to have Magistrate Illinois tell her that her child is going to be "The Duck Who Quacks Like No Other," and sure, it was nice to be thirteen and pregnant, just like the vast majority of her fellow Easterrabbitarian thirteen-year-olds, but the vomiting, the constant urination, and the nonstop cravings for oats and carrots drove her to distraction.

Ivan Drago seemed to like the lump in her midsection, as born out by the fact that he took her to the center of town to have sex three times a day instead of the typical two. Those who watched Loly and Ivan Drago do their thing had taken to chanting throughout the act; their cries of *KER-BANG-ER! KER-BANG-ER!* could be heard from the rivers to the mountains. Thanks to the ducklike pregnancy and the incessant outdoor lovemaking, Loly had become the most beloved KERBANGER in Dork's long history. But not everybody was enamored with the ruler.

"You have become *so* conceited," Vladymyr ranted. "You think you're Miss Thing, but the fact is, you're a hot mess. And can we talk about that top you've got on? Two words, darling: *Puh-leez*. All I see is tits and gut, tits and gut, tits and gut. Cover that stuff up, girlfriend."

By now, Loly was immune to her brother's clothing suggestions, so she addressed the one thing that had been bothering her for days: "Vladymyr, are you wearing makeup?"

He touched his face, pursed his lips, and purred, "So what if I am? I'm fabulous, and this just brings out my fabulousness."

By now, Loly was immune to her brother's incessant need to call himself *fabulous*, so she addressed the one thing that had been bothering her for months: "Vladymyr, are you gay?"

Vladymyr Targetpractice looked to the floor, shuffled his feet, and croaked, "So what if I am?"

"Frankly, brother dear, if you are, I think it would be better for everybody if you admitted it."

"Why?" he asked, still staring at the floor.

"Because you don't need to spend your life hiding. Your family will always love you, no matter what." She stepped down from the throne, put her hand on his cheek, and whispered, "I'll always love you."

He met her eyes, and she noticed that a single tear had cut a path in his makeup. Clearing his throat, Vladymyr admitted, "I'm gay." And then he smiled, and repeated, "I'm gay!" And then one more time: *"I'm totally, totally gay!"*

With a spring in his step that Loly had never before seen, Vladymyr ran from the castle and skipped across town crying, "I'm gay, Dork, I'm gay!" With each skip, more and more Dorkis followed him, and they took up the chant: *KER-BANG-ER's brother is here! KER-BANG-ER's brother is queer! Get used to it!* Loly and Vladymyr were so caught up in the moment they did not consider the fact that the Dorki population was forming a complete English sentence, with nary an *ooga* or a *booga* to be seen.

Once the Targetpractices, accompanied by Magistrate Illinois, made it to the center of town, Ivan Drago picked up Vladymyr and tossed him in the air in such a manner that he landed on the man/horse's back. "Ooga booga! Let's celebrate KERBANGER'S brother's coming out of the closet! Ooga booga! A grand feast for all at Javytz! Ooga booga!"

As they galloped over to the Javytz Conventyn Centyr on the Eastern outskirts of Dork, Vladymyr asked Ivan Drago, "Hey, Big Sexy, when did you guys learn to talk for real?"

Coughing, Ivan Drago asked, "What do you mean? Oonga boonga, boonga oonga?"

Chuckling knowingly, Vladymyr uttered, "Your secret is safe with me."

It seemed like the entire population of Dork was waiting for the Targetpractices at the Centyr, waiting with a sense of anticipation that was palpable. There was singing, and dancing, and neighing, and ooga booging; all in all, it was the most festive, flamboyant celebration that this book had ever seen. On the far end of the room, there was a large, raised stage on which sat a boiling cauldron. Ivan Drago pointed at the pot and roared, "Boogie googie foogie *gold*!"

Illinois explained to Loly and Vladymyr, "They're making a golden statue of Vladymyr. Apparently he's the first human to declare his homosexuality in the history of Dork, and the horse-people—a good number of whom are either gay or bi—are quite impressed." She paused, then added, "FYI, they're probably going to want Vladymyr to have sex in the middle of the city, in full view of everybody."

Vladymyr leered, "Honey, I'm counting down the seconds."

Ivan Drago tapped Vladymyr on the shoulder and gestured to the stage. "Wowie wowie woo woo woo."

Illinois translated, "He wants you to go stand by the pot, so the master Dorki sculptor can replicate you."

With a grin that could melt an onion, Vladymyr lisped, "Sssssssuper," and navigated his way to the other side of the room. He jumped up onto the stage and jogged to the cauldron, then tripped on his shoelace and fell in.

Over the crowd's deafening silence, the master sculptor reached into the pot and gently pulled out the KERBANGER's brother, who was completely encased in bright, gleaming gold. Everything about the statue was undeniably breathtaking—the detail was astounding, naturally—but its most notable feature was the beatific, contented smile frozen on the face of Vladymyr Targetpractice.

As Loly stared at her brother's lifeless yet life-affirming grin, she thought, *I should probably go check in on my eggs. I haven't mentioned them in a bunch of chapters, and they might be ready to hatch.*

HEADCASE

Lord Headcase Barker asked Tinyjohnson, "Why doesn't anybody just admit it?"

"I told you," the possible eunuch answered, "because there's nothing to admit."

"For Gods' sake, just call a spade a spade already!" Head demanded.

"I shall do no such thing. You can yell at me all you want to, but my answer shall not change."

"Tinyjohnson, look at this thing," Head ordered, then rose from the throne. "It's a toilet, pure and simple. There's a ring, and a hole, and I'm pretty sure I can see a tampon in there."

"That is not a tampon, m'Lord. That's, um, that's a magical ruby."

"A magical ruby, eh? Seems to me that it's silly for a ruby to sit at the bottom of a"—here he did finger quotes—"'throne,' so maybe you should reach in and grab it. As acting King, I give you permission to sell it and keep the profits."

Tinyjohnson cleared his throat, then claimed, "I am perfectly solvent, m'Lord. No need for me to take something that doesn't belong to me."

Head removed his ridiculous temporary crown—it was made from a thick type of paper, and imprinted with the words *Burgyr Kyng*—tossed it across the room, then said, "Let's get this thing started. What is it called again?"

"A town hall meeting, m'Lord."

"Right. How does it work?"

"Simple. Any resident of Capaetal Ceity can approach the King—or, in this case, the acting King—and ask for aid or advice for their problems."

"That doesn't sound too bad. Send in the first favor-asker!"

A strapping young man without a shirt approached the throne. "Good morning, Lord Barker. I am Anklebracelet Beetbox of Gigglesworth Road. The front yard of my house is covered with mud. I'm hoping you can help."

"Begging your pardon, Mr. Beetbox, but the front yard of everybody's house is covered with mud."

"But I'm more special than everybody." He pointed at his stomach, then boasted, "I mean, look at this six-pack. These abs deserve the royal treatment."

Head leaned over to Tinyjohnson and whispered, "How would Bobbert handle something like this?"

Tinyjohnson whispered back, "Depends on his mood. Good mood, ask him politely to leave. Bad mood, hit him with a raven."

"Do we have any ravens?" Head asked.

"No," Tinyjohnson claimed.

Head turned to Beetbox and said, "I will politely ask you to leave. Good day, sir."

Beetbox jeered, "You suck, Barker," then strolled from the room.

The next favor-asker entered, a pretty, round-faced woman with a remarkably ugly baby. "Good morning, Lord Barker. I am Wilhelmina Concertina of Ringworm Road, and this is my child, Dilbert."

Head leaned forward and patted Dilbert on the noggin. "My, such a lovely child," he fibbed.

"Please, m'Lord," Wilhelmina countered, "let's be honest here: This is the ugliest baby in Cap Ceity. I'd like to trade it in for something more attractive."

"Um, I'm afraid that's impossible. Your child is your child."

Ignoring Head, Wilhelmina continued, "I tried to shove him back up there, because I thought maybe if he cooked some more, he'd turn out tastier. But either he was too big, or I was too small. Or maybe it was both, I don't know. Point is, I'm wondering if you have any cute babies hiding somewhere in the castle."

"We don't have any cute babies hiding in the castle. I will politely ask you to leave. Good day, ma'am."

After she was gone, Tinyjohnson said, "You're a natural, m'Lord. I believe we only have one hundred seventy-three people left."

Over the next eight hours, Headcase had requests for new houses, new wives, new horses, new clothes, new onions, new sequels, and something called a nuclear-powered Gantry robot. Unable to grant a single request, he was depressed and grouchy, so he turned to Tinyjohnson and asked, "Since I'm the King, can I make a decree?"

"Of course."

"Great. I decree that whoever brings me the head of Jagweed Sinister receives one million dollars."

"That might not be a good idea, m'Lord. Sur Jagweed is the Queen's brother. That's the kind of rash decision that could get you murdered."

Off in the distance, Juan Nieve's direpanda, Fourshadow, could be heard growling.

SASHA

O h. My. Gods. I, like, totally hate you! *Totally!*"

"I hate you more!" Malia Barker told her sister.

"Well, I hated you first, because I'm, like, older!" Sasha Barker simpered.

"And *stupider*."

"What*ever*. I'm *totally* smarter than you."

"Oh yeah? What's five plus three?"

"Fifty-three. Like, *duh*."

Malia shook her head and grumbled, "Yep, you're a regular Einstein, Sash."

"A regular *what*-stein?"

"Forget it."

Sasha claimed, "If you don't tell me what a mine-stein is, I'm totally tattling on you."

"Oh, that's *real* mature, Miss Older Sister," Malia sneered.

Sasha opened the bedroom door and yelled, "*Daaaaaaaad!* Malia's being mean! Again!"

Malia then yelled, "*Daaaaaaaad!* Sasha's being an idiot! Again!"

Headcase roared, "It's midnight! Both of you pipe down and go to sleep."

Sasha called, "She totally started it!"

Head stomped down the hall into the girls' room. "Started what?"

Turning to Malia, Sasha asked, "Like, what did you start?"

Malia scratched her head, then noted, "I don't remember."

"Gods almighty," Head growled. "You two are driving me nuts, and exchanges like this—and there are too Godsdamn many of them—bring this Godsdamn story to a Godsdamn grinding halt, and the last Gods-damn thing we need in this Godsdamn story is a Godsdamn grinding halt! So pack up your things! You're going back to Summerseve tomorrow! I'll let Bobb deal with this garbage." And then he stomped away.

Sasha whispered to Malia, "He's been totally grouchy since he got into the poo fight with Jagweed."

"Totally," Malia agreed.

HEADCASE

Lord Headcase Barker felt horrible about yelling at Sasha and Malia, but the pressure of being a King—even for a day—was weighing on him. After he finished with the girls, he found himself in desperate need of grog; being that he was in Bobbert Barfonme's house, he figured finding libations would not be a problem.

He was wrong. After an hour-long hunt, Head determined that Bobbert had either hidden the grog in some secret compartment, or had drunk every last drop. Irked and on edge, Head walked back to his room, opened the drawer of his nightstand, and pulled out the last of the heroyne.

Recalling the manner in which Bobbert had ingested the powder, Head took a tiny pinch, brought it to his nostril, and took a tentative sniff, then climbed in the bed with his head in the clouds, and was gone.

It was hot, hotter than the hottest of Summers. The mud was gone, and in its place, sand, miles and miles of sand, sand as far as the eye could see, the nose could smell, and the ear could hear. Head walked through the desert, naked and sweating, at once feeling light and heavy, black and white, awake and exhausted. He came across a man, a dark-skinned man cloaked in a multicolored blanket, a feathered headdress atop his skull.

Head asked the man, "Do you have a message for me?"

The man regarded Head with a skeptical eye for what seemed like hours, then droned, "You are a Caucasian man amongst Caucasian men, yet you are a fighter amongst fighters. You are ready now. You have always been ready. You have never been ready. Go out and stroll with the misery of the Earth.

Stroll to the end of the hurricane and break it for all, as you were meant to do. You are the Stone of Oliver. You are the Kilmer from Val. You are the King. The temporary King. The Lizard King."

Staring into the dark man's eyes, Head was overcome with a sense of peace unlike anything he had ever experienced. A light called him from above, and as Head floated toward it, the sense of calm tripled, as did the size of his erection. The light kept calling, and calling, and calling . . .

"I've been calling and calling and calling, and you haven't answered, and I was worried. Are you alright, Head?"

Head grunted, then groaned, then moaned, then belched, then said, "What're you doing here, Queen? And what are you wearing?"

Cerevix looked down at her body, blinked, and chirped, "Ooh, goodness gracious me, it appears that I'm wearing nothing." Sighing, she added, "Bobbert hasn't seemed too impressed with this, and it makes me lonely. So I ask, Mr. Temporary King: Do *you* like what you see? And do you want to keep me company?"

"We've been down this road before, Cerevix, and if I was so inclined, I'd tell the story via flashback, but it wasn't that great, so why bother?"

"It was great for me," she purred. "You sure lived up to your name, Head." She hopped onto the bed, straddled him, then breathed, "Ooh, goodness gracious me, it appears that somebody's ready for action."

"That was here before you showed up, Cerevix." He could not, however, deny the fact that the Queen's grinding felt magnificent. Head felt his willpower drain away, and, against the King's specific wishes, he touched her boobies.

The faster she grinded, the louder her noises became; after several minutes, her grunts became full words: "Yes . . . yes . . . right there . . . that's it, baby . . . oh, wow . . . you're so hard, Jagweed . . ." At that, Head shoved her off. "Hey, I wasn't finished," she complained. Gesturing at the clean sheets, she added, "And apparently neither were you."

"We're done here, Cerevix. Go back to your room, please."

Cerevix pouted. "This was because I called you Jagweed, wasn't it?"

"To quote my oldest daughter: *Duh!*"

"What's the problem, Heady? You're well aware that's the way us Sinisters do these things. We keep it in the family. This has been going on for, what, like ten generations now. We're about three generations away from becoming a master race."

"You think?"

"I don't *think,* sweet cheeks, I *know.*"

"What about Goofrey?" Head asked. "That kid's not exactly master race material."

"Ah, right, Goof, that's a whole other story. You'll find out about him in the not-too-distant future."

"I don't really care to find out about Goof, Cerevix."

As she slinked from the room, she sang, "Oh, you'll care soon enough, Heady. You most certainly will."

JUAN

Juan Nieve, Snackwell Fartly, Otter, Pinto, Bluto, Flounder, and D-Day became sworn members of the Fraternity of the Swatch in a long, boring ceremony that can be explained via another of those awkward metaphors that populate these pages: Ever watched *Anymal Housse* while sipping on grog, gnawing on a turkey leg, and rubbing a cheese grater across your stomach? It was a lot like that.

HEADCASE

King Bobbert Barfonme staggered into the throne room, puddles of blood and bodily fluids spurting from dozens, if not hundreds, of wounds that dotted his entire body. Lord Headcase Barker hopped off the royal toilet—er, the royal throne—and ran to his friend, managing to catch him before he fell to the floor.

"My Gods, Bobbert," Head exclaimed, "what happened?"

Bobbert plucked a slender, pointy piece of wood from his left eye, then said, "Barky-Boy, they got me with my tee . . ." He then removed a shoe with a spiked bottom that was stuck to his backside. ". . . and my spikes . . ." He then took off his shirt and plucked five small, white, dimpled orbs from his chest. ". . . and my balls. Godsdamn it, *they got me with my own balls.*"

"Bobbert, what is all this, this, this *paraphernalia*?"

"It's the accoutrements of a game, Barky-Boy, a game of Kings. And this game has killed others of my kind. I don't know why I play, Head." He coughed tragically and put his shirt back on, then repeated, "I don't know why I play."

Queen Cerevix traipsed into the room, gasped, and dramatically—some might say *too* dramatically—cried, "Oh my Gods! Bobbert! What has happened to you? Tees in your eyes, spikes in your butt, and balls in your chest? Who would do such a thing? Who would commit such a heinous crime? I have never been so upset or surprised in all of my life!"

Head asked, "How did you know about the balls in his chest, Cerevix? He has his shirt on."

Cerevix blinked, then stammered, "I . . . um . . . I . . . er . . . a wife can sense these things. Especially one who loves her husband above all others."

After spitting up a huge blop of black blood, Bobbert coughed, "Just stop it, Cerevix. You're embarrassing both of us."

Cerevix blinked, then stammered, "I . . . um . . . I . . . er . . . *Headcase touched my boobies!*" And then she sprinted from the room.

As they watched her go, Bobbert croaked, "The dumb bitch totally had me whacked."

Nodding, Head agreed. "Totally."

"She wants Goof on the throne. I shudder to think." And then, deep in thought, he shuddered. After heaving up another heap of hemoglobin, Bobbert ordered, "Barky-Boy, take a letter." Once Headcase rustled up some paper and a quill, Bobbert dictated, "To whom it may concern: First of all, Cerevix had me whacked, so if somebody could kill her, that would be greatly appreciated. Secondly, I shall be replaced on the throne not by my son, Goof, but rather by my brother, Slobbert."

Head stopped writing. "Wait, I've known you for eighteen Summers, and you never once said anything about having a brother."

"I've been keeping him under wraps just for such an occasion."

"What kind of occasion?" Head asked.

"An occasion when I can introduce him into a story in a dramatic, surprising fashion."

Nodding, Head said, "Okay, okay, I get it, I get it. A little soap opera-ish, but not bad at all. But why should . . . um, what's his name again?"

"Slobbert. And as if that's not bad enough, our sister is named Knob-bert."

"Ouch. So why should Slobbert be the King? Isn't Goofrey next in line?"

After vomiting up another chunky mass of red and white cells, Bobbert opined, "Goofrey is a moron."

"How can you say that about the product of your own loins?"

"I can say it simply because it's true. The boy is dumber than mud. But Barky-Boy, here's the thing: Not only is Goof a moron, but he's also a jerkoff." Bobbert paused, then noted, "That's not exactly true. We know who his father is. The guy's just been kind of absent."

"It's Jagweed, isn't it?"

Bobbert laughed, hacked up some more fluids, then said, "Ah, if only it was that easy. No, Goofrey Barfonme's father is . . ." Another cough.

". . . is . . ." A deeper cough. ". . . is . . ." A rattling cough that shook the castle. ". . . is . . ." And then, a tragic cough that signaled the death of King Bobbert Barfonme, the eleventh King in the long history of Easterrabbit to die of golf-related injuries.

As Lord Barker wept over the corpse of his oldest friend, Tinyjohnson crept into the throne room, put his hand on Head's shoulder, and whispered, "He's in a better place now." The possible eunuch let Lord Barker cry for a bit longer, then, once Head regained some semblance of control, asked, "You're coming to Incest Boy's swearing in, aren't you?"

"But what about Slobbert? Bobbert decreed that he take the throne."

Tinyjohnson asked, "Who the hell is Slobbert?"

"Bobbert's brother."

"Let me get this straight: Bobbert has a brother that nobody knew about, and we're supposed to let him take the throne just to keep Goof from being King? Screw that *deus ex machina* crap. It's Goof's gig."

Holding up the note with Bobbert's dying words, Head said, "But Bobbert dictated . . ."

Tinyjohnson ripped the page from Head's hands, tore it into itty-bitty pieces, and growled, "Bobbert didn't dictate a Godsdamn thing. Now that little shit Goof is taking the throne tomorrow afternoon, and if you don't like it, you can take your sorry ass back to Summerseve. I'll meet you there."

"You'll meet me where? At the swearing in?"

"No, in Summerseve."

"But how can you be at the swearing in and in Summerseve?"

Tinyjohnson huffed, "I . . . I . . . I . . . *fuck you, Headcase! Long live King Goof!*"

As the little man stomped out of the room, Head yelled, "Or long *die* King Goof!" After a pause, he mumbled, "Wait, that doesn't make sense. Maybe *short* die King Goof? No, that's also weird. How about *quick* die, King Goof? Or *quick death* to King Goof? Man, I could go for another direpandaburger . . ."

FREON

Out of breath and practically dying of hunger, Freon arrived at the court of his father, King Seabiskit. "Father," he burbled, "I am here to lead your ships into battle!"

His face redder and shinier than an ancho pepper in a Summer rainstorm, King Seabiskit roared, "You fool! That's not supposed to happen until the next book!"

"The next book?" Freon asked.

"*A Crash of Bling: A Sonnet of Slush and Soot, Book 2*. Coming March 27, 2138."

HEADCASE

Please direct your attention to the front of the room, where, for the first time, his Grace, Goofrey of the Houses Barfonme and Sinister, Thankfully the First of His Name, King of the Anuses and the Ryebread and the Fat Fathers, Lord of the Who-Knows-How-Many Kingdoms, and Protector of the Protractor, takes his rightful place on the throne!"

Lord Headcase Barker stood in front of the dais, glaring at Lord Petey Varicose Bailbond as he introduced the new King to the apathetic audience. It took all of Head's strength to keep from leaping onto the stage and trying to throttle Goof, Tinyjohnson, and Queen Cerevix. (Yes, his leg was still brown and smelly, but righteous anger trumps a poo'ed leg.) But even if he did leap upon the stage and try to throttle Goof, Tinyjohnson, and Queen Cerevix, he likely would not have succeeded, as Tinyjohnson had hired Grandstand and Sandstorm Leghorn to protect Goofrey. Headcase was good with his fists, but he was aware that going up against two men who had a combined total of seven arms might prove problematic.

Goof plunked gracelessly on the royal toilet, er, the royal throne, and raised his arms above his head in triumph. Three people in the crowd of three hundred responded with claps, and three others with yawns, while the rest shuffled their feet uncomfortably. The new King frowned, turned to the Queen, and asked, "Mom, why's everybody being so quiet?"

She whispered into his ear, "They just need to get to know you. They need to feel confident that you can rule them. So read the decree."

Brightening, Goof said, "Oh, right." He pulled a parchment from under his cape, unfurled the document, and read, "Today, on the fifth day of the fourth week before Winter is coming . . ."

Cerevix loudly cleared her throat, leaned over, and whispered, "It's *Summer* is coming, Your Highness."

"I said *Summer*," Goof whined.

"No, honey, you said *Winter*. Don't worry about it. Everybody makes mistakes. Just keep reading."

Goof read, "Today, on the fifth day of the fourth week before *Summer* is coming, I declare that the rights to the plot of land to the West of Mount Cheeryos will . . ."

Again, Cerevix loudly cleared her throat, leaned over, and whispered, "It's *East* of Mount Cheeryos, Your Highness, not *West*."

"Fine," Goof sneered. "The rights to the plot of land to the *East* of Mount Cheeryos will reburt to Sur Anglophile Pointystick of . . ."

Again, Cerevix loudly cleared her throat, leaned over, and whispered, "It's *revert*, Your Highness, not *reburt*."

Goof threw the parchment at his mother's chest and whined, "If you're so smart, why don't you read it yourself?"

"I'm just trying to help you out, honey," Cerevix explained.

"I don't need your help," Goof whined. "I hate you. I hate you, and I hope you die." He stomped out of the room, after which the crowd delivered a lengthy standing ovation.

After the noise died down, Head jumped onto the stage and, ignoring the pain in his wounded, fetid leg, roared, "You have just applauded the departure of a false King! Before he died, King Barfonme declared the new ruler to be his brother, Slobbert!"

In unison, the crowd cried, *"Who the hell is Slobbert?!"*

Head answered, "The rightful heir to the throne!"

In unison, the crowd cried, *"Why haven't we heard of him until now?!"*

"One of Bobbert's dying wishes," Head explained, "was that Slobbert be introduced into the story in a dramatic, surprising fashion!"

In unison, the crowd cried, *"That's a really good literary device! But that doesn't mean this Slobbert guy should be King!"*

"I agree," Head agreed. "But do you want young Goofrey ruling the roost?"

In unison, the crowd cried, *"Not particularly! He's kind of a dick!"*

"I know, right?" Head said. "So how about we give this Slobbert fellow a chance?"

Tinyjohnson said, "How about you shut your mouth before Sandstorm cuts off your lips."

In unison, the crowd cried, *"Ooooooooh!"*

Tinyjohnson pointed at Lord Barker and, addressing the audience, yelled, "People of Capaetal Ceity, do you want to see this man executed?"

In unison, the crowd cried, *"Not really, but we don't have anything else going on this afternoon, so go for it!"*

Tinyjohnson turned to Head and pointed out, "The people have spoken. Are you ready to die?"

"As a Lord, I am always ready to die, eunuch . . ."

"I'm not a eunuch!" Tinyjohnson screeched.

". . . but before you begin the execution proceedings, I'd like you to taste this."

And then Head reached behind the throne and picked up an onion cream pie, which he threw across the room with the speed, accuracy, and élan of a snake coiling and uncoiling.

And then the lunacy began, lunacy that ended in the arrest and possible death of Lord Headcase Barker.

MALIA

Wordless screaming, incessant curse words, and rapid-fire splats: For the life of her, Malia Barker could not figure out what the noises from the throne room signified. Part of her wanted to open the door and look, but the other part of her wanted to track down her father and finish preparing for her return trip to Summerseve, and yet the other part of her wanted to divorce herself completely from the proceedings, as the page count was starting to pile up, and even though Malia was not much of a reader, she knew there was a point when enough is enough . . . for instance, when you get to, say, page 527, it might be time to call it a day. Finally, after much deliberation, for the first time in years, Malia took the path that would keep her out of trouble.

Or so she believed.

On the way to the staircase that led to her and her father's respective bedchambers, Malia was stopped by ten men clad in full Knight regalia. "Halt!" the commanding officer commanded. "State your name and your business!"

The Knight to his left mumbled, "Sur, you already know her name and business. It's the youngest Barker girl and she's looking for her father so she can finish preparing for her return trip to Summerseve."

The lead Knight bonked his subordinate on the top of his headgear, then explained, "I know how to read, Sur Whalewhipper. I'm just following Goof's orders to detain and question everybody named Barker." At that, all ten Knights broke down in laughter, after which the leader chortled, "Ahhhh, Goof Barfonme giving orders, what a joke. The kid's an idiot. I give him a week."

"If that," the subordinate giggled.

Once the laughter died down, the lead Knight ordered, "You are to come with me. We have been ordered by good King Goofrey . . ."

One of the Knights in the back whispered, "You mean *dumb* King Goofrey."

". . . to put you in a nice room with a comfortable bed."

The Knight to his left mumbled, "Sur, we were ordered to bring her to the basement and flog her so she wouldn't stop us from murdering her father."

The lead Knight bonked his subordinate on the top of his headgear, then explained, "That *comfortable bed* thing was supposed to be misdirection, Sur Whalewhipper. The girl knows how to fight, and if she becomes aware that we are going to jail her, then murder her father, she might engage us in a battle. Whereas if she believes she's being taken into a nice room with a comfortable bed, she will be less likely to . . ."

Malia interrupted, "I will *not* be imprisoned, *never!*" To the head Knight, she called, "You: What Pittsburgh Pirates player had exactly three thousand career hits before dying in a plane crash?"

The Knight asked, "Who?"

"*Wrong!* Roberto Clemente." At that, the Knight gagged and died.

To the second Knight, Malia called, "You: What franchise has lost the World Series a record twelve times?"

The second Knight asked, "What's a franchise?"

"*Wrong!* The Dodgers of both Brooklyn and Los Angeles. But I would have also accepted if you had just answered Dodgers." At that, the Knight keened and croaked.

To the third through ninth Knights, Malia called, "You seven: name the first five players elected to the Hall of Fame."

At once, all six Knights said, *"Um, I don't know, maybe Jesus Chryst?"*

"*Wrong!* Ty Cobb, Babe Ruth, Honus Wagner, Christy Matthewson, and Walter 'Big Train' Johnson." At that, the six Knights retched and kicked the bucket.

Malia and the lone remaining Knight stared at each other, then finally, the Knight brandished his sword and pointed it at the girl. With a noticeably unsteady hand, the Knight nervously stuttered, "You'd . . . you'd . . . you'd best stand down before I . . . I . . . I attack!"

Malia took one step closer, and asked, "Would you like me to be merciful, dear Knight?"

The Knight fell to his knees and wept, "I beg you, m'Lady, for the love of Gods, please be merciful! If you're going to kill me, show a modicum of compassion! If you have a kind bone in your body, you will not ask me a question about baseball!"

Nodding, Malia murmured, "I shall show you compassion, good Sur. Put down your weapon and remove your headgear." After the Knight followed Malia's requests, she pulled Syringe from her dress and stabbed the Knight in the face 412 times.

With his dying breath, the Knight gasped, "Tis far more noble to have perished by the miniature sword than by the trivia battle!" At that, the Knight retched and expired.

Malia regarded her good work, put Syringe away, then called, "I'm coming for you, Father!" And then she began a journey through the castle that might or might not end in the death of a main character.

LOLYTA

Lolyta Targetpractice's womb was so stretched that she felt as if she were going to give birth to a horse, which stood to reason, because chances were quite good that she *was* going to give birth to a horse.

As Loly lay in bed, barely able to sit up, Ivan Drago held her hand, kissed away her tears, and sadly repeated, "Ooga booga. Ooga booga. Ooga booga."

With a brave smile, Loly said, "Thanks, honey. That's sweet of you to say." She took a deep breath, then continued, "I'm frightened, Ivan Drago. This thing in me is so big, and it's going to tear me up on its way out, and I'm so scared, and I feel so clueless, and I think if I knew how it all worked, I might feel a little comforted. Oh, how I wish you could explain it all to me, darling. I see the wisdom and love in your eyes; if only there was a way you could express it in words."

Ivan Drago walked to the other side of the room, peeked out of the window, then closed the curtains. He said, "Okay, here's the deal, babe: Childbirth—which is also referred to as labor, birth, *partus,* or parturition—is the culmination of a human pregnancy or gestation period with the birth of one or more newborn infants from a woman's uterus. The process of childbirth is categorized in three stages of labor: the shortening and dilation of the cervix, the descent and birth of the infant, and the birth of the placenta." Ivan Drago then went on to explain in lengthy, graphic detail about the machinations of having a baby. After he finished, he asked, "Now that that's out of the way, what do you say we go to the village, grab some grog, and have sex in front of everybody, like Dorkis have always done, and Dorkis always will do, even up through books six and seven, which might or might not eventually be written."

Poleaxed by both her birthing lesson and the newfound knowledge that the husband she had previously believed to be a monosyllabic idiot was actually a verbose genius, Loly agreed, even though the last thing she wanted to do in her physical state was get stabbed in between her legs by her husband's enormous Dorki love-sword.

When the KERBANGER and Ivan Drago arrived at the center of town, the crowd, sensing some voyeurism in their near future, buzzed with anticipation. A Dorki woman tapped Loly on the shoulder and said, "Yowza, yowza, yowza, KERBANGER. Chuckle chuckle doo."

Ivan Drago told the Dorki woman, "Back off on the yowzas, Ivan Betsy. She knows."

Ivan Betsy smiled at Ivan Drago, then said, "Oh. That's cool." Turning to Loly, she added, "KERBANGER, I look forward to watching you guys get it on. I don't know if you're taking requests, but I'd love to see some ass play, and possibly . . ."

"Alright, Ivan Betsy," Ivan Drago growled, "that's enough. Be gone. I'll see you at the meeting tomorrow night." He raised a fist to the sky and said, "Power to the people."

With a fist in the air, Ivan Betsy answered, "Power to the people," then trotted off.

When they were again alone, Loly asked, "What was that 'power to the people' business about?"

"You've had enough schooling for the day," Ivan Drago claimed. "We'll go over Communism tomorrow."

An elderly manhorse galloped over and panted, "Ivan Drago, Ivan Drago, waggle gaggle maggle! Boo boo boo boo! Fraggle fraggle . . ."

"Chill, Ivan Dirk. She's cool."

"Thank Gods," Ivan Dirk sighed. "I was running out of nonsense syllables."

"Yeah, me too. So what's up?"

"Word at the trough is that somebody wants the KERBANGER dead."

Nodding, Ivan Drago pointed out, "Old news, Ivan Dirk. We've known about this for months."

Loly cleared her throat and growled, "Um, what do you mean by *we,* kemosabe?"

Grimacing, Ivan Drago hemmed and hawed. "Yeahhhhh, I was going to tell you eventually, babe, but I figured our lines of communication weren't quite open yet, and I didn't think it would be the most romantic thing in the world for 'There's a price on your head' to be the first real words you heard come out of my mouth."

"I'd say saving my life is pretty romantic," Loly pointed out.

"Ahh, don't worry about it. Nobody's going to kill you." He pointed to one of the vendors and said, "Let me grab you some grog."

Motioning at her gigantic gut, she noted, "I can't, Ivan Drago. Grog isn't good for the baby."

"That's what the powers that be will have you believe," he argued. "It's all a big conspiracy. The Illumynati's behind that one. We'll also discuss that tomorrow." He took a mug from the vendor, handed it to his wife, then cajoled, "Bottoms up."

She sniffed the grog, wrinkled her nose, and noted, "It smells funny."

The vendor gave her an offended look. "Pardon me if this is disrespectful, KERBANGER, but I sell only the finest grog. If I may." And then he removed the mug from her hands, chugged it down, and grunted, "Mmmm, deeeelicious, best grog I've had the pleasure of tasting. A fine vintage if I've ever . . ." He then grabbed his stomach, moaned, "Ooooooohhhhhh, crap, I forgot about the poison," and promptly dropped dead.

Gawking at the dead man, Loly whispered, "Ivan Drago, please take me home. I need to be alone with my eggs."

As they trudged back to the castle, Ivan Dirk called, "Yo, KERBANGER, does this mean you guys won't be screwing out on the lawn?"

SASHA

Oh. My Gods. What is, like, going on there? It sounds totally like a pie fight. With, like, onion cream pies. *Grrrrrrrosssssss.* And not to mention deadly to the max." Sasha Barker then raised her eyes to the heavens and sighed, "Dear Gods, please keep Goof safe from the pies. You know I'm, like, radically in love with him, and we're totally getting married, but he won't be a good husband if he's, like, dead."

Sasha sat down on the floor beside the throne room door, rested her back against the wall, and contemplated not a whole lot, because Sasha was not the kind of girl who contemplated. Just when she was about to come up with a complex idea —and this would be the first complex idea that Sasha Barker had ever had, so it was a good thing she was interrupted, for complexity would have literally burnt her cortex into ash—she felt a tap on her shoulder. "Mind if I join you?"

Sasha sat up a bit straighter and said, "Like, totally, Queen."

Cerevix Barfonme hunkered down next to Sasha and explained, "I had to get out of there. The boys weren't playing nice." She then whispered conspiratorially, "It's important for boys to play nice, right?" Sasha nodded, then Cerevix added, "It's important for girls to play nice, too. Especially if they're going to be the Queen someday." Again, Sasha nodded, then Cerevix continued, "You know how to play nice, don't you, Sasha?" Again, Sasha nodded, then shook her head, then shrugged. Cerevix draped her arm around Sasha's shoulders and explicated, "If you want to play nice, well, when two people love each other very, very much, they get certain feelings, feelings of excitement, and their private parts—the man's is called a penis, and the woman's is called a vagina—become sensitive to the touch . . . but in a good way."

"Oh, I totally know all about that junk, Queen," Sasha noted. "At first I thought it was, like, totally gross, but then I did some stuff in between my legs with my hands, and I decided it's totally awesome."

"It *is* awesome, isn't it," the Queen agreed. "And you know when it's even more awesome? When that person you love very, very much is somebody you've loved for your entire life. Now who have you known for your entire life, Sasha?"

After a bit, Sasha answered, "Like, my mommy and daddy."

"Right, of course, but loving your mother or father in that special way would be weird. On the other hand, loving your one or all brothers in that special way, well, that would be magical."

Frowning, Sasha asked, "When you love someone in that special way, you have to get, like, naked with them, and I totally don't want to get naked with Bobb. He's gross."

"What about Allbran?"

"Like, yuck. He farts."

"What about Dickoff?"

"Like, double yuck. He's a baby. Plus he's, like, not even a fully formed character."

"Well, how about the jerkoff?"

"Juan? *Triple* yuck. He's a jerkoff."

Cerevix removed her arm from Sasha's shoulders, took the girl's face in her hands, and leaned forward so their noses were practically touching. "Listen, here's the deal, missy," she hissed. "If you're going to be Queen, there are certain sacrifices that have to be made, and one of them is banging your brothers, so next time you see Bobb, or Allbran, or any of those other snot-noses you share DNA with, you tear off your clothes, and you lie down, and you spread your legs as wide as they'll go, and you tell them to stick their throbbing member in there, or, by the order of Queen Cerevix Barfonme, their throbbing member will be guillotined off. If you and your brothers don't make the beast with two backs, you will never, ever, *ever* marry my son. Got it?"

Sasha threw up in her mouth a little bit. As a single tear rolled down her cheek, she stuttered, "G-g-g-g-got it."

Before the girl exploded in tears, Cerevix said, "But if you don't want to screw your brothers, there's something else you can do for me."

"Like, *anything*," Sasha moaned.

She took a parchment from her cleavage, which she then unfurled and placed on the floor, after which she reached farther down her cleavage and pulled out a quill, which she then handed to Sasha. "If you put your John Hancock on this thing, you can be Goof's wife."

"Like, John who-cock?"

Ignoring her, Cerevix pointed at an empty line on the top of the document and ordered, "Don't read it. Just sign here." Sasha obeyed. Cerevix's finger moved down the document: "And here." Sasha obeyed. "And here." Sasha obeyed. "And here." Sasha obeyed. Thirty-seven "and heres" later, Cerevix rolled up the parchment, took back her pen, and smiled. "Thank you, Sasha. I'll put in a good word with Goof for you."

As the Queen stood up, Sasha asked, "Like, what did I just sign?"

Queen Cerevix explained, "Nothing too important. Just a declaration that you have proof your father is trying to usurp the throne from its rightful owner, and if he continues with his rabblerousing, he is to be executed. Toodles."

After Cerevix was out of sight, Sasha scratched her head and asked herself, "Like, what's *usurp*?"

JUAN

As the sun ducked beneath the horizon, Juan Nieve and Snackwell Fartly stared at their smoldering campfire. After fifty-three minutes of silent contemplation—and their contemplation was silent because the only actual action in the chapter was the Wall melting some more—a raven dive-bombed their campsite, staggered around for a bit, then cawed, "Head might be dead! Head might be dead! Head might be dead!"

Snack screwed up his face and wondered aloud, "I didn't know ravens could talk."

"Me neither, *jefe*,"[48] Juan intoned. "Me neither."

---

48. Dude.

ALLBRAN

After he read the ravengram, Bobb Barker's face turned red, and he made an odd gurgling sound in the back of his throat. Eventually, he whispered to himself, "Well, now. How about that."

"What is it, Bobb?" Allbran asked, struggling fruitlessly against the straps his brother had used to secure him to his bed.

Bobb explained, "Apparently Father is temporarily indisposed—or maybe permanently indisposed; it wasn't really clear—and I'm to head up an attack on the Sinisters, who are wandering around somewhere between here and Vailcolorado."

"Gosh, Bobb, I'm really happy for you," Allbran lied. "You probably have a lot to do. So maybe you could go ahead and do it, you know, *now*."

"I'm supposed to watch over you. But now that I'm in charge, I could get somebody else to watch over you. Or I could leave you on your own." Clearly eager to be on his way, Bobb asked, "You'll be okay by yourself?"

"Yes, Bobb."

"Great! If you need anything, feel free to . . ." Bobb then hustled out the door so quickly that Allbran could not hear the rest of the sentence.

Once he was certain that Bobb was out of earshot, Allbran closed his eyes, took a deep breath, clenched his buttocks, and emitted a high-pitched fart that was not audible to the human ear. However, it was right in the direpanda auditory range, so mere seconds after gas whiffed from his hindquarters, Hinky was at his bedside. An empathetic and intelligent animal, Hinky immediately discerned that his master wished to be released from his shackles, so after one slick paw swipe, Allbran was free.

Allbran tiptoed from his bedroom to the top of the stairs, but three steps down, he heard Bobb droning to somebody: ". . . and I've been drawing up this plan for a while. I've honed it, and honed it, and I tried to show it to Father, but he laughed and told me to go back to the drawing board, but I knew it was perfect—I just knew it—and now I finally get to show everybody what I can do because *I'm in charge!*"

"Very good, m'Lord." It was Maester Blaester. "Hand over your plans and I shall deliver them to the proper officers."

"Oh, no no no no no, Blaester. I will deliver these, and see that they are executed to perfection, because it's my plan, and nobody will be able to explain it better than I."

Blaester drily offered, "It's good to see that your newfound power hasn't gone to your head, m'Lord."

"Just keeping my eye on the prize. If you don't pay attention, you get killed, and since I'm in charge, nobody wants me to get killed, plus I'm a key player in the sequel, and everybody knows that the sequel is where the big bucks are."

Allbran shook his head sadly, then he stalked down the stairs and out of the castle, in search of somebody who could tell him where the hell his mother had been for the last fifty or so pages.

GATEWAY

A dirty, filthy, grimy, unclean, grubby, sullied Lady Gateway Barker trudged toward the Barker castle, bone-tired from her second journey of the book. Not yet ready to face whatever weirdness was awaiting her at home, she plunked down under a tree and pulled the last bit of Godsweede from her cleavage, then lit up, took a deep toke, closed her eyes, and, for the first time since before her first journey of the book, smiled.

Just as Gateway was on the precipice of the best nap in Easterrabbit history, she felt and heard a rumbling. She opened her eyes and looked over her left shoulder. Seeing nothing, she stood up, turned to her right, and was almost run over by a cavalry led by her son Bobb.

Bobb's horse came to a screeching, neighing halt directly in front of her; the horse immediately behind Bobb crashed into his horse, then the horse behind that horse crashed into that horse, then the horse behind *that* horse crashed into *that* horse, and so on, until Bobb's steed was the only animal left standing. Unfazed by the pile of fallen animals and Knights to his rear, Bobb exclaimed, "Mom! You're home just in time to see me lead men into battle!"

She smiled and said, "That's wonderful, Bobb. What's your battle plan?"

"I left it with Blaester," Bobb explained. "Figured I'd wing it." Cocking his thumb over his shoulder, he said, "I've got the best of the best on board, so we'll be fine."

Looking at the pile of horses and Knights trying to extricate themselves from the gummy mud, Gateway thought, *I wouldn't go that far,* then she asked, "Anything I can do to help?"

With a condescending smile, Bobb said, "I'm in charge."

Nodding, Gateway agreed, "Of course you are. But some sort of plan might be useful."

Bobb gave her a dismissive wave. "We've got it. Go home and take a bath."

Ignoring him, Gateway quickly spat out, "It would be best to attack decisively from the rear with a heavily concentrated strike. Focus on destroying their small pockets of resistance, and then when your reinforcements arrive—and I'm assuming there *will* be reinforcements, because without a proper second wave, the first wave is all but pointless—you can retreat and simultaneously tend to your wounded—and no matter how strong your attack-slash-defense is, there *will* be wounded, make no mistake about it—and form a perimeter, enabling your second wave to triangulate their primary targets. Once a goodly number of their men are felled—somewhere between thirty and fifty percent is acceptable—close the perimeter, destroy or detain their remaining soldiers, commandeer their weapons, then take the hell over. In terms of an exit strategy, plan to leave one fifth of your unit there for thirty to sixty days to protect against any uprisings." She took a huge toke of her Godsweede, then asked, "You get all that?"

Bobb gawked at his mother for a bit, then turned to his mostly fallen unit and said, "To battle, men! Glory awaits!" And then he rode off by himself.

Gateway glumly watched her son gallop off to certain death, then turned to the writhing heap of men and beasts, held out her roach, and asked, "This won't end well, on either the page or the small screen. Anybody want a hit?"

TRITONE

Tritone Sinister and Sur Crayola Burntsienna stood at the top of a low peak, staring down upon what appeared to be a bustling town; the odd thing was that it was bustling in the middle of nowhere.

As the stars twinkled in the sky, Tritone opined, "Looks like a dump."

"A pit," Burntsienna added.

"A hole."

"A pigsty."

Tritone pointed out, "Maybe they have some food."

"Good call. All of a sudden, it looks lovely."

"Gorgeous."

"Sumptuous."

"Breathtaking."

The duo tiptoed into the itinerant camp, Tritone's lips buttoned shut for a change. The vast majority of the group was curled up in the mud, snoring happily, befouling the area with their onion breath. On the far end of the field, a fire sparked and popped; Burntsienna gestured to the flame and proposed, "We should head over there, because if there's food, it'll be by the fire."

Tritone said, "You're a regular Einstein, Crayola."

"A regular *what*-stein?"

"Forget it."

Burntsienna claimed, "If you don't tell me what a mine-stein is, I'm totally stabbing you."

Heading toward the fire, Tritone offered, "Temper, temper, temper. Looks like somebody didn't get enough hugs when they were growing up."

There was a single individual seated beside the flame; their back was turned to Tritone and Burntsienna, thus Tritone quietly cleared his throat so as not to scare the person. The stranger said, "Whoever that is, you smell so bad that you make onions cry. *Zzzzzzing.*"

Tritone whispered, "Father?"

The man turned around and smirked, "That's my name, don't wear it out." He offered his hand to Burntsienna, then said, "How's it going, Henny? Tutone Sinister, owner of Sinister Mortuary. You stab 'em, we slab 'em! *Yowzah, yowzah, yowzah!*"

Burntsienna turned to Tritone and said, "I didn't know you had a father."

"What, you thought I was a jerkoff?"

"Kind of."

"Where'd you get the idea I was a bastard?" Tritone asked.

"Oh, no," Burntsienna answered. "I thought you were just a jerkoff in the truest sense of the word."

"Thanks a lot, Shecky."

Burntsienna said, "It's just you'd think with all this stuff we all know about you, Cerevix, and Jagweed—not to mention the incessant tales of your family's issues with the different Houses—it would be logical that somebody somewhere would've mentioned your father."

"Yeah," Tritone drawled, "but logic doesn't always rule the day in the story of Easterrabbit, now does it? Little logic, and lots of dead spots. Why anybody buys this crap, I have no clue."

Tutone—who was as fat as Tritone was tall—said, "Boys, this is fascinating stuff, but I have to go back to staring at the fire." And then he went back to staring at the fire.

After a beat of silence, Tritone grunted, "Hey, Pops?"

Without turning around, Tutone grunted, "Hey, son?"

"Anybody ever tell you that you're so stupid that you couldn't even pour mud out of your boots if the instructions were written on the heel?"

"How dare you . . ."

"Did you study to be that ugly, or did it come naturally?"

"Wait a sec . . ."

"You're so fat that your shadow weighs fifty pounds."

"Hey, that one was pretty good."

Tritone paused, then asked, "Did you just say something nice about me?"

Looking around as if to make certain nobody heard him, he offered, "It'll probably be the last time, because you're so dumb that you think a riverbank is where fishes keep their money. *Hi-yo!*"

Tritone chuckled. "Classic material, Dad, just classic."

"Tell me something I don't know, Henny."

In an impressive bit of subject changing, Tritone gestured at the dozens of sleeping bodies and asked, "What's going on here?"

"We're taking down House Barker."

"Why?" Tritone asked.

"Don't tell me you didn't read *Why All the Houses Hate Each Other So Godsdamn Much* by that Flaysh guy."

"Okay, I won't tell you I didn't read *Why All the Houses Hate Each Other So Godsdamn Much* by that Flaysh guy even though I didn't read *Why All the Houses Hate Each Other So Godsdamn Much* by that Flaysh guy. Give me the gist."

Tutone admitted, "I didn't read it either, but if there's a book about the Houses hating each other, then all the Houses hate each other, and who am I to buck tradition? So how about you help us kill Headcase Barker and that Godsweedehead wife of his?"

"I don't know, Pop. Head's a good guy, and . . ."

Tutone put his hand on Tritone's shoulder and intoned, "Listen, everybody knows that the reason you do stand-up is because you crave acceptance, since you didn't get enough of it from your father, just like Jeffrey Ross. If you help me bring down House Barker, I'll accept you, and your daddy issues will be solved. *Capice?*"

Tritone said, "Daddy issues? Me? Come on, Pop, I'm a bastion of mental health." And then the tall Sinister pulled the fat Sinister into an odd embrace and wept onion tears until he could weep no more.

SASHA

"Oh. My. Gods. Goof is, like, so Kingly."

Sasha Barker leaned against the wall at the far end of the throne room, alone with her two or three thoughts, gazing lovingly at the boy she believed would be her future husband. The emotion from the look she gave Goof was the antithesis of what every other person in the room was feeling—the crowd wanted him drawn and quartered.

King Goofrey pointed at the fifth person in the third row of the audience—a woman with blond, matted hair and a dirty face—and demanded, "State your name!"

"Ginalollo Wackypack."

"Ginalollo Wackypack, do you swear your allegiance to me, Goofrey of the Houses Barfonme and Sinister, Thankfully the First of His Name, King of the Anuses and the Ryebread and the Fat Fathers, Lord of the Who-Knows-How-Many Kingdoms, and Protector of the Protractor?"

"Do I have to?" she asked.

"Just like I told the person before you, and the person before him, and the person before her, and the person before that, *yes,* you must swear your allegiance."

"Can't we all do it at once?" Ginalollo Wackypack wondered.

"Just like I told the person before you, and the person before him, and the person before her, and the person before that, *No! No no no no no!*"

"Why?"

"Because I'm King, and I want to do it this way, and whatever the King says, goes, so *nyah, nyah, nyah!*" He turned to his right and asked his Foot,

Lord Petey Varicose Bailbond, and his Other Foot, Sur Jagweed Sinister, "That's right, guys, right? Whatever I say goes? Right? *Right?!*"

Tinyjohnson rolled his eyes and grunted, "Whatever."

"I don't like your attitude! Uncle Jagweed, you're promoted! Tinyjohnson, you're fired! You're not my Foot. I'm de-Footing you! I don't need your help! I hate you! I hate you, and I hope you die!"

Tinyjohnson grabbed his tiny johnson and snarled, "Bite this, Your Highness."

"I would if you had any junk, but you don't have any, because you're a eunuch!"

"You know what?" Tinyjohnson asked. "Let's put this eunuch business to bed right now." He pulled down his pants, laid down on his back, spread apart his legs, and called, "Get a good look, people! There you go! The full package! Live it up! Tell your friends!"

Goof knelt down and stuck his nose right in front of Tinyjohnson's man parts. "Loyal subjects, he's right! The full package is there! It's really, really small, but it's there!"

With wide eyes and an open heart, Sasha whispered, "Oh. My. Gods. Goof is, like, so Kingly."

"You really think so?"

Sasha looked up: Queen Cerevix. "Like, totally. He's way tubular."

"If he doesn't settle down," Cerevix mumbled, "one of these people is going to put him in a tubular and bury him in ten feet of mud."

"Queen, you're, like, so mean sometimes."

Cerevix asked, "You want to see mean? Watch this." She cupped her hands over her mouth and roared, "Hey, Goof, your Uncle Tritone's really your father!" She told Sasha, "And if you think that was mean, check this out." Then she roared, "Hey, Jagweed, I'm making it a law that everybody has to call you Sur Impotent." Over cries of her betrayed family and the amused crowd, she said, "*That,* young Miss Barker, is mean. Welcome to the family."

"Oh. My. Gods. You're, like, a total bitch."

"You want to see bitchy? Goof told me to have you arrested, and even though I don't have to follow his command . . ." In a perfect impression of Sasha, she continued, ". . . I'm, like, totally going to."

As the Leghorn brothers dragged Sasha Barker to her cell, she called to Cerevix, *"I don't care how many potential HBO royalty checks I'm blowing with this decision, but I'm, like, totally not marrying him now!"*

TRITONE

With his giant head resting on Sheastadium's dwarf breasts, Tritone Sinister replayed that morning's conversation with his father:

"Listen, Henny," the fat Sinister had intoned to his son, unsuccessfully attempting to put his arm around the giant's shoulders, "I'm demoting you."

"Demoting me from what?" Tritone had asked. "You have to be given a job before you lose it."

"I'm demoting you from guy-who-might-or-might-not-join-us-in-our-fight-with-the-Barkers to guy-who-stays-at-homebase-and-has-sex-with-a-prostitute-so-he-doesn't-screw-anything-up-on-the-battlefield."

From the waist up, Tritone was insulted—just because he had never fought did not mean he lacked the ability to fight—but from the waist down, he was elated. "Well, Pop, you know how they say, *Now is the time for all good men to come to the aid of their country?* In my case, now is the time for all good men to come. *Ring-a-ding-ding!*"

Nodding appreciatively, Tutone asked, "You come up with that off the cuff?"

"Nah, I've had that one in my back pocket since last night. So where're the hos at?"

Tutone cocked a thumb over his shoulder and said, "Fifth tent to the right. Her name's Sheastadium. She's the perfect size for you." He paused, then admitted, "Tritone, as a father, I've never been there for you . . ."

"No shit, Sherlock."

". . . but I'd like to remedy that. I'd like to impart the wisdom that every father imparts to his son." He took a deep breath and said, "When two people love each other very, very much, they get certain feelings, feelings of excitement, and their private parts—the man's is called a penis, and the woman's is called a vagina—become sensitive to the touch . . . but in a good way."

After twenty more minutes of unnecessary biology lessons, Tritone patronizingly patted his fat father on the top of his head and stated, "Thanks for clearing that up, Shecky. Let me go put this newfound knowledge to work." All of which is how he ended up with his giant head resting on Sheastadium's dwarf breasts.

Just as he and his hooker were about to go for a second time—unlike his brother, Tritone did not have potency issues—the entrance to the tent flew open and a man roared, "Sinister, we're sustaining more casualties than anticipated! Put away that insanely huge dong of yours, find some armor, grab a weapon, and get fighting!" The man sounded to Tritone like he had three arms, so he assumed it was Sandstorm Leghorn, but since his giant face was buried in between Sheastadium's dwarf thighs, he could not confirm or deny his supposition.

Tritone sat up, gave Sheastadium a regretful look, and said, "We'll always have Paris, darling." Still naked, he sprinted from the tent and toward the armor tent, ready and eager to come to the aid of his country.

There were only seven suits of armor: six mediums and one large. (Tritone had never been fitted for a Knight's outfit, but he rightly assumed that he would need an XXL, extra long, a size that nary a House produced.) He picked up the bottom half of the large and attempted to pull it up his long legs; somehow, someway, Tritone was able to yank the armor pants up to his waist. Unfortunately, they ended at his knees—his calves and ankles were exposed—and he was not able to take a full step without having his manhood squashed. He squeezed into the top half with a similar result, then wondered, *Is it too late to go AWOL?* Tritone then snatched up the biggest available sword and waddled out of the tent toward what turned out to be a chaotic battle.

There were a dozen or so small, awkward skirmishes on the periphery, but the main action was in the middle of the field, where Bobb Barker was surrounded by six of Tutone's men, all of whom were taking turns bopping Barker on the head. From what Tritone could tell, Bobb's response of

"Ouch, quit it . . . ouch, quit it . . . ouch, quit it . . ." was not endearing him to his troops.

The Barker-boppers seemed like they were having a good time, so Tritone sauntered toward the fracas nearest to him, on the way to which he tripped over a hardened mud ball, fell, and rolled into the legs of a Barker soldier's horse. Domino-like, the horse fell down, knocking over another Barker horse, who fell and knocked over another Barker horse, who fell and knocked over another Barker horse, and so on, until the only Barker horse left standing belonged to Bobb. Bobb shook his head, sighed, and rode off, head hanging like a snake coiling, then uncoiling. (Last snake metaphor, we promise.)

The Sinister army gawked at Tritone, then one of the Surs broke the silence with a cry of "The giant has given us victory! Long live the giant! Long live the giant! Long live the giant!"

While the rest of the Knights took up the chant, Tritone extricated himself from the mud puddle, pulled himself to his knees, and answered, "Thank you very much, ladies and germs! That's all for me this afternoon. Tip your waitress, and try the veal with onions, and please always remember, and please never forget, wherever you go, there you are!" He walked off of the battlefield to a raucous round of applause, and a chant of "Tri-*tone*! . . . Tri-*tone*! . . . Tri-*tone*!"

On his way to Sheastadium's tent for a celebratory round of two people loving each other very, very much, he ran into his father, who put out his arms and uttered, "Henny."

"Shecky," Tritone answered.

"Henn-uh-luh."

"Shecky-sheck."

"Henny hen hen hen."

"Sheck-a-doodle-doo."

And then the tall Sinister pulled the fat Sinister into an odd embrace and wept onion tears until he could weep no more.

HEADCASE

T he wounds he suffered during what the residents of Capaetal Ceity had taken to calling the Great Onion Pie Massacre were becoming more painful by the second, and Lord Headcase Barker was not happy. "Guards," he called, wincing as he wiped the drying blood from his neck, "where's my heroyne?! You can't imprison me without allowing me my opiate!"

Tinyjohnson sauntered over and said, "Lord Barker, I'm afraid your guards are otherwise occupied incarcerating your daughter. But I'm here to help."

"Wait, I thought you were in Vailcolorado."

"Enough of that business already! I was there then, but I'm here now!"

"Which begs the question," Head questioned, "what *are* you doing here now?"

"I just wanted to let you know what's going on in Summerseve," Tinyjohnson explained.

"How do you know what's going on in Summerseve?" Head asked. "I thought you were in Vailcolorado, then here."

Ignoring him, Tinyjohnson explained, "House Barker and House Sinister are about to engage in an epic battle that will result in six or seven more books. I don't want that, and I know you don't want that, so let's figure out what we can do to put an end to this mess."

Head explained, "I can't do anything about it from in here, and I doubt that Cerevix is going to be freeing me anytime soon, so you're on your own." After a pause, he sighed, "You know what, Tinyjohnson? I hate House Sinister more than anything in this Godsforsaken world."

"Anything?"

"Anything."

"More than the New York Yankees?"

"They buy championships, they don't build them. It goes against the spirit of professional sports. If baseball would adopt a hard salary cap, it wouldn't be those Godsdamn Yankees year after year after year. But yeah, I hate the Sinisters more."

"More than broccoli?"

"Why is it that the healthiest vegetables taste the worst? Put the Selenium in something people will eat. Like apples. Or onions. But yeah, I hate the Sinisters more."

"More than J. R. R. Tolkien?"

"Oh, come on, I don't hate Tolkien. He's just overrated."

Nodding, Tinyjohnson agreed, "I agree. But I didn't come here to discuss sports, nutrition, or literature. I spoke with Cerevix, and I negotiated a deal for you. I can get you out, so long as you call off Bobb and make sure that this is the last book of this series. But on one condition." He pulled a white burlap short-sleeved shirt from his pocket and showed it to Head. "You are free to go only if you wear this at this afternoon's rally in the center of town." He then threw the shirt at Head and said, "It's your decision, Lord Barker."

After Tinyjohnson exited, Head read the slogans on the shirt.

On the front, in big black letters: HOUSE BARFONME RULES.

On the back, in bigger black letters: HOUSE BARKER SUCKS DIREPANDA COCK.

Lord Headcase Barker dropped the shirt to the floor, fell to his knees, covered his face, looked to the heavens, and wailed, "Noooooooooooooo-ooooooo!"

GATEWAY

So. How'd it go? Did your no-plan plan work out like you thought it would?"

"I don't want to talk about it."

Lady Gateway Barker shook her head sadly and grumbled to Bobb Barker, "Did you attack from the rear like I told you to?"

"I said I don't want to talk about it," Bobb repeated.

"How many of your guys survived? Twenty? Thirty? Fifty?"

Again, Bobb said, *"I don't want to talk about it!"*

She stared silently at her son for several seconds, then asked, "You lost all of them, didn't you? Great, now the HBO casting director has to set up another audition for extras, and the budget for the show was already blown after the third episode, so we'll probably have to get non-union people, and that'll be an insurance nightmare." She paused, then added, "We'd better get a whole buttload of Emmys for putting up with this crap."

Bobb stomped toward the front exit, bitching, "Oh, Miss Know-It-All, you think you're sooooooo great, don't you, Mom? Miss I'm-So-Cool-Because-I'm-a-Bully. Miss I'm-Married-to-a-Tactical-Genius. Miss-I-Am-Woman-Hear-Me-Roar." At the door, he stopped, spun around, and said, "I bet you can't do this, Miss Fancy Pants Weedehead." And then he left.

Gateway slumped onto the floor and thought, *Speaking of weedehead, I'm dry, and Bobb got Sur Thaistik Skunkafornia killed, so I'll be dry for a while.* As she contemplated life without her righteous bud, she heard the front door open, followed by the familiar clatter of armor. "Hello," she called, then stood up and asked, "Can I help you?"

"The question, Mother, is, Can *I* help *you*? And the answer is a resounding *Yes.*" And then Bobb entered the room holding a prisoner: Sur Jagweed Sinister.

Staring at the Not-Kingslayer, Gateway asked Bobb, "How did you find and capture him so quickly, Bobb?"

Tightening his chokehold on Jagweed, Bobb explained, "In Easterrabbit, events generally unfold with the speed of a heavy onion rolling through the thick, thick mud, but once in a rare, rare while, things happen quickly. This, Mother dear, is one of those times."

"But you were gone for only three minutes."

"Mom, you're overthinking this."

"I thought he was in Cap Ceity. Goof made him his Foot. What would he be doing three minutes away from our castle?"

"Let it go, Mother."

"Or maybe this isn't Jagweed. Maybe it's his lookalike."

Bobb roared, "I don't have to take this! I'm in charge, and you don't speak to leaders this way!" He let Jagweed out of the chokehold, then ordered, "I order you to leave."

Jagweed turned to Bobb and said, "Wait, let me get this straight: you're telling me to go?"

"I am."

"You're releasing your best possible bargaining chip, just like that."

"Just like that."

"Why?" Jagweed asked.

"Why not?" Bobb answered.

Jagweed looked at Gateway and queried, "How do you feel about that?"

Shrugging, she answered, "He's in charge."

The Not-Kingslayer clapped Bobb on the shoulder and told him, "Keep up the good work, buddy. Now if you'll excuse me, I have a rival to execute and a twin sister to screw." And then he ran from the castle, leaving Bobb and Gateway to prepare for their respective appearances in *A Crash of Bling: A Sonnet of Slush and Soot, Book 2,* coming March 27, 2138.

MALIA

After being ignored by everybody in the book for days, Malia—who was sick to death of Cap Ceity and its moronic political infrastructure—decided to steal a horse and trek her own way back to Summerseve, unconcerned for her safety because she was a Barker, and Barkers were all about trekking safely to and from Summerseve.

There was, however, a problem with her plan: what with all the wars being fought, Cap Ceity was short on equines, so she decided to walk, figuring she could bum a ride along the way. (That would not be as difficult as it might sound, as this was Easterrabbit, and there was always somebody journeying from one place to another.) On her way out of town, Malia happened upon a mob, an angry mob, a mob she sensed was looking for blood. Considering her mood at the moment, bloodlust was something she could get behind.

The audience was facing some sort of makeshift stage, which Malia could not see, as she was really, really short. Her oversized suitcase in tow, she navigated her way through the crowd, toward the front. When she was halfway there, the crowd began to chant in unison: "House Barfonme rules! House Barker sucks direpanda cock! House Barfonme rules! House Barker sucks direpanda cock!"

After contemplating the fact that the denizens of Easterrabbit did a whole lot of unison chanting, she continued toward the front, her suitcase bashing annoyed mob members in the knees. Eventually she got close enough to see the stage to see what was going on . . . and she did not like it one bit.

King Goofrey stood next to Queen Cerevix Barfonme, who stood next to Sur Jagweed Sinister, who stood next to Sandstorm Leghorn, who stood next to Lord Headcase Barker. Cerevix stared at Goof with an annoyed look on her face. Goof stared at Head with a confused look on his face. Jagweed stared at Cerevix with a lustful look on his face. Sandstorm stared at Head with a violent look on his face. And Head stared at everybody with a pissed-off look on his face.

Queen Cerevix roared, "Lord Headcase Barker, have you anything to say before we execute you for reasons that are not quite clear or logical?"

"Gods yes, I have something to say: the rightful heir to the throne is Slobbert Barfonme! Goofrey Barfonme's father is not Bobbert Barfonme, but rather it's Tritone Sinister! Goof is the product of incest and should not be allowed to rule!"

The crowd was silent. And then there came a murmur. And then a wave of sound. And then, unsurprising to Malia, came yet another chant: "Incest is *best*! Incest is *best*! Incest is *best*!"

Head moaned, "Seriously?"

"Incest is *best*! Incest is *best*! Incest is *best*!"

"Really?"

"Incest is *best*! Incest is *best*! Incest is *best*!"

"Come on, now, people."

"Incest is *best*! Incest is *best*! Incest is *best*!"

Anger welled up in Malia's soul, an anger that tasted of blood and smelled of onions. She pulled Syringe from the side pouch of her suitcase and stabbed the man to her left 167 times, then the woman next to him double that, then the man next to her triple that. Malia's killing spree would have continued had she not heard Queen Cerevix yell, "Sandstorm Leghorn, I order you to chop off the head of Headcase Barker."

Leering at Head's neck, Sandstorm growled, "With pleasure, Your Highness." The three-armed man then unsheathed his sword and advanced on Head. As he wound up for the neck chop, Head kicked him in his stomach, then snatched his weapon.

Head kneeled down and roared, "If I am going to die, it is going to be on my terms! If I am going to die, it will be my way! If I am going to die, it will be by my hand! *Summer is coming!*" And then he stabbed himself in the midsection, and died a gruesome death that scarred his daughters for life.

The silence was deafening. After two minutes of utter quiet, King Goofrey Barfonme said, "Whoa. That sucked. I was totally gonna pardon him."

SASHA

Oh. My. Gods. This is, like, the grossest jail ever."

The guard gazed impassively at Sasha Barker and said, "You've mentioned that."

"I know, but it's grosser than gross. Like, how do you deal?"

"I already told you," the guard said with infinite patience, "I get paid."

"I totally want to go home. If I show you one of my boobies, can you let me out?"

"I already told you, if you escape, the Barfonmes will have me killed."

"Both boobies?" After the guard shook his head, Sasha added, "That's, like, so rude. I totally hate the Barfonmes."

From the opposite end of the corridor, a peevish voice called, "Do you hate *all* the Barfonmes?"

Sasha yelled, "I don't want to see you, Goof! You suck to the max!"

Goof sashayed over to Sasha's cell, dismissed the guard, and gloated, "I have a gift for you." He pulled a bouquet of flowers from behind his back.

If they were not coated with mud, they probably would have been the most beautiful flowers Sasha had ever seen, but she did not want to give Goof the satisfaction of seeing her smile, so she turned around and squealed, "*Ewwwwwwww,* those are grotty to the max. Take them away before I, like, throw up all over the place."

Goof asked, "You don't appreciate my flowers? Fine." He sprinted away and returned a minute later with an ornate macaroni sculpture in tow. "I made it myself," he explained. "It's a bust of your head. I think it captures your true beauty."

Sasha gave it a quick peek, then retorted, "I think it captures, like, your true lameness or something."

Goof growled, then sprinted away and returned a minute later with a large painting in tow. "I also made this myself. It's a self-portrait. It was going to be my wedding gift to you, but I want you to have it right now."

Without giving the canvas a glance, Sasha said, "I want you to stick it up your butthole right now."

"Okay, fine, watch this." Goof then did seven push-ups, then puffed, "Pretty extraordinary, right?"

"Totally *not* extraordinary. You're, like, way out of breath."

"Okay, listen to this: Five plus five equals ten. Ten plus ten equals twenty. Twenty plus twenty equals forty. Are you impressed now?"

Sasha, who had no idea if Goof's calculations were correct, sneered, "You totally got all those, like, wrong."

"Aaaargh," Goof moaned, then stomped away.

When the guard returned a bit later, Sasha asked, "If I show you one of my boobies, can you get me some Godsweede?"

Grinning, the guard said, "Now *that* I can do. And you save that boobie for the right guy, sweetheart."

When Goof returned to the jail later that day, Sasha was thoroughly baked, and understood exactly why her mother was such a proponent of the pungent plant. "Gooooooooof," she slurred, "I hate you sooooooo much."

Puffing up his chest, Goof boasted, "Well, Sasha Barker, I'm about to show you something that'll make you love me forever and ever."

"Like, whatever."

"Oh, you won't be *whatever*-ing me when you see this," Goof claimed, then called, "Sandstorm! Grandstand! Bring them in!" The Leghorn brothers marched in lockstep toward Sasha's cell. In each hand, they held a long post, and at the top of each post sat a severed head. The heads were fresh, so fresh that the blood dripping from each was still warm. "This, my future bride, is what House Barfonme does to deserters. How cool is that?"

For a moment that seemed to go on forever, but was, in reality, about forty-five seconds, Sasha Barker gave King Goofrey Barfonme a look that could have frozen mud. Finally, finally, finally, Sasha broke the thick silence: "Oh. My. Gods. I, like, totally love you. Let's, like, totally get married."

And they lived happily ever after. Or at least for another book or two.

LOLYTA

Don't wake the ducks, Loly," Vladymyr ordered. "If you have your baby, the ducks will awaken, and it's very important that you do not, under any circumstances, awaken the ducks."

"Why?" Lolyta Targetpractice asked. "What happens if I wake the ducks?"

"Trust me, you don't want to know," Vladymyr simpered. "It won't be pretty."

Loly peered at Vladymyr's face and declared, "You don't know what'll happen if I wake the ducks, do you?"

Vladymyr claimed, "I absolutely know what will happen if you wake the ducks." After a lengthy staring contest, Vladymyr admitted, "Okay, fine, I don't know what'll happen if you wake the ducks."

"I didn't think so," Loly said.

"But don't you think just to play it safe, you shouldn't wake the ducks? I mean, what do you gain by waking them? They'll probably just make a mess, and this castle is fabulous. Do you want it covered with duck droppings?"

"Vladymyr, I miss you and all, but this dream is a total waste of time. I mean, there's no correlation for it on the page or the small screen. I'm waking up."

"Wait, wait, wait," he said, "before you do, there's something I should tell you: Never before has a Dorki mated with a human. Their bodies are not compatible. Your baby is going to have the head of a horse and the body of a human."

Loly hissed, "Go away, Vladymyr. I'm waking up."

And then she woke up.

When Loly regained her faculties, she was hungrier than she had been during her entire pregnancy. "Illinois," she screeched, "I need food!"

Magistrate Illinois hustled into the KERBANGER's bedchamber and asked, "What can I get you? Anything you want is yours."

"I'm having cravings, Illinois. Pickles. A salt lick. Cheeze Whyz. Fried and oiled potatoes. You know, the kind of things that pregnant women all over Easterrabbit crave."

Looking away, Magistrate said, "Yeah, about that. Here's the thing . . ." And then she trailed off.

After a silent moment, Loly asked, "Here's what thing?"

"Well, while you were asleep, you gave birth."

"I *what*?!" She felt at her stomach, and sure enough, it was flat. "Where's my baby?"

Looking away, Magistrate said, "Yeah, that's the other thing . . ." And then she trailed off.

After two silent moments, Loly asked, "What other thing?"

"The baby had a horse's head and a human's body. The body couldn't support the weight of the head, and, well, it wasn't pretty. I'll spare you the details."

In a span of two minutes, KERBANGER Lolyta Targetpractice experienced every emotion in the spectrum: denial, anger, depression, acceptance, numbness, exhaustion, horror, shame, hunger, thirst, horniness, confusion, hunger again, anguish, more hunger, and then more hunger yet. When she felt somewhat composed, she took a deep breath and ordered Magistrate Illinois, "Bring me my eggs."

Magistrate said, "Yes, KERBANGER." She curtsied and left the room.

Off in the distance, Juan Nieve's direpanda, Fourshadow, could be heard growling.

JUAN

The Wall had melted to the point that Juan Nieve could step over it without straining himself. The Others could probably do the same, but Juan was too overheated, overtired, and over-booted to care. As he tried to figure out his next move—Go home? Become one of the Others? Kill Otter and D-Day for sport?—he felt a tap on his shoulder. He spun around and was greeted with the most repulsive sight of his life.

Despite the fact that they each had two arms, two legs, and heads with two eyes, one nose, and one mouth, the two beings were not men, but Juan thought that they might have been at one time. After all, despite their rotting limbs, they were able to move, and despite the oozing sores on their lips, they were able to speak.

"How's it hanging, pal?" the taller being asked.

"How's tricks?" the younger one queried.

"Um . . ."

The taller thing explained, "Listen, we won't keep you. I'm Jarhead, and he's Airhead, the two of us used to be Swatchmen, but we got murdered in the prologue, then reanimated by the Others . . ."

From the distance, a voice cried, *"We're not the Others! We're the Awesomes, asshole!"*

". . . and then we dropped off the face of Easterrabbit, and we want to find out why."

Despite their hideous appearance, Juan could hear the pathos in their voices, and he wanted to help. "There's only one thing I can tell you, gentlemen: *A veces en nuestro mundo, algo que ocurre, y nada se resuelve.*"

In unison, Jarhead and Airhead asked, "What does that mean, jerkoff?"

"Sometimes in our world, little happens, and nothing is resolved."

LOLYTA

A side from Loly Targetpractice (aka Lolyta Tornadobutt, Princess of Duckseventually) walking into a raging campfire with her eggs balanced on her shoulders, and coming out of said fire with a bunch of baby ducklings in her hair—ducklings rather than baby dragons, mind you, and you should have seen that coming, because it had been foreshadowed for many, many chapters—little happened and nothing was resolved, but as was always the case when

You can read the remainder of that sentence and much, much more in *A Crash of Bling: A Sonnet of Slush and Soot,* Book 2, coming March 27, 2138.

ACKNOWLEDGMENTS

The author wishes to thank Benjamin R. R. Franklin, Thomas R. R. Jefferson, James R. R. Madison, Alexander R. R. Hamilton, John R. R. Adams, John R. R. Jay, and his beloved wife, Martha R. R. Washington.

The author also wishes to thank his editor, Peter R. R. Joseph, for his patience, his kindness, and his wisdom in advising him to trim 916 pages from the first draft of this book.

The author also wishes to thank everybody at St. Martin's Press and Thomas Dunne Books, most notably Thomas R. R. Dunne, Margaret R. R. Smith, Loren R. R. Jaggers, and Joe R. R. Goldschein.

The author also wishes to thank his readers Susan R. R. Smith and Kush R. R. Mangat, who have ten or eleven more *Sonnets of Slush and Soot* to look forward to. Maybe twelve.

The author also wishes to thank his literary agent, Jason R. R. Allen R. R. Ashlock of Movable Type Management for his excellent swordsmanship, marksmanship, and penmanship.

The author also wishes to thank his other wife, Natale R. R. Rosenberg, for her love, support, and the mighty tasty direpandaburgers with grilled onions.

Finally, the author wishes to thank the wonderful, kind, handsome, brilliant, adorable, handsome, hilarious, handsome, handsome, charming gentleman who made this all possible—the man of the hour, who makes the ladies wanna shower—Alan R. R. Goldsher. Here's mud in your eye, and an onion in your mouth.